it's a Tracey Richardson book but I was really drawn to the characters over and above the storyline itself.

-Les Rêveur

Delay of Game

There are so many things to love about this book. There are great characters working to be together in a seemingly impossible situation. The scenes on the ice were wonderful and visceral, but without slowing down the story. I've heard it said that in some sport romances, the sport scenes can get in the way of the plot, which is definitely not the case here. The action on the ice is as important as what happens off the ice, both in terms of character and plot development.

-The Lesbian Review

With a story set around the very real rivalry between the Canadian and US women's ice hockey teams, this book has a realistic edge to it to go along with the romance that is the main focus of the tale. Although the romance is given slightly more weight, there's enough of the hockey story to keep sports fans truly interested. Richardson clearly knows hockey, and all the scenes around practice, training, and actual matches come across as very authentic.

-Rainbow Book Reviews

Thursday Afternoons

Other Bella Books by Tracey Richardson

Blind Bet
By Mutual Consent
The Campaign
The Candidate
Delay of Game
Heartsick
I'm Gonna Make You Love Me
Last Salute
No Rules of Engagement
Side Order of Love
The Song in My Heart
The Wedding Party

About the Author

Tracey Richardson is the author of twelve previous novels, all of them lesbian romances with Bella Books. Her best known novels include *No Rules of Engagement* and *Last Salute*, both of which were Lambda Literary Awards finalists, along with bestsellers *The Candidate*, *By Mutual Consent*, *Delay of Game*, and *I'm Gonna Make You Love Me*. Tracey is a first-place Romance Writers of America Rainbow Romance winner, and has written several short stories, one of which won second place in an international competition. Tracey worked for nearly three decades as a daily newspaper journalist, but now writes fiction full-time. She lives in the Georgian Bay area of Ontario, Canada, with her wife, Sandra, and their dogs. Visit www.traceyrichardson.net for more information about her books and to connect further.

Bella Books, Inc.
P.O. Box 10543
Tallahassee, FL 32302

Printed in the United States of America on acid-free paper.

First Bella Books Edition 2019

Editor: Medora MacDougall
Cover Designer: Sandy Knowles

ISBN: 978-1-64247-055-0

Thursday Afternoons

Tracey Richardson

BELLA
B O O K S
2019

Acknowledgments

Health care is under siege around the world. The price of health care goes up constantly, while governments and insurers are inclined to spend less and less on this vital service. I've been privy to an inside perspective on health care from my years as a health reporter, and I hope this novel helps give readers a bit of insight into the growing pressures and demands that hospitals and staff face every day. Let me be clear, however, that this is a fictional story, and I've taken some artistic license. I remain indebted to our hospitals and to our dedicated health care workers. Without our health, not a lot else matters.

I'm also indebted to readers of lesbian fiction. Your loyalty gives us, the writers, a home for our creative outlet, and it's an honor and a privilege to write for you. Thank you, as always, to the Bella Books team, and to Linda and Jessica Hill for continuing to serve lesbian readers and writers. Thank you to my fabulous editor, Medora MacDougall, for sharing her expertise with me and making my work better.

Dedication

To those who've devoted their lives to working in health care. And to my wife, Sandra, who retired recently from thirty years of exemplary service as a police officer. Those who make a living helping others are true heroes.

CHAPTER ONE

Amy Spencer presses the button for the hotel's ninth floor even as she tells herself it's not too late to back out, as if she has a choice. Which she does, except she's not the kind of person to bail at the last minute. If anything, she's the opposite—the last one to turn out the lights, even in the most hopeless of situations. Disappoint someone? Fall short of fulfilling an obligation? Not in her DNA.

She unlocks the door and opens it, a rock settling into her stomach. Which of course is anatomically impossible, she reminds herself. It's a hotel room that's not unlike the endless hotel rooms she's stayed in for medical conferences—a king bed, a dresser, a loveseat and chair surrounding a neat but plain coffee table. The familiarity dulls the edges of her anxiety for a moment, until a parade of questions stampedes through her mind, the biggest one being, *what the hell am I doing here?* She's about to meet a stranger, a woman she met on a lesbian dating app with only a first name—Ellen—for an afternoon of mutually satisfying, hot sex. Well, sex anyway...the hot part and the satisfying part she can debate later. At thirty-nine, it's a little too soon to blame a midlife crisis for this crazy idea. But she hasn't had sex in more than three years and if she remains celibate for even one more month, she really will go crazy. This, she reassures herself, is the way to do it. No strings, no expectations, no demands on her time and attention, which lord knows she has so little of at the end of a long day at work.

She goes to the minibar and gives serious thought to opening an airplane bottle size of Jack Daniels, even though it probably costs ten bucks. It would calm her nerves, grease her introversion, but she dismisses the idea because it's an hour's drive home and she's most certainly *not* spending several hours here, even though technically the room is hers—theirs—until tomorrow morning. The sooner she can slink away with her shame and her post-sex glow, the better.

She takes a long, deep breath. Reminds herself it's only sex, and if this Ellen woman—which of course probably isn't her real name, just as Amy is using the name Abby—is half as hot as her photo, it's all good. Provided, of course, that Ellen is not a sadist, a nut job, or, like, some kind of serial killer. But really, what are the chances of that? And as for this Ellen's motives for an afternoon tryst, well, who cares? *It's not like we're going to become friends,* Amy tells herself. *After today, I'll never even have to see her again.*

A quiet knock on the door spins her around. *Oh shit. She's really here.* She takes her time getting to the door because it wouldn't do to answer out of breath, showing herself to be too eager (code for desperate). Plus, she still isn't entirely convinced she wants to go through with this. And, oh yeah, what if this woman is nothing like her photo? The possibilities of what the real Ellen might look like play havoc with Amy's imagination even as she places her hand on the door handle. Fuck, it never occurred to her before that her "date" might have used someone else's photo.

When she opens the door, she's dumbstruck—because Ellen looks exactly like her photo. Long, thick, reddish blond hair that's like a flaming sun sliding into the horizon and viridian green eyes that her dark framed glasses can't hide. At the edge of her left eyebrow, there's a very small and very faint scar—the only flaw (if you could call it that), as far as Amy can see. Ellen is gorgeous, and Amy exhales her held breath.

"Hi," the woman says in a low voice that somehow manages to sound sultry and sexy while also shy. "I'm Ellen." She elegantly offers her hand and Amy shakes it like they're conducting a business transaction. Which they kind of are, minus the exchange of money.

"A…ah… I'm Abby. Nice to meet you."

Ellen sheds her bright spring vest and makes a beeline for the minibar. She roots around, grabs one of the little bottles of Jack, retrieves a can of soda water from the bar fridge. "Mind if I fix a drink?" Her nervousness is a good sign, because in their email exchange, she too claimed never to have done this before.

"Please do." Amy watches Ellen take tiny sips by the minibar, shakes her head no when Ellen asks her if she'd like one too. "Should we, um, talk first or something?"

Lips that have been painted with a soft and slightly glossy pink lipstick curl slowly into a smile that seems equal parts flirtatious and bashful (*how does she do that?*). The woman tosses back the rest of her drink in two swallows, peels off her glasses, which land with a soft thud on the coffee table. A clear signal, Amy supposes, that pretenses and small talk are over.

"Come here," Ellen says.

A low rumble begins in Amy's stomach as she stands before her soon-to-be-lover, noticing instantly that while Ellen is tall, Amy is still a good inch taller in spite of the two-inch, strapless sandals Ellen is wearing. Amy's height has always given her confidence, though nobody would accuse her of lacking any— at least, not at the hospital, where a simple glare is often all she needs to make her point. It's in her personal life, in moments like these, that she's a little lost. With her sophomoric gestures and words—lack of words, more like—she might as well scream out that she's a loser when it comes to women.

But Ellen doesn't seem to notice. She quirks a finely shaped eyebrow, tilts her chin up. *God*, Amy thinks, *those eyes!* They look like exotic jewels...emerald or jade or the rare green sapphire she once saw at a jewelry store—she'd been surprised to learn that not all sapphires were blue. "Kiss me?" Ellen phrases it as a question, and Amy almost declines because who said any of this was about kissing?

"All right." She's wrestled patients from the jaws of death, but saying no to a beautiful woman standing in front of her, asking to be kissed? She doesn't stand a chance.

The kiss is tentative at first, their lips meeting as softly as the brush of a butterfly's wing as they become accustomed to the taste and feel of one another. It's been awhile since Amy has kissed a woman, but instantly the sensation is familiar, swamping her with a deliciousness that's like a returning to herself. *Oh, I've missed this*, she thinks as she deepens the kiss, surprised by her newfound bravery. But it feels good, especially when Ellen's hand slides up her back and presses softly. Such an intimate, affectionate gesture that is completely contradictory to the fact that they're about to have meaningless sex. Amy's only had casual sex once before and it didn't suit her. And yet... there can be no other alternative, not if she ever wants sex again with another human being.

Sex. How easy it is when you're young—when you think about it all the time without really reflecting on it. So concerned about when and how and with whom that you forget to wonder what it means. Well, this one is easy. This won't mean anything, she decides, even though it feels...okay. Better than okay.

Ellen pulls her mouth away, traces a finger along Amy's jaw, and it's right there in her eyes that she's trying to be brave too, that she's playing a role that isn't entirely comfortable. Her apprehension gives Amy the courage to take her hands and gently lead her to the bed.

"Should we...undress each other...or undress ourselves?" Ellen asks.

No way is Amy up to undressing a stranger, especially one who looks like she's stepped out of a fashion magazine—her beauty as intimidating as a supervising surgeon calling on a medical student to answer a complex question. Oh, Amy remembers those days—her mouth as dry as her armpits were drenched while she struggled to make something out of the mush gumming up her brain.

Amy swallows and says, "Let's do our own disrobing." She unbuttons her dress shirt, her slacks, modestly turning her back to Ellen, who's doing the same thing. She can see that the woman's clothes, now folded in a neat pile, are expensive—the fabric fine, the shoes designer—confirming that she's a fellow professional. Maybe another doctor, though Amy has never seen her before.

They both make a dash to get under the covers, as though it's freezing cold, and Amy is tempted to ask Ellen why she's meeting a stranger for sex—why in hell she *needs* to meet a stranger for sex looking the way she looks—at Windsor's riverfront Hilton Hotel on a Thursday afternoon. She's guilty herself of failing to fit the profile of someone into anonymous hookups. Women, men too, take one look at the stethoscope around her neck and her ring-less left hand, and she has to beat them off. But there's an unspoken agreement that she and Ellen are not to ask personal questions. Probably a good thing, because she doesn't need to take on somebody else's burdens. She's shouldered plenty of them in her life, some hers, mostly not, and it's for damned sure she doesn't need any more.

The first touch from Ellen ignites a trail of fire down the center of her chest, and Amy slams her eyes shut.

"You're even more attractive than your picture," Ellen whispers, her breath ruffling the short hair above Amy's ear. "I didn't quite know what to expect, but…"

"You're satisfied?" It matters, for some reason, and Amy opens her eyes to stare into Ellen's.

"Yes, very." Her smile appears nervous, but her dimples reassure that she's being genuine.

"Good. Me too. You're…beautiful, Ellen."

It's the most words they've exchanged, Amy realizes, and while the idea of lying naked together and talking some more has its appeal, she worries Ellen will get the wrong idea. Or, hell, that *she* will get the wrong idea and think this is some kind of date or something. A get-to-know-you session when the only thing Amy wants to know is the feeling of her orgasm ripping her apart. Gently, slowly, she climbs on top of Ellen, giving her a chance to back out, to protest, to say this isn't at all what she wants. But she doesn't. Instead, Ellen parts her lips, reaches for Amy's mouth and claims it with another kiss. *God, her mouth tastes good*, Amy thinks as she loses herself in the kiss—a kiss that's one part exploration and three parts lust. And then she remembers the fire raging in her belly as she slides her mouth down to Ellen's throat, to her collarbone, where she plants little kisses, licks the tender, smooth skin, and tastes its faint saltiness. There will absolutely be no oral sex today, and she hopes there's no need to spell out that it would be too risky, given that they're strangers. Being a doctor sucks sometimes.

Amy brushes her hand beneath a breast. They're fabulous breasts, perfect really, a little bigger than average but not too big. The curve of them, the slight heft, feels just right in her hand, and she can't wait to put her mouth on them because she's suddenly ravenous for them. Which comes as a complete shock because she's not supposed to be so into this meaningless sex stuff. Amy prefers love to go with her sex, same as she likes cream with her coffee, butter with her toast. Sex is always sweeter when love's involved. But there's a flip side too, when the love dies, when it becomes an invasive disease that destroys the sex and mows down everything good in its path—ruthlessly, categorically. Yes, love is cruel, love is disappointing, which is why Amy is not going there again. Ever. Sex is sex now, a release. And since when did she become a breast woman?

She's so hard and wet for this woman that she refuses to think about anything that's going to throw cold water on her libido. She lets it all fade away as she takes a nipple into her mouth, stiff as a pebble, and when she sucks urgently, Ellen moans and nearly levitates off the bed. It shocks Amy how excited she feels making love to this woman, how much she's getting off on the little touches, the little kisses, the taste and smell of Ellen. It should feel mechanical, weird, but it doesn't. Perhaps it's the illicit nature of it, the fact that they're sneaking around in a hotel room in the middle of the afternoon, using fake names as if they're cheating on a spouse, that kindles this fury of arousal in her.

Ellen moans louder, arches her body into Amy for more friction. Amy complies with the silent demand, moves her hand between them and dances her fingers over Ellen's velvety wetness. She's so swollen and slippery that Amy feels her own wetness coat her inner thigh.

"Oh God, yes!" Ellen cries out as Amy's fingers lightly press on her clitoris, trace tiny circles over it, around it. She's not sure if she should enter Ellen, because it's an intimate gesture, almost as intimate as placing her mouth down there. She wants to go inside, but she's not sure of the rules, other than no oral. Maybe they should have talked about it first? Maybe she should—

"Please, I want you inside me."

The raw need in Ellen's voice sends a quiver of excitement through Amy. She swallows a moan back down her throat. She can't resist letting her mind go to that place where she imagines Ellen wants her, really and truly wants *her*, that it can only be Amy giving her such pleasure. It's a fantasy, which is exactly what this whole thing is, one giant fantastical experience. She pushes a finger into Ellen, curls it inside her, adds another, and only then does she sneak a look at Ellen's face, at the taut muscles of her throat, at her head thrown back. It's a picture of pure ecstasy—her lips muttering unintelligible things, her eyes squeezed shut as she rides Amy's hand hard, pushing against it, speeding up the pace, meeting her thrust for thrust. When she comes, she trembles violently and all the air whooshes out of her lungs. She calls out Amy's fake name one final time before her body collapses, her muscles limp and quivering.

"Wow," Ellen says slowly, like she's emerging from a fog, and opens those unforgettable eyes to stare right through Amy. It's almost unsettling, and then Ellen shifts until they are side by side, facing one another. She strokes Amy's side, around to her rib cage, flutters her long and painted nails across her abs. "You're very fit. And very talented." If this were a real date, Ellen would surely start asking her questions, personal questions, but

Ellen seems as intent as Amy to keep from going there. If sex isn't considered too personal, that is.

Amy closes her eyes as a finger trails up to the underside of her breast, follows its natural curve. Oh, she wants Ellen to fuck her; she can almost taste the release now. But she doesn't want to get ahead of herself. She wants to suck every last strand of enjoyment out of this because it's most certainly the first and last time they'll see one another. And the last time she'll be having sex with anyone again for a long while. As fun as it's been, she's not going to make a habit of slinking around hotels with strangers. She'll take this memory and wring every drop of pleasure out of it for days, weeks, months.

Ellen gently squeezes her nipple, and before long she's sucking on it, moaning like it's the tastiest thing she's ever put into her mouth, and it drives Amy wild. She's so turned on; she's crazy with desire. She knows it won't take much, and it doesn't. Ellen's hand moves down to her sex, and Amy traps it there with her thighs and grinds into it until the colors explode behind her eyelids, her orgasm thundering through her like a herd of wild horses. She feels like she's splitting in half, coming apart, with only Ellen's lips and hands keeping her together. And oh, it's so glorious. Her heart rate continues to pound and the doctor in her counts its beats, estimating she's at more than 140 a minute. *Good God!*

Ellen plants a final kiss on her chin, smiles at her before moving away because the spell that's enraptured them both is broken now. It's time to put an end to this little afternoon delight, and they both seem to sense it. The shutting down of this liaison is as sudden as the commencing of it was, and while it's jarring, Amy doesn't question the need for it. She knows it's right to end this, and the sooner the better.

She climbs out of bed, her limbs still a little shaky from her orgasm, and reaches for her clothes. Ellen's watching her, a question in her eyes.

"You're welcome to stay," Amy offers. "The room is ours for the night."

"No need for that, but I'll take a shower, if that's okay."

"Of course."

Ellen has the sheet wrapped snugly around her, as if Amy hasn't seen her naked, hasn't touched her everywhere, hasn't been the architect of her orgasm. "Um, Abby?"

"Y-yes?" She can't quite get used to her fake name.

"What are you doing next Thursday afternoon?"

CHAPTER TWO

Ellis Hall gives in to the urge to linger in the shower, even with the pressure of having to be somewhere else in about thirty minutes. The warm water sluicing down her arms and chest, and the surprisingly nice (for a hotel) soap that smells of lemon and rosemary make it difficult to leave. And then there's the memory of Abby's kisses—her strong body against Ellis's, her sure but gentle touch, her uncanny ability to know exactly where and when and how much pleasure to give. *God, those hands! They belong to a magician.*

Ellis closes her eyes and luxuriates in the memory of her orgasm moments ago, its sweeping ecstasy that was like the slow but steady release of a pressure valve. It had been exactly what she needed, and oh, what a relief to not have to pretend they were embarking on a relationship. Relationships are past tense for her. Dating too, though that's a more recent development. Her job sucks away all her attention and energy, and while admittedly her job is not as fun as it used to be, it doesn't leave much time for anything or anyone else. Placing her work ahead of everything has become too much of a pain to explain and to excuse and too much to bear for potential partners. Even casual dating is next to impossible. Her long days, the distractions, the stress, and now a new city to call home for the next ten months or so have thoroughly convinced her that she's far better off alone. Except alone no longer has to mean celibate, thanks to the enchanting Abby and her talented hands and lips.

Ellis shuts off the water, wraps a thick towel around her midsection, and tries to resist the pull of wondering who Abby is, of what brought her to this hotel room to meet a stranger, and what her actual name might be. She pictures Abby's collar length, light brown hair with its roguish swoop over her forehead, the square jaw, the sharp nose, the prominent cheekbones that give her…not so much an air of severity as a statement of competence and singular focus. Abby looks the type who wants to be in charge and is good at it. Not unlike Ellis herself. But in Abby's eyes, a shade of pearl gray that almost resembles translucent smoke, there'd been an unexpected shyness, a trace of vulnerability that had made Ellis do a double take. And then pretend she hadn't noticed. In Abby's defense, who wouldn't feel a tad vulnerable, meeting up with a stranger in a hotel room for anonymous sex? Ellis certainly did. She almost hadn't shown up, worried that she'd blow it with her sophomoric ways, her self-doubt, that she'd be unveiled as an amateur. It was a delight to see Abby act every bit the novice.

Ellis finishes drying herself, decides it is not necessary to wonder about Abby's motives, because their deal was no personal chitchat, no questions. Aside from mild curiosity, it's better this way, because Ellis doesn't want to come under another woman's microscope either. Doesn't want to have to go through the motions of pretending to be interested in what her "date" does, thinks, who she is and where she's been, what she wants out of life, what her politics are, and all that time-consuming drivel that's more likely to drive a wedge between them than offer up common ground. This little arrangement is appealingly facile, exceedingly efficient. And Ellis, if nothing else, is all about efficiencies and bottom lines.

Slipping her watch on her wrist, she notices the time. *Shit.* She's got fifteen minutes before she's supposed to pick up Mia for their dinner date. She'll have to step on it and hope that traffic is light, because she hates being late for anything. She also hopes that Mia, for a change, isn't full of attitude. Or mute sullenness. It's always one or the other, which doesn't give Ellis much to work with and means their time together isn't exactly pleasant.

Minutes later, when Mia slides into the passenger seat of Ellis's car, Ellis can see that her mood is as black as the heavy kohl eyeliner she's wearing. *How can anyone think that crap is attractive*, she wonders, and then reminds herself not to bring it up, because bringing it up will surely lead to an argument, and kohl eyeliner is definitely not worth the trouble. *Ugh!* She's exhausted thinking about the next ninety minutes or so that this dinner's going to take, finds her mind drifting to the glass of wine back at her apartment that she could be having right now. She's almost salivating at the thought, can almost smell the chilled sauvignon blanc. *Wait.* She wrinkles her nose, sniffs in Mia's direction. Marijuana. Faint, but there. *Dammit.*

She clamps her mouth shut, congratulates herself on not blowing up, which is exactly what she would have done a couple of years ago. Something about settling into her forties has softened the lines she used to so definitively and so quickly draw in the sand. Her way or the highway has become more "let's share the road." She's more patient in her middle age, more contemplative, which, honestly, scares the hell out of her, because she knows she can't do her job with the same zeal, the same sharpness, the same penetrating precision, if she pauses to consider too many other angles. Particularly the emotional ones. Getting soft is okay for the bedroom but not for the boardroom. And so she's been carefully walking a line these days.

"The usual?" she says to Mia and gets a curt nod in return. The "usual" is a Chinese buffet restaurant on Windsor's east side, where the food is passable, nothing particularly special, but Mia likes it. Or at least, she doesn't complain about the place. It's the third time they've met for dinner, though Ellis has also taken Mia to the mall a couple of times. She's only been in the city for five weeks and trying to build a relationship with Mia has been…challenging.

What she wouldn't give to still be in that hotel room with Abby, stretched out naked with her on the bed. And not in a hurry this time. Staying for a second round would have been… ooh, heavenly…but probably too much for their first hookup. They've agreed to a second time, next Thursday, and Ellis is already looking forward to it, though she's not greedy enough to expect a third liaison.

She waits until she and Mia have found a table and selected their food before she brings up the marijuana. *Tread carefully and do not get upset,* she reminds herself, taking a page from her parents' book. They were academics—both of them professors— and older when Ellis was born. They never got too excited when Ellis went through her teenaged years of rebelling against the rules, figuring there wasn't much they couldn't reason their way through. They'd been mostly right.

"Mia, how often are you smoking marijuana?"

Brown eyes swing toward her, eyes as resistant as a brick wall. "What do you care?"

"I care, okay? Especially since you're only fifteen."

A shrug. "Sixteen in a few months. Besides, it's not like you're my mother."

No, Ellis thinks, *I'm not.* But she was a stepmother to Mia for a while. So long ago now that Mia probably barely remembers it. "I don't have to be your mother to want what's best for you. And marijuana is dangerous, okay? It's very harmful to developing brains."

Another piercing glare. "Spare me. Like, you never do weed?"

"I don't." *Honesty, Ellis. The kid isn't dumb.* She lets up her guard for a moment. "Not more than a couple times a year." *Sheesh.* The last time was about seven months ago. She and a colleague she was chummy with were hanging out on his back patio when he lit up a joint. Ellis shared it with him. Took a cab home when he lit up a second joint.

"See? I *knew* it!"

"Recreational cannabis is legal in Canada. For adults. And as much as you'd like to think you're an adult, you're not. And I'm not trying to talk down to you, I swear I'm not." Ellis takes a moment to gather herself, to reinsert some calmness. Dealing with a mercurial teenager is a lot of damned work. "I'm worried about you, Mia. I don't want you throwing away your future, doing…things that you can't always make up for later on. I know these last couple of years have been hard on you, losing your mom and all."

"I don't want to talk about my mom. Especially not to you."

Ouch. Okay, I probably deserve that.

"Fine. We don't have to talk about your mom. But I do want to talk about you. There's so much waiting out there for you, so many good things, so many opportunities, experiences. You haven't even scratched the surface yet. I don't want you to be cheated out of anything, that's all. I don't want you to hurt yourself."

Mia rolls her eyes, doesn't even try to hide her derision. If Ellis could simply get up and walk out right now, she'd do it, because she really doesn't need this bullshit, especially when she's only trying to help. But guilt is a funny thing. Guilt makes you stand there and take it on the chin over and over.

"Can we cut the lecture on life, please? Like, what do you know about it anyway? You're married to your job. Same as always."

Indignation ratchets up the pounding of her heart, except the kid is right. Ellis is an expert at putting her job above everything else, at letting it consume her. Knows all about failing at personal relationships, too. But hell, they're talking about Mia here. She'll be damned if she lets a fifteen-year-old hijack the conversation and turn it into a judgment of her own life.

"I'm good at my job, Mia." So good, that her services demand mid-six figures a year. "I only hope you find something you're as good at. But this…" She makes a smoking gesture. "Isn't the way to go about it. Look. Why don't you tell me one thing you enjoy, all right? One positive thing in your life that makes you feel good."

Mia exaggeratedly plows into her food and shovels it into her mouth. "I enjoy eating," she mumbles around the food. "Happy now?"

No, Ellis thinks, *I'm not happy at all*. She decides to finish her meal in silence, before her frustration ruins everything, makes her say or do something she can't take back. She can endure anything with enough willpower; she'll endure this too.

An hour later, when she drops Mia at the curb in front of her grandparents' house, Ellis reminds her that they're seeing a movie together next week.

"Whatever" is Mia's response, right before she gets out and slams the car door shut. She doesn't look back.

Ellis eases the car away, resists the urge to squeal the tires and peel off in a cloud of dust. For not the first time, she wonders what the hell she's doing here. And whether it's worth it.

CHAPTER THREE

The morning can't move fast enough for Amy. Rounds and paperwork, then it's off to her afternoon tryst with Ellen. Mysterious Ellen with the liquid green eyes and the waves of red hair highlighted with early summer blond. Then there's her lips that are so soft and ridiculously kissable, hands that are long and slender and—

"Dr. Spencer?"

"Yes?" Time to pause the sexy daydreaming, which is just as well, because it's only making the time crawl.

A look of distress is firmly entrenched on the face of Erin Kirkland, a family medicine resident who's doing a sixteen-week surgical rotation at the hospital. She's young, though not as young as some because she took a year-and-a-half off between medical school and her family medicine residency to have a baby. She's in her second and final year of residency, after which she can hang her shingle as a primary care physician. Amy hesitated to take her on at first because she's a single mom of a three-year-old. She's probably exhausted much of the time, which doesn't exactly bode well for handling the demands of an operating room—being on your feet for hours and hours at a time, plus the stress of sometimes working overnight. Erin assured her that she was up for it, said she had lots of family help with her daughter, and so Amy came to her senses when she asked herself if she'd have the same concerns about a male resident with a young child at home. It's hard enough for women docs without getting crap from other women docs. Two weeks into her rotation, Erin has been nothing but a model resident. She's diligent, professional, keen to learn. But right now she's trying to hide her exasperation that probably has more to do with exhaustion and the emotional free fall that comes with the onslaught of so much new information.

"It's Mrs. Kenney." Erin inclines her head in the direction of the door down the hall that is their next stop. Yesterday at this time Amy was doing a bowel resection on the sixty-year-old woman, and she's looking to discharge her today as long as things look good. Erin has been on duty since yesterday morning, responsible overnight for the six in-house surgical patients, plus sharing responsibility with another young resident for the fifty or so medical patients who are being lodged. Along with all of that, she would have helped out in the ER if anything remotely surgical came in.

"Is there a problem? She's set to be discharged shortly." Amy hadn't been paged overnight or accosted at the door this morning, so she assumed everything was in order with Mrs. Kenney. The surgery went as well as expected, and Mrs. Kenney should be moving around by now and eating a liquid diet—two benchmarks Amy insists on before she will release her patient.

"There's a bit of a problem with the orders you gave me last night."

A list of complications runs through Amy's head—infection, the incision breaking open, internal bleeding—and her heart rate begins to pick up. "Why wasn't I called," she's about to bark, when Erin softly shakes her head.

"She won't get out of bed," Erin clarifies in a tone that indicates she's embarrassed by such a simple problem.

"Did you explain to her why she needs to get moving around?" Unlike years past, post-op patients aren't allowed to languish in bed for days because of the risk it poses for pneumonia, clot formations, other infections. Numerous studies have shown that patients decondition at an alarming rate for every day they remain in hospital. Amy has already explained all of this to Erin. And to Mrs. Kenney.

"I did, but she refused."

Amy huffs out a frustrated sigh as she strides purposefully to Mrs. Kenney's room. "Follow me," she says needlessly to Erin, who's like a puppy dog on her heels.

"Good morning, Mrs. Kenney," she calls out to the patient, who is a giant inert object under a flannel blanket. The woman's eyes drift open and she responds in kind.

Instead of berating her patient, Amy makes small talk. Asks her about her grandchildren, asks about the complicated quilt she knows the woman is anxious to get back to making. In the same mundane tone, as if she's going to start talking about the weather next, Amy simply says, "We'd really like for you to be able to go home today, Mrs. Kenney. It's time to get out of bed now."

The patient stares at her for a long moment, and Amy fears she's going to refuse. She holds out her hand for Mrs. Kenney and is surprised when the woman takes it, tosses the blanket aside with her other hand, and swings her legs gingerly over the side of the bed. With Amy's assistance, she hauls herself up, shuffles a few feet over to a chair, and plops down. "Well, that wasn't nearly so bad."

After checking the woman's incision and asking a few questions, Amy steers Erin into the hall. It's time for Erin to go home and Amy doesn't want to delay her any longer than necessary. Erin needs sleep. And some time with her baby girl.

Together they walk toward the staff lounge, where Erin has been assigned a temporary locker. "When I started my surgical residency, I thought the job of a surgeon entailed diagnosing, cutting, and sewing. That's it. I had almost no idea how to talk to patients, how to manage them." Amy rolls her eyes for good measure and smiles at her exhausted resident because she knows exactly what it's like to feel that you don't have the know-how or the authority to get patients to cooperate. "Shows how little I knew. As a general practitioner, your bedside manner will be ten times better than mine in about three years. It takes time and some experience, that's all. You'll get there."

"Thanks," Erin replies, relief smoothing out her frown lines.

"Sure. Now go home and kiss that girl of yours."

"I will." Erin beams and can't make her exit fast enough. "Thank you."

"There you are." Kate Henderson intercepts Amy outside the staff room. Kate is a scrub nurse, the best in the hospital if you ask Amy, although she doesn't wait to be asked before extolling her best friend's virtues. It's a mutual admiration society, because Kate seems to think Amy is the best damned surgeon she's ever worked with. "We could be rock stars in the big city," Kate likes to joke. To which Amy replies, "Naw, we'd only be the opening act. *Here* we're the rock stars." Now Kate eyes Amy's scrubs and says, "I thought today wasn't a surgery day for you."

"It's not, but a seventy-year-old woman was brought in this morning after a bad fall. Tibia fracture at the medial malleolus. Michaels is on it. He asked me to stand by in case he needs another pair of hands. Diabetic. Circulation issues." What she doesn't need to spell out is that if an amputation is needed, she will be called on. So far, she's heard nothing, but if things go south, she knows her afternoon plans will be jeopardized. It's all she can do to keep her thoughts from spiraling.

Paul Michaels is the orthopedic surgeon on staff. The thing about a small hospital like this with its fifty-eight inpatient beds is that there aren't many other surgeons to fight over the three operating room suites. Amy is one of three general surgeons, plus Michaels, plus a gynecologist, a urologist, and an ENT who occasionally need an OR suite. The schedule isn't always pretty, but they manage.

"How's the young Dr. Kirkland doing?" Kate is just starting her shift and hasn't worked much with Erin yet.

"I think she's going to be okay. A little confidence is all she needs."

"Well, then, looks like she's learning from the best when it comes to that."

"Is that a backhanded insult, Hendy?"

Kate smiles, and Amy feels the familiar tug of relief, the way she always does when Kate smiles. Kate lost her wife to cancer twenty-one months ago, and Amy knows she's a long way from healing. Smiling is a good thing. Smiling means she'll get through another day.

"I wouldn't dream of insulting our Chief of Surgery." Kate pulls a face. "Mostly because I'd like to keep my job in the OR."

"Nice try. You're not afraid of me."

"You're right, hon, I'm not. Hey, would you like to catch dinner after work? Cooking for one holds about as much appeal as mowing the lawn. Which I also need to do."

Amy winces. Normally she'd take Kate up on her offer, but she doesn't expect to be back home from the city until later in the evening. "Can't, sorry. I've got something that I can't get out of." Not a total lie, and since she's crappy at lying anyway, it's best this way.

Kate glances at her watch. "Time for lunch later in the cafeteria?"

"Always."

Over a grilled cheese sandwich for Amy and mushy meatballs for Kate that look like they've been extracted from somebody's abdomen, Amy tries to keep her mind from wandering to where it really wants to go: sex with Ellen in a few hours. It's not like the best sex she's ever had—not yet anyway—but there's something about its forbidden nature, the anonymity and secrecy of it, that excites her. She doesn't realize she's smiling and staring off into space until Kate calls her on it.

"You need to spill whatever's making you look like the cat that swallowed the canary," Kate admonishes. "Cuz I'd like a taste of that catnip!"

Amy won't confess what she's up to with Ellen because she knows Kate won't approve. Kate's a romantic who's only ever had one love. Not Kate's fault that Anne left her a widow, but she doesn't believe in casual hookups. Ever. In Kate's mind, sex is two-thirds brain. Her conclusion? Casual sex is only one-third as satisfying as sex that's part of a loving relationship. "So why settle for a bite instead of the whole meal," she's said on more than one occasion. Amy knows her friend is probably right, but damn, that one-third with Ellen feels pretty fucking amazing. Or maybe she's simply that desperate for another woman's touch. Whatever. She's not quite ready to toss Ellen to the curb yet.

"Wait." Kate points an accusing finger at her. "You didn't meet someone, did you?"

Amy tries to ignore the sudden dryness in her throat. "Nope. Haven't met a soul lately that isn't a patient or a colleague."

"You'd tell me if you did, right?"

Yes, she'd tell Kate if she ever met anyone worthy of a committed relationship. Or even worthy of dating. "Of course I would. But you know me, I never go anywhere, so the odds of meeting somebody are—"

"Ah, yes, but it's always when you least expect it." Kate met her future wife at the local YMCA after they'd unceremoniously collided while swimming laps.

"Probably true, but I'm keeping my head down and my pants on, so there'll be no trail of broken hearts in my future."

Kate clinks coffee cups with her, but the bonhomie falls apart when Kate looks at her with that mix of empathy and sadness that Amy knows all too well. "I know, sweetie. I know exactly how it is." They're both still firmly on their life rafts, hunkered down as though the storms they'd once endured continue to rage around them.

* * *

Ellis knocks softly on the hotel room door. Different room than last week, but inside it's pretty much identical.

"Hi," Abby says, looking crisp and neat in a collarless white shirt and grey tailored jacket that's the same shade as her eyes. "Please, come in."

A professional. Definitely. The fabric of her jacket is expensive and so is her cologne. There's a trace of nobility in her bearing, all of which reassures Ellis, because she needs to be careful that a stranger like Abby isn't after her for her money. Well, that's her official excuse, but now she's super curious about what Abby does for a living. Banker? CEO? Lawyer? Professor? It's academic, though, because it's understood they're not to discuss such things.

Ellis slips off her shoes. Reaches for the zipper at the back of her skirt.

"Wait." Abby says. Smiles to show she's not calling the whole thing off. "Join me for a drink first?"

"All right." Ellis claims the solo chair, leaves the adjacent love seat for Abby. They may have had sex once, but it doesn't mean they're bosom buddies or confidantes or lovers who want to share everything, including space. When they're not in bed, that is. "Jack and soda please."

"Coming right up." Abby fixes two, deposits one in front of Ellis and sits down. "So." She sips, eyes Ellis speculatively over the rim of the chunky crystal glass. "How was your week?"

Ellis feels her eyes widen in surprise before she schools her expression and shrugs lightly. Crappy, if she's honest. Mia has been recalcitrant. Her new job is demanding—meetings, thousands of pages of reports to review, budgets to analyze line-by-line, more meetings. God, she needs a good roll in the sack. "All right," she answers evasively, knowing Abby is simply being polite, nothing more. "Yours?"

Abby's brows draw tightly together, and for a moment she looks like she's going to answer honestly. But after another sip, her mouth curves into a rakish smile. "Let's just say that this is the highlight of my week by far."

Good answer, Ellis thinks, and tips her glass in salute. Abby scoots over to the cushion closest to Ellis's chair.

"Your drink okay?"

"Perfect." She's more of a wine drinker, but the Jack Daniels helps her relax quicker. And judging by the fresh glint in Abby's eyes, it's helping her relax as well. Helping embolden her, too, which Ellis can appreciate.

"Last week," Abby says, "here. Was it okay? Was it…should we do anything different?"

Her gentle inquisitiveness confirms for Ellis that, like her, Abby is new at this. Not that it really matters, because Ellis isn't looking for girlfriend material, but at least it's indicative of Abby's honesty. "Last week was great." Her breath catches a little as she remembers Abby on her. Abby in her. Abby's a handsome woman, no doubt about that, and her body is firm, muscular, athletic. She could be her type, Ellis supposes, except it's a moot point. She can't even imagine how she could date anyone right now, what with Mia's issues and the demands of her job consuming her. Plus there's the fact that she has absolutely no idea how to do an actual loving, committed relationship. She thought she did once, only to walk away when she suddenly couldn't stand the shackles of being a live-in partner and a stepmom.

Abby's fingers edge onto Ellis's knee, begin a slow slide north, past the hem of her skirt, and it sets Ellis's skin on fire. Time for talking is clearly over. She settles her head back against her chair, closes her eyes, allows Abby's touch to electrify her. God, those fingers are so talented. Perhaps she works with her hands, does something…magical with them. She moans as Abby's fingers dance closer and closer, and she spreads her legs a little to grant her lover more access. *Lover.* Does what they're doing make them lovers? *Probably not,* Ellis decides, because there's likely an element of affection or at least something more than a casual connection that defines being lovers. If this ended right now, today, Ellis knows her life would resume its usual shape and she'd probably not give Abby more than a passing thought. But oh, this is *not* going to end right now, because Abby is stroking her through her Victoria's Secret underwear, leaning over her, her breath warm against Ellis's chest and neck. She wants to kiss Abby. Wants to come from Abby's touch. Wants to get naked with her and feel Abby's nakedness sliding softly and wetly against her skin.

Ellis moans again, louder this time, reaches down and stills Abby's hand. Her voice sounds low and thick when she says, "Abby, I need you on the bed." God, does she ever.

They move to the bed, this time Ellis letting Abby undress her. Up and over her head goes her blouse. Then Abby, with gentle yet efficient hands, removes her bra—black and satiny, which Ellis hopes makes her hair look even more aflame, more vibrant. Forget how her hair looks. The way Abby is looking at her breasts, ravenous and unblinking, is enough. Oh, how Ellis has missed having another woman look at her like this, like she wants to eat her right up. Which would be quite incredible, except she's not a fan of engaging in oral sex with someone whose history she's unaware of. And she suspects Abby feels the same. Still... She fantasizes about Abby going down on her while stimulating her with her fingers, and it makes her incredibly hot, incredibly turned on. It makes her a bit crazy, actually.

They lie facing one another, Abby running her finger along the curve of Ellis's hip, until Ellis can no longer wait to kiss Abby. She moves her head toward Abby's, presses her lips to Abby's. Ellis has always loved kissing, always loved the way it feels to have another woman's mouth sliding over hers, all hot and demanding, then alternately sensual and tender and teasing. Abby's lips push back against hers and they deepen the kiss until tongues begin exploring one another. It's so powerful, having a part of Abby inside her, that Ellis feels the pressure building in her womb, a slow, liquid spreading of pleasure that soon races like an electrical current through her blood, up her spine, down her legs and back up again.

"Please," she begs, not caring that she's being so needy. Out of this bed, this room, she'd never exhibit such raw vulnerability, such transparent neediness, to another person. In the boardroom, she's ruthless, tough, in charge. But here, with this woman who possesses such capable hands, whose rainwater eyes are yielding, trusting, protective, and not to mention hot with desire, Ellis forgets who she is and allows herself to simply feel. She wiggles out of her skirt, sliding her underwear with it down her legs.

"Oh yes," she groans as Abby's hand finds her. She rocks against it before fingers trace her lips and the wetness coating them. Ellis's chest feels like it's going to explode as Abby enters her. One finger. Then another before Ellis's hips reach up to meet the rhythmic thrusts. They move together as one. When Abby's thumb finds her clit, all other thoughts flee from her mind as she concentrates on her own breathing, on the way her pleasure climbs higher and higher. She's dizzy with want, with the need to come. It's entirely perfect, except for the fact that Abby's mouth isn't, and can't be, on her. But she imagines Abby licking her, sucking her, and in an instant her breath leaves her lungs in a whoosh as her orgasm sweeps up her legs with the power of an earthquake. Her body quivers violently, but Abby stays with her, rides her until Ellis is completely spent.

Ellis arrives at the part where she wants to be held, wants a gentle landing from which to come down. Is it cool to ask Abby to hold her? To nestle against her? Probably not, but she chances it anyway, her hand touching Abby's shoulder and motioning her forward. Wordlessly, Abby curls her body into Ellis's, and the sensuality of the act is enough to evoke another post-orgasmic tremble.

Goddamn, Ellis thinks with what little brainpower she has left. *Where has this been all my life?*

CHAPTER FOUR

Amy's sister, Natalie, rushes into the restaurant as though being carried in on a windstorm. If you didn't know her, you would think she did it for the attention, but it's really because her life is in a constant state of chaos and drama. Three teenaged kids, an underemployed husband, and on top of that, she works full time as a receptionist for a busy gynecologist in Windsor. Getting her to sit down for an hour is a major victory.

"God, I'm sorry I'm late," Nat says as she sits down, immediately noticing that Amy has already ordered a glass of wine for her. "You're an angel, Ames." She picks up the glass and takes a long sip. Almost long enough to make Amy worry that her sister has developed a drinking problem, which she does not need on top of everything else.

"Long day?"

"Aren't they all? At least it's Friday. Thank *God!*"

"Friday for you but not for me. I'm on call all weekend."

"That sucks." Nat eyes Amy's soda and lime. "That explains the non-alcoholic drink. Damn, I thought we were having dinner together to let our hair down. I could use a bit of that. Actually, a lot of that."

It's Amy's default to feel sorry for her sister—and to sometimes be pissed off at her. But she loves her too. Three years older, Nat should have been the role model Amy idolized. But the truth is, they were opposites from day one with Nat always flitting from boyfriend to boyfriend as a teenager, blowing off school whenever she could, fighting with their parents over everything—big and small. At twenty-two she married Tim. They settled in Windsor, and even though she's only an hour's drive from her parents, she might as well be in another province. It's Amy who shoulders the burden of helping them. Four years ago, she returned to practice surgery in their hometown on the shores of Lake Erie. Not so much because she was homesick or nostalgic to return, but because her parents had begun needing more and more help. And Natalie, well, let's just say that their parents haven't been her priority. But still, Amy doesn't want to have to make all the decisions about how to care for them— their dad in particular.

"I thought you said Tim was finally able to get out more?"

Amy admires Nat's dedication to her husband, but it's been a struggle. Tim can only manage to work part-time at a liquor store outlet. He's a severe introvert and suffers from occasional crippling anxiety, leaving Nat to do all the heavy lifting at home as well as financially. Amy tries not to judge, but man, there are times when she'd like to slap her sister upside the head, demand that she start salvaging something of her own life, her own dreams. Nat always wanted to be a lounge singer, and she's got the vocal chops to do it, but with her need to earn a consistent living, well, shower singing is about the only singing in her immediate future.

Nat takes another sip of wine, shakes her head, but doesn't elaborate on her husband. "What about you, you having any fun lately?"

The question catches Amy off guard, too late to halt the blush she feels crawling up her cheeks. She evades, says she's working a lot (what else is new), but Nat isn't buying it.

"You look different."

"No, I don't."

"You do, actually." Nat leans closer, lowers her voice to a whisper. "Is that a *sex* glow I'm seeing on my baby sister?"

"A *what*?" Her assignation with Ellen is more than twenty-four hours old. Surely she's not still glowing, even though it was hotter sex than their first time. They even stayed long enough for a second round—in the shower. Buckling knees, warm water cascading over them, slippery skin, urgent moans that drowned out everything else. Taking a shower will never be the same again for Amy.

Nat grins and laughs like she's learned the juiciest gossip she's heard in ages. "Who's the lucky lady?"

"Nobody. You need more sleep, because you're way off base." Amy is not going to confess her crazy affair with Ellen. She doesn't need to be teased or, worse, lectured. Natalie has never exhibited the same patience for Amy's romantic choices (or choice, to be more accurate, since there's only ever been one major one) as Amy has with Nat.

"Ah jeez, Ames. I wish you'd find somebody. It's long past time, don't you think? You're more than settled in your career now and…" Nat has never understood why Amy is so reluctant to enter into another relationship, but then, she's always been better than Amy at scattering problems and heartbreaks into the wind. Or ignoring them altogether, as Nat has often done in her own life. "Can't you let what happened with Lisa go? I mean…"

They haven't talked about Lisa in years and Amy has no idea what's inspired her sister to bring up her ancient past. Her jaw tightens and she has to squeeze out the words, "You don't just forget that stuff." Going through more than three years of hell with someone isn't exactly a memory you can simply file away forever, never again to feel its sadness, its wretched frustration.

"I know, I know. It was an awful time for you, and I'm sorry for bringing it up, but you'd be so good for someone. You're kind, you're super smart, you're extremely loyal."

Amy raises her glass in mock salute. "Nobody can question the loyalty of the Spencer sisters, that's for sure."

Nat accepts the jab with a casual shrug. "So you're not drinking tonight and you have nothing exciting to confess. I was hoping for a fun distraction."

"Actually, I have a distraction for you, but it's not fun." It feels like they're lurching from depressing topic to depressing topic.

"Is it Mom and Dad?"

"It is." Both eighty now, both failing but for different reasons. Their mom recently had a hip replacement and arthritis is giving her daily pain, while their dad is succumbing more and more to dementia. Neither sister can quite accept that their once vibrant, incredibly intelligent father can't remember something as simple as what he had for breakfast. Most recently, he's begun getting lost on neighborhood walks when he ventures too far. "They need more help, Nat."

"I know they do. But I can't do it, Ames. You know I'm at my max."

Amy sighs quietly, bites back a sarcastic retort. Why should she have to carry more of the load because her sister chose a difficult life? *Stop it*, she commands herself. *You're the one who chose to be a surgeon, which means you're not around much either. And now you're stepping out on Thursday afternoons when you could be helping Mom and Dad instead. Okay, but so what? Is it a crime to want a few hours a week to do something pleasurable for myself?* "I know you are," she says. "I am too."

Natalie blows out an exasperated breath, even though it's Amy who lives less than ten minutes from their parents and has been the one trying to organize paid help for them. "Why can't they see for themselves that they should be moving to an assisted living place? I mean, isn't it obvious? They can hardly do anything for themselves anymore...the lawn care, the house cleaning, preparing decent meals. What else can we do?"

Their server, a perky young thing who's a little too perky, a little too young, a little too cute for Natalie's sour mood, takes their order. Natalie practically barks out her choices, asks the server to put a rush on another glass of wine.

Amy suggests a family meeting. "You, me, them. See if we can have an honest discussion about their limitations, what else they need going forward."

"You mean an intervention?" So far, their parents have resisted the idea (which has only been benignly suggested) of moving to a retirement home or even an apartment.

"Call it what you want. But we—" Amy suddenly can't speak because her heart is in her throat. It's Ellen, walking in with an older couple and a teenaged girl who looks…dour, to say the least.

"What?" Natalie's gaze follows the path of her sister's. "Wow. Who's *that*?"

"Who?"

"The woman you can't take your eyes off of, darlin'. Long reddish blond hair? Looks like a model or actress or something? My God, she's a dead ringer for the star of that television show that was on the air a couple years ago. *Nashville*. Dammit, what's that actress's name again?"

Amy ignores her sister and fantasizes about pretending to go to the washroom and then sneaking the hell out of here. Which is not very surgeon-like of her. Or very sisterly. What is she afraid of? Okay, not so much afraid as definitely uncomfortable at seeing the woman she's…screwing…out of context like this. Amy knows she has nothing to be uncomfortable about, has done nothing wrong. Unless… What if Ellen is married? This could be her parents or her in-laws and her child she's having dinner with. Maybe her husband is joining them later. Amy feels sick. *Goddammit. I'm fucking around with a married woman.*

Nat must have noticed the blood draining from her face because suddenly she's *in* Amy's face. "What's wrong? Do you *know* her?"

"No, I, ah…thought I did but…"

Nat gives her a look that says she's gone nuts, but before the conversation can go any further, their food mercifully arrives.

By the time she notices Abby at a quiet table with another woman, Ellis has already ordered her meal and is in the middle of a conversation with her ex's father about the latest dip in the stock market. He's always trying to pick her brain about the markets, assuming because she works in business, has a degree in business and a master's degree in health care management and policy, that she must have some sort of insider knowledge or expertise. He doesn't seem to get, or maybe he doesn't want to, that what she's really good at is finding efficiencies for health care providers. More like imposing them once she identifies where the money can be saved. When budget deficits begin to swell, Ellis is sent in as the pin to deflate the balloon. Messy work sometimes, but she likes to think of it as saving hospitals, clinics, and institutions from self-destructing under their own weight.

"I'm sorry," she says to Ed. "I don't—"

"Man, those cannabis stocks are going crazy lately. I'm tempted to pull out of my Big Pharma investments and go with the cannabis. That's the future. Right, Marjorie? All you have to do is look at all the marijuana greenhouses out in the countryside. They're popping up like weeds!" He laughs at his own joke while Ellis and Marjorie cut furtive looks at Mia, who's staring blankly at a distant wall. Probably high, if Ellis has to hazard a guess. Marjorie, by the look of judgy displeasure on her face, has figured out exactly what her granddaughter does in her spare time. Not Ed, apparently. Ed can't get his mind off the almighty dollar.

That's when Ellis notices Abby at a nearby table. And loses every single thought in her head and anything she is about to offer by way of conversation to her dinner companions. Abby almost, no, definitely, looks like she's trying to hide from her, having angled her chair slightly away from Ellis's line of sight. Except she hasn't succeeded, because Ellis can see Abby and her girlfriend clearly. *Huh.* Why does Abby need these little weekly trysts with her if she has a girlfriend? Or a wife? The idea appalls Ellis. They'd double-checked with one another in their limited online conversations about being single before starting up their...affair. If that's what it is. Abby, like Ellis, said she was single. She lied, obviously. The last thing Ellis wants is some jealous girlfriend or wife coming after her. No, wait. The last thing she wants, truth be told, is a sexually transmitted disease. Followed by a jealous girlfriend or wife. *Jesus Christ, this is a nightmare.*

"So," Marjorie says, glancing nervously from Ellis to Mia. "About this summer."

Ellis can't focus on anything but Abby right now. Is she happy with her girlfriend? She doesn't look it, exactly. They're not touching or acting romantic. In fact, they seem to be in a pretty heavy conversation, judging by the grim expressions, the tautness in Abby's shoulders. Ellis can tell Abby is tense; her neck and shoulders look nothing like when Ellis's lips and tongue are tracing abstract patterns on them. No. Abby is the epitome of a woman in the throes of ecstasy when Ellis is having her way with her. Whoever this woman is sitting across from her, she's definitely not giving her the kind of pleasure that Ellis gives her. *Well, well.*

"Ellis?" Marjorie's voice rises a notch. "This summer?"

"Sorry? What about this summer?" Is it terrible that she wants to slip a note into Abby's hand asking her to meet her in the washroom? She's never had washroom sex before, but for Abby she'd gladly make an exception. Girlfriend or not, Abby is hot as hell, and Ellis knows that resisting her is futile, that her moral objections don't stand a chance against Abby's sexiness, Abby's exquisite lovemaking skills. *Bring it on, sign me up, because I want more of that, consequences be damned!*

"Mia," Marjorie continues. "We were hoping you could take Mia for the summer."

The salacious fantasies in her head come crashing to a halt. "What? Sorry, I don't follow."

Ed looks like he's swallowed something he can't, well, swallow. He leaves it to his wife to pitch the idea to Ellis that Mia stay with her for July and August, as soon as school's out. Which is only a month away. To give everyone a nice change, is how Marjorie words it, but what Ellis hears loud and clear is that it's to give Marjorie and Ed a break from their rebellious granddaughter.

"I, ah…" Jesus, did they have to ambush her like this? And right in front of Mia? "I'd love to, but my job is going to keep me extremely busy. I'm not home until well after six each night and I usually end up working from home on the weekends. I may have to travel a bit as well."

"Mia could easily stay with us when you have to be out of town. And she's becoming quite an independent young woman who can even cook her own meals. Isn't that right, Mia?"

Mia gives her grandmother a death stare before going back to fixating on the wallpaper. Well, that went well. *Not.*

The idea of being saddled with a kid for two months, and a difficult one at that, is not something Ellis wants to commit to. But she understands it must be tough for her ex's parents to be raising their granddaughter at this point in their lives. And then there's Mia. Motherless, father an unknown sperm donor. The kid has no one in this world except for her grandparents. And Ellis. It's what drove Ellis to take the ten-month consulting contract in Windsor with the Essex County Regional Hospital Services Corporation, made her uproot and sell her pricey condo in Toronto. Because she owes Nancy. And Mia. Only took her nine years to figure out that it was time to repay old debts, but at least she's here, dammit. Trying.

She clears her throat, tries to get Mia's attention. "What about you, Mia? What are your wishes on this?"

The kid's eyes widen, the question clearly catching her by surprise. It's like she inherently knows nobody wants to be saddled with her. She shrugs as though her answer doesn't matter anyway. And yet, what could matter more than being wanted or not wanted?

"Whatever," she finally grumbles, and it doesn't fool Ellis, who's inwardly freaking out. She's not prepared to take Mia for nine or ten weeks, no matter how desperate Ed and Marjorie are. She wants to say no. She's still settling into her new job, still in the early stages of assessing this massive review and cost-cutting project that's going to take months. Plus, a full-time kid is absolutely not what she signed up for. She wishes she had someone to talk to about it, people other than Ed and Marjorie, but she's on her own.

"How about this. How about we all think about it, then discuss it again in two or three weeks. We still have a month before school's done, right, Mia?" Cowardly of her, but it's the best she can come up with, especially with Mia sitting right here.

Marjorie answers for all of them. "I think that sounds very doable. Doesn't that sound good, everyone?"

Ellis feels sorry for Mia, having to live with people she doesn't feel close to, who treat her like she's an interloper without wants, needs, opinions. But she can't snap her fingers and fill Nancy's shoes, can't be this girl's mother figure. It sucks that Mia's been orphaned. Sucks too that Ellis was naive enough to think she could step in and somehow help out, that taking the kid out to dinner or a movie once a week could make amends for walking out on her and Nancy all those years ago. Okay, so she underestimated things, but she's here, if not with both feet, then certainly with one. *I'll just have to figure it out,* she tells herself and glances once more in Abby's direction. This time Abby sees her looking, gives her the slightest, most minuscule nod of acknowledgment.

Frosty, if Ellis has to describe the gesture, and she begins to wonder if Abby's coolness will extend to next Thursday afternoon for their third…date? Assignation? Nope, definitely feels like a date, and the tickle in Ellis's throat makes her want to giggle.

CHAPTER FIVE

Amy rushes to the operating suites, where she's been summoned via her pager from the hospital parking lot. Her escape for the day will have to wait, because her gut tells her it's Dr. Don Atkinson who's in trouble. Atkinson, like Amy, is a general surgeon at the hospital. There's only the three of them, but Atkinson has been her albatross for the past few months. Mistakes, tardiness, he hasn't been on the ball, and it looks bad for the entire surgical service. He's only sixty-one or sixty-two, not exactly ancient, but his skills have definitely gone downhill lately.

She curses under her breath as her suspicions are confirmed. Atkinson had been performing an emergency gall bladder removal a little while ago when things began to go south. One big thing, to be exact. He severed the common bile duct, a very serious complication that will make the patient very sick and can even prove fatal. It's the most feared mistake for a surgeon when it comes to a cholecystectomy.

As hastily as she can, Amy scrubs up, steps into the operating theater, and lets a nurse glove her and wrap her in a sterile gown. She glances at Atkinson, who's sweating profusely, but his relief at seeing Amy is unmistakable. She steps up to the table, her eyes finding the monitor Atkinson was looking at while he operated on the patient via laparoscopy. She doesn't need to ask all the details of what happened, not yet. Right now, the patient is the priority.

She takes the tools from his trembling hands, her eye catching a wisp of yellow liquid seeping from underneath the patient's liver.

"I-I don't know what the hell happened," Atkinson sputters. "This patient was such a mess, I couldn't see the field properly. I—"

"Please step back, Dr. Atkinson."

The best thing, the only thing, she can do right now is to drain the leaking bile from the patient's abdomen and complete the removal of his gallbladder, which she does over the next fifteen minutes. She orders a nurse to call the nearest big teaching hospital in London, Ontario, which is a good ninety-minute ride away by land ambulance. The patient is going to need bile duct reconstruction surgery, which she's not prepared to do here because she, the hospital, and its staff are not equipped or trained for such a specialized procedure.

Once her patient is wheeled out of the OR and into the small ICU to await transfer, she takes her colleague aside in the hallway. Not for the big talk that she, as chief of surgery, is going to need to have with him (that will come later, probably tomorrow), but to find out everything she can about the patient before they talk to the family. The patient is a retired cop in his late fifties; an infected gall bladder brought him to the ER earlier in the day, and Atkinson was the surgeon whose turn it was to take emergencies. Amy performed a scheduled mastectomy this morning before diving into a pile of paperwork for the afternoon. If she'd been this patient's surgeon, she too might have made the same mistake, but probably not. She's done hundreds of laparoscopic cholecystectomies and has never sliced through the common bile duct. Atkinson, on the other hand, has made several serious mistakes the last few months. Two weeks ago he perforated his patient's bowel during a regular colonoscopy; a few weeks before that he nicked a bladder. His once solid reputation for competence is increasingly in tatters, his mistakes no longer a matter of coincidence or bad luck. Amy knows something must be going on with him, though now isn't the time to figure out what.

Atkinson remains in denial, a stream of excuses falling from his mouth. "I didn't even feel anything when I cut through it. Somehow I—"

"How well did you prepare the family for complications?"

The better prepared, meaning the more details that have been shared about what could go wrong, the better the bad news will go down with the family. The worst is when the family and the patient are expecting the procedure to be a breeze. And then it isn't.

"I…I told them there's always the risk of complications with any surgery."

"Specifically, did you discuss a severed bile duct as a complication?"

Atkinson is pale. He shakes his head. "I don't think so. I can't be sure."

Goddammit. "All right, let's go find them." Every surgeon strives for that moment of looking into a loved one's eyes and saying that everything went well, that everything's going to be fine. This won't be one of them.

Days later as Amy drives to the city for her weekly rendezvous with Ellen, she's still grumpy as hell and can't shake her bad mood. Dr. Atkinson broke down and cried in her office the day after the botched surgery. He couldn't shed any light on why he's been less than stellar in the OR. Said he's sleeping fine, isn't having marriage or financial difficulties, said his memory is fine, that he doesn't feel unwell. But Amy isn't so sure. His skills might be declining because of his age, but there could be something more sinister responsible. After a private meeting with the chief of staff, the director of human resources, and one of the hospital's lawyers, she was forced to place him on light duties and ordered him to get a full medical workup before he'd be allowed back in the OR. And then she went home and poured a huge glass of wine.

She thinks now of her father, a family practitioner for more than forty years in the town this very same hospital serves. He didn't retire until he turned seventy and only because he too was starting to slip. That was a decade ago and six years before Amy decided to return home and take a surgical position at the hospital. She knows firsthand how distraught her father was at having to give up medicine, how difficult it was to give up something that so deeply defined him. Now he barely remembers that he was a doctor. Could the same thing be happening to Atkinson? She hopes not. Hopes there's a simpler explanation, but regardless, patients come first and she will not let Atkinson become a greater liability. It isn't the lawsuits she is afraid of, but the very integrity of the hospital's surgical service. She's fully aware that small hospitals such as this one struggle to meet targets set out by the government, struggle to keep their accreditation. If a hospital doesn't perform a certain number of particular procedures in a year and perform them well, funding for those procedures can be cut. And if their funding is cut, that means the entire department—the surgical service—is left vulnerable.

She doesn't want to be the kind of hard-ass supervisor who doesn't appreciate what her colleagues might be going through. Doctors aren't machines. People aren't perfect. She knows this all too well. All she has to do is look at her father, at the immense pride he used to have in being a doctor. When Amy was a kid, it struck her that medicine was the noblest profession on earth, that doctors and nurses were true heroes because they saved people's lives. All she wanted to do was to join that elite club. To help people, to be a hero like her dad. No one told her, until it was far too late, about the failures, the mistakes, about the people you can't help or can't help enough, about all the grey areas in a profession she once naively thought was mostly black and white.

Amy pulls into the hotel parking lot, parks her SUV, and sits for a minute, contemplating what the hell she's doing here. First off, she's not really in the mood for sex. Secondly, she's not even sure she wants to keep seeing Ellen. Ellen who's probably married and shouldn't be having hot, dirty sex in a hotel with an almost-stranger. *I'll break it off with her,* Amy decides on the spot. *In person. Right now. I'll tell her that what we're doing is wrong and that we'll never see each other again. There. Problem solved.*

Ellen's ready to confront Abby for lying to her about being single, but she waits until Abby's fixed them a drink first. It's become their little ritual—a Jack and soda or cola, just one drink, and then sex. Except there'll be no sex this time, and this will be the last time they'll have a drink together, though she could use the hit of bourbon before she breaks off this *thing* with Abby. So she takes a long, bolstering sip and gathers her courage.

Abby beats her to it. "So," she starts. "The other night at the restaurant."

Good, Ellis thinks, they're on the same page about this. Maybe Abby will save her the trouble of being the bad guy and confess that she's been two-timing on her girlfriend or wife, that she was wrong to do so, and that they can't keep doing this.

"Was that your daughter with you?" Abby asks pointedly.

"Not…exactly. More like stepdaughter. Mia is her name. She's fifteen."

"And the older couple? In-laws?"

Ellis nods.

Abby has an aha look about her, like she's caught Ellis at something. "Your husband. Or wife. I was expecting them to join your family gathering. Something delay them?"

Ellis is in no mood to humor Abby's poor attempts at an inquisition. "What is it that you're trying to get at?"

"I'm trying to *get* at the fact that you're married and have a family. That we've been…that you've been unfaithful to him.

Or her. With me. And that's not cool, Ellen. I'm not okay with that. I will never be the other woman."

"Wait. What?" *She thinks I'm the one who's two-timing?* Ellis jumps up from the sofa, sets her drink on the coffee table and paces. She tries to keep the anger from her voice but isn't very successful. "You think I'm the one who's married? Who's being unfaithful? What about you?"

"What about me?" Defensive, but then, so is Ellis.

"You lied before, when you said you didn't have a girlfriend."

"I didn't and I don't." Abby gets up and walks over to Ellis, but Ellis can't stand still. Fury keeps her moving.

"It sure looked like a date you were on," Ellis accuses.

"You're changing the subject. And that was my sister."

A leak has sprung in the well of Ellis's anger, but she holds onto every last drop of it. "I'm not changing the subject. You accused me of being married. And guess what? You were wrong."

"All right. So you really are single?"

"Yes. But what does it matter to you?" It's not like this thing they're doing is going to lead anywhere.

"It matters."

"I see. So it's okay for us to show up here every Thursday afternoon and fuck like it's our last day on earth or something when we hardly know each other. And that's okay as long as we're single?"

"Yes. I don't want anyone to get hurt."

Dammit, Abby's being so fucking calm, so reasonable, so infuriatingly in control. And it's in such contrast to the tears Ellis feels pressing behind her eyes. Because you know what? This screwing-a-stranger-in-a-hotel doesn't feel so good anymore. It feels like, okay, they're not lying to a third party, to a spouse or girlfriend or whatever—they've cleared all that up at least—but it sure feels like they're lying to somebody. Because what Ellis really wants, even the pretense of it for ten minutes, is for Abby to care for her. To care *about* her. To not be a stranger. To not have to hide this thing they're doing, to not have it feel so dirty. Perhaps the whole anonymous sex thing has grown old already, but if she's being honest with herself, it's only part of what's bothering her. Hooking up with Abby once a week is every bit as shallow and empty as her pattern of drifting from job to job every year or two, as unsatisfying as moving to different cities and having to travel regularly for business. And then there's the disheartening mess with Mia and Ellis thinking she could repair something that's so obviously irreparable. There's barely anything about her life right now that she feels good about.

"What is it that you want?" Abby whispers, stepping closer. So close that Ellis has to stop her pacing or she'll step on Abby's feet.

"I..." Ellis is being selfish. And weak. She doesn't need anything more from Abby than what she gets. That was the deal, after all, the deal they both agreed to in advance. No-strings sex. And she's not about to try to change the rules now. "Nothing. It doesn't matter." A tear, a single, stupid, betraying tear rolls down her cheek, horrifying her. Pissing her off. She can't even remember the last time she acted so weak in front of anyone.

Abby reaches out a thumb to Ellis's face and wipes the tear away, the act so tender, so kind, that another tear chases the first one down. *Goddammit!* The one thing in her life that was supposed to be uncomplicated is turning out to be anything but.

"It's okay," Abby whispers, and then her lips are on Ellis's. Lips that are as soft as the petals of a rose—velvety with exactly the right amount of moisture. Warm too, and tasting slightly of the honeyed bourbon. Ellis sinks into the kiss and then into Abby's arms. *Yes*, she thinks with relief and wonder. *This is exactly what I need because it feels...safe, reassuring, perfect in its own uncomplicated way.* Abby deepens the kiss, tightens her embrace, and Ellis has never wanted another woman this way, this much, before. It's as though Abby is some kind of lifeline and Ellis, Ellis who doesn't normally need lifelines, is grabbing on with all her might.

Abby's voice is against her ear, sending warm pulses up and down Ellis's spine. "You feel so good. I want to touch you. Can I touch you?"

Something bursts inside Ellis. Something warm and full of want. "God. Yes, please. Please touch me."

"Here?" Abby's mouth slides down to her throat, sucks gently.

Ellis's eyes snap shut. She wants all her powers of concentration on what Abby's doing to her. "Yes, there."

Abby unbuttons Ellis's blouse as her mouth trails kisses down her chest. "Here too?"

Ellis swallows, can barely speak. "Yes. More."

Her bra is released and Abby's mouth is on her breasts, on her nipples, doing glorious things that make her want to beg. She needs Abby to be the one in charge, and Abby does not disappoint. She backs Ellis up against the wall, hikes up her skirt, and then looks at her with those stormy grey eyes that pose a question, as though she doesn't entirely want to assume what Ellis wants. Ellis nods because she can't speak.

Abby unceremoniously drops to her knees, pulls Ellis's panties down—bright red silky ones that Ellis figured would be a waste of time because they were supposed to be ending this little affair. Except they aren't doing any such thing now, and all Ellis can think about, can anticipate, is Abby's mouth on her. Oh, she's so wet already, vibrating like a tuning fork, and then Abby's tongue finds her. *Yes yes yes yes.* Abby's giving it to her with her mouth—sucking, licking, running her tongue over her clit fast, then slow, then fast again, then mashing her mouth against her. Ellis puts her hand against the wall for support. *This whole oral thing, Jesus, what a surprise,* she thinks, *what a fucking spectacular surprise!* And Abby, of course, is as adept as this as is she is with her hands.

Ellis gives herself over to the power of her arousal, to the pure bliss, the joy Abby's mouth offers. For a moment she's untethered from everything: from the stresses of her job, the stress of Mia, even this room. She's floating, her body turning to something intangible, something fluid, with a kind of abandon she hasn't felt in years. And then her orgasm sends her ever higher before it crashes over her, through her, bringing her back to the present with an insanely pleasurable jolt. She has to work at keeping her knees from buckling, moves her hands to Abby's shoulders not only for support but because she needs to touch Abby, needs to dig her fingers into the muscles below her collarbone, needs to root herself.

Abby looks up at her with a grin that's not so much cocky as knowing. "Was that okay?"

"No. It was a thousand times better than okay. Come here." Ellis pulls Abby to her feet and steers her toward the bed, holding her hand. "Now that we've broadened the menu, I can't wait to sample you."

Abby laughs, and it's the most relaxed Ellis has seen her. They've come a long way from their first time, when they were all nerves and lame bravado. She takes her time now removing Abby's clothes. She wants to savor every second of this, wants it to be enough to help get her through the next week.

CHAPTER SIX

Amy has had to fight to keep her Thursday afternoons and evenings free, thanks to Dr. Atkinson being on the shelf while the hospital figures out what to do about him. Amy knows it means he'll probably be given a no-refusal incentive to retire, and then it will be more months before a replacement is hired. She and the other general surgeon on staff, Judy Warren, are picking up the slack, doing the work of three. And it couldn't come at a worse time. On Amy's to-do list is figuring out how to get more help for her parents because there's not much more she can give. She's used to not having a life for herself, but she won't—can't—give up these Thursdays with Ellen. She can't even say why. Sex is a big part of it, and while it's good sex, Amy has gone months, even years without sex. She and Ellen hardly even talk, know almost nothing about one another, and yet... their time together represents something precious, something weirdly necessary to Amy. It feels like some crucial connection to the outside world—to sanity—that she can get nowhere else, while at the same time it's a cocoon that's anything *but* a connection to the outside world. It's her salvation, the thing that reminds her she's human, and she's pretty sure Ellen feels the same way.

She thinks back to their last assignation two days ago, when Ellen had looked at her with such need, with such raw emotion, it had set Amy's heart thudding like a runaway motor. Ellen had even shed a few tears, and the display reached in and touched something inside Amy that had gone dormant. For that moment at least, she'd wanted to be Ellen's rock, Ellen's comfort. Wanted to soothe and pleasure her, and she'd done so, using her mouth on Ellen for the first time. They were both single and otherwise celibate, so it was safe, or reasonably so. And oh, how sweet Ellen had tasted, how intensely she'd responded to Amy's lovemaking. And when Ellen had made love to her, using her mouth as well, Amy had completely let herself go, holding nothing back. The resulting endorphins had made her fall asleep afterwards, and she'd awakened an hour later in Ellen's arms. Ellen's warm, soft arms. And to those green, misty eyes, there to catch her. It was too much, too wonderful, and Amy resorted to cowardice, muttering a lame excuse for having to rush out.

If Ellen was hurt by Amy's quick exit, she covered it well, but there was no mistaking that something of a deeper dimension had begun inserting itself in their time together, a bond that went much deeper than sex. If it got much deeper, there was no question Amy would have to end things. Oh, she'd had the kind of love people dream about, beg for, spend all kinds of time and money and energy trying to find. And keep. The rush of excitement, the endless string of sacrifices you make without thinking or caring, the branding of your soul that is both thrilling and terrifying. Oh, she'd had it once. And it'd nearly destroyed her. She would not be somebody's rescuer again, and the thing is, she knows so little about Ellen. Does she need rescuing? Saving? Amy's too good at doing the saving, and that's the problem.

The pager on her hip chimes, saving her from further brooding. She's the surgeon on call for the weekend and has already repaired a man's thigh ripped up from the slip of a circular saw. So much for her plans for a quick visit with her parents followed by a quiet dinner at home.

"What have you got?" she says into the nearest wall phone. A seven-year-old boy, the nurse explains, shot in the head with a .22 while he and another boy were playing with a gun they'd found in a barn. ETA five minutes out.

She spies her young resident, Erin Kirkland, exiting a patient's room and flags her down. "Come with me," Amy says, explaining the case while they sprint down a set of stairs, her voice echoing in the cinder block void. Mike Connors is the ER doc on duty today, but a case like this demands all hands on deck. Mentally she goes over what she knows about neuro and about gunshot wounds to the head. She did a year of trauma surgery at St. Mike's in Toronto as part of her surgical training, plus another year as a surgical fellow at Cook County Hospital in Chicago. But those two hospitals have experienced neurosurgeons on staff. Such specialized help for her now is in the city of London. Windsor, a little less than an hour's drive away, has neurologists on staff but no neurosurgeons. Air ambulance is an option, but you don't get a chopper in the air in ten seconds. The bird also has to come from who knows how far away, since none are stationed locally. She is going to have to be it until a transfer is available.

Erin. Right, she's the mom of a toddler, so this case won't be easy for her. She's already pale and her voice trembles when she asks Amy questions. Amy places a steady hand on her forearm. "This kid needs our help, okay? We need to be at our best today, because we're all he's got right now. Focus on what we can do, not on what we can't do."

His name is Jeffrey. He's unconscious, and Dr. Connors is in the process of placing a tube down the boy's throat, which will be connected to a ventilator. Amy takes a turn listening to the patient's lungs—breath sounds on both sides, which is good. But his blood pressure is low and his pulse fast and thready. He looks so small. And so pale. Like he's waiting to die. Connors gives her the slightest shake of his head. He doesn't think the boy will make it, and Amy can't disagree. But they're not giving up.

"Have you alerted University?" she asks Connors. University Hospital - London Health Sciences Center has the expertise and the equipment to give the boy a fighting chance. Connors nods, says the medevac helicopter team has been placed on standby, but they won't make the trip here and transfer Jeffrey until he's stable.

Abby carefully examines the child's head. There's a small entry wound on one side, a much larger exit wound on the opposite side. Each hole oozes a darky, gooey substance that is blood and brain matter and bone. *Shit.* She pinches the skin on the boy's chest to see if he reacts. Nothing. Next, she lifts each eyelid, shines her pen light in each eye. There's no reaction. *Double shit.*

"CT is ready for him." It's Amy's friend Kate, who has answered the all-hands-on-deck code and come to help.

Amy, Connors, Erin, Kate, and another nurse rush the bed to diagnostics, where the CT scanner resides, then step out to let the technicians do their job. Jeffrey looks so vulnerable, so tiny, Amy thinks as she watches through a window. If she had to operate, she could, but it's a neuro case and a pediatric one at that. Her ego is healthy enough, but she's a realist, and she understands that the kid's best chance of survival does not lie with her. She'll do everything she can to help stabilize him, and if he doesn't make it, she knows she'll still find a way to blame herself. She's not one of those surgeons who can file away every unsuccessful case, who can move on simply by propelling herself onto the next case and the next and the next. She'll mull over every tiny detail for days, examining what she might have done differently, what she could have and should have done differently. It's always been her way.

For now, though, there's a kid fighting for his life. As his scan images start popping up on the computer monitor, she can see bullet and bone fragments traversing the brain from side to side. Not good, but not the absolute worst she's ever seen, though she's only ever seen adults with gunshot wounds to the head, not kids. She explains to Erin, Erin who's clearly struggling to keep her composure, what they're looking at.

Kate tugs on Amy's sleeve. "The helicopter's grounded now because of the storm coming in."

"What storm?" Amy says absently. She's so focused on the patient that she's momentarily forgotten what day it is, let alone the weather.

"A bad storm's minutes away. Coming in off the lake."

Connors says the neurosurgeon from London is on the phone and wants to speak with her. He's already seen the scans, thanks to a secure network between hospitals across the province, where doctors can tap into patients' test results in a matter of seconds, no matter which hospital they're in.

"You're going to have to do it, Dr. Spencer," the neurosurgeon says flatly. "This isn't going to wait a few hours. I'll be on speaker and I can walk you through it."

Amy swallows against her dry throat, against the momentary rise of panic in her chest. The boy's vitals are worsening—his oxygen saturation level is dropping and so is his blood pressure. The London doc is right. Jeffrey won't survive a land transfer and can't wait for the helicopter to be cleared. "All right," she says into the phone and motions to Erin that she'll be scrubbing in. Erin looks like she wants to flee, but she doesn't. Extra points to the young resident for hanging in there.

Twenty minutes later, scrubbed and prepped, it's Go Time for Amy, Connors, Erin, Kate, an anesthesiologist, and an OR technician. The London surgeon remains on speakerphone, telling them that the situation is extremely grim, that generally speaking gunshot wounds that cross the midline of the brain are almost always lethal. But he adds that it's a small caliber bullet, and since the boy is so young, his chances of survival are better than most. Treatment has to be aggressive, he cautions. Amy isn't afraid of being aggressive.

For the next two hours, she carefully removes portions of the boy's skull on both the left and right sides, then meticulously removes the tiny burned and pulverized bits of irreversibly damaged brain tissue. She irrigates the bullet's path with saline solution, thinks how surreal it is as she watches the liquid pour out the exit wound.

"Doing okay?" she says to Erin, who's even paler than she was a half hour ago.

Erin nods. "What happens next, Dr. Spencer?"

The boy's brain is extremely swollen and angry looking, given the trauma it's sustained and continues to sustain from Amy's instruments. It looks like rising bread that's expanded beyond its bony confines. "We won't get the pieces of skull back on for some time. Not until the swelling is gone."

Kate whispers close to her, "Good job, Doc. He's a tough kid."

Amy passes her friend a look that says "I hope it's enough." Hope is always the final tool in her tool kit, after she's exhausted everything else.

An hour later, Amy sags against a stairwell wall, the cinder block rough against her thin cotton scrubs. She wipes her sweaty forehead, cheeks, with the back of her hand. It's up to the boy now, or some divine being, if he's to survive. She tells herself this but doesn't entirely believe it. There's always something else that could have, should have been done. Had they dithered too long deciding whether to transfer him or keep him here? Had she excised too much brain tissue? Not enough? Nicked something she shouldn't have? Taken too long in the OR, where his exposed brain might have picked up an infection? And if Jeffrey does survive, how much function will he regain?

In an instant, she's back into that rabbit hole of guilt and uncertainty and self-flagellation that she learned so well—too well—from her years with Lisa. She can still remember how, blind with exhaustion from the endless hours of studying, she'd help Lisa study, because Lisa would have probably—no, definitely—bombed out of med school much sooner without the crutch of Amy there to help her. There were times she'd beg Lisa to get off the couch and see a counselor when depression and inertia kept her there for days. Hiding Lisa's liquor bottles, flushing her pot down the toilet and whatever else she was using to self-medicate. Taking notes for her when she couldn't drag herself to class. But nothing worked for very long, and so Amy would aim higher, vow to do more—sacrificing sleep, sacrificing friendships, shutting everything out but Lisa and her own school work. But nothing seemed to halt Lisa's spiraling or Amy's quiet desperation. Mental illness doesn't fight fair—it's a hell of an opponent and one Amy wishes she'd never had to go up against. She vividly remembers the day she decided she could no longer be with Lisa. She literally woke up one morning and couldn't move, could barely breathe, just lay there curled up like a bean as she saw herself becoming a carbon copy of Lisa. Saw her dreams of becoming a doctor going quickly down the toilet. It scared her so badly that when she could finally get up, she called Lisa's parents and asked them to come get her. And they did, all the way from the west coast. It was the last time she ever saw Lisa.

Until then, Amy had never quit anything. Her problem, she knows all too well, is that she doesn't know when it's time to stop trying. When it's time to pull the plug.

* * *

Ellis sits down at her desk for the first time all day and pulls up a house rental website. She was told in a meeting this morning that as her project becomes more intense over the next few months, more of her time will have to be spent in a small town on Lake Erie, almost an hour's drive away. And while she could simply keep residing at her rental apartment in Windsor, the idea of a nearly two-hour round-trip commute each day, on top of long work hours and on-site meetings, is less than ideal. Moving certainly won't be as convenient for making her Thursday afternoons at the hotel with Abby. Hell, that should be the last thing on her mind, but it isn't. Spending a couple of hours in bed with Abby once a week has become her week's highlight, the thing that keeps her sane or at least her stress levels manageable. It's been the one thing she looks forward to. No matter what she has to do, she will keep those appointments with Amy. Or as many of them as she humanly can.

Her cell phone chirps. She decides to ignore it until she glances at the screen to see who's calling. It's Marjorie Hutton, Mia's grandmother. *Shit, now what?* she wonders with only a modicum of patience. Then she remembers they still haven't resolved the issue of who Mia will be staying with this summer.

"Hello, Marjorie," she says into the phone. "How are you? Is something wrong?"

"Something's wrong, all right." Marjorie's voice is pitched with exasperation, a breath away from tears.

"Oh no, is Mia okay?" *What the hell has that kid done now?*

"No, Ellis, she is not okay. We're at the police station. She's been arrested."

Aw fuck. Immediately, she thinks it must be the pot Mia's been caught with. "What happened?"

"Shoplifting. A leather bracelet or something and some other stuff. Plus...she had a joint in her pocket, Ellis. A joint, for God's sake. Marijuana!"

"Is she being charged?"

"I...yes, but the police seem to think that because of her age, there's some sort of diversionary program so she won't end up with a record. Ellis..." She can hear Marjorie suck in a deep, ragged breath before whispering frantically into the phone. "We need your help. Please. We don't know what else to do. You've got to help us."

"I understand, Marjorie." *Goddammit.* Of course Mia has done something to draw attention to herself, to cry out for help. The kid is a mess and probably in much more need than Ellis and certainly the Huttons can give her. Ellis's first urge is to run away. Again. Use her career as an excuse. Like always. To say she's sorry but she can't help.

Before she can utter a refusal, she pauses to wonder what Nancy would do in this situation. Nancy, who doted on Mia, who protected her and sheltered her and loved her. They both had, in the three years Ellis was part of their lives. She remembers how Mia would reach for her hand before crossing a street. How Mia wanted Ellis, and not her mother, to teach her how to ride a bike. It'd nearly cut her in two the day she explained to Mia that she had to leave, that her mother and she couldn't be together anymore. Six-year-old Mia had cried and cried and then refused to speak to Ellis ever again.

Ellis knows she's being a coward and that she's scared. But Mia doesn't have her mother anymore, and her grandparents are most definitely in over their heads. If she doesn't at least try, Mia will surely end up on the trash heap of lost causes—she's well on her way to it now. "What do you need me to do?"

"Will you come with us before the judge next week?"

"Yes. Absolutely." She'll figure out a way to clear her schedule.

"And…"

"Yes?"

"Ellis, we really need you to take her for the summer." Marjorie's voice hitches. "We…it's too much for us."

Well, Ellis thinks, at least's it out in the open now, the fact that Mia's grandparents are abandoning her, too, for the summer at least, and that Ellis is the girl's only recourse. She wants to protest, to say she didn't sign up for this, but instead she sighs in resignation. She may have walked out on Nancy—and Mia—all those years ago, but she won't walk away this time. Walking away is getting damned exhausting. "All right, Marjorie. All right. Text me when you know more."

CHAPTER SEVEN

"I'm so very sorry, ma'am, but there's a plumbing issue on the ninth floor and we've had to evacuate everyone."

Oh please no, no, no, Amy thinks. Not on a Thursday afternoon. She needs this today, needs this pleasurable escape more than she's needed it at any time in the last three weeks. "Um, I'll take another room on a different floor please," she tells the desk clerk, who frowns immediately and shakes his head.

"I'm afraid we don't have any other free rooms right now. There's a big convention in town. But you're welcome to wait. It shouldn't be more than an hour. Ninety minutes at the most."

What if Ellen can't hang around and wait that long? And if she does, what are they going to do while they're waiting? Knit? Play Scrabble? Have a long, personal heart-to-heart? *Absolutely not.* "Thanks," she says to the desk clerk. "I'll let you know what I decide." It's unreasonable, this sudden melancholy over events beyond her control, but it pulls her down like an invisible weight.

She wanders over to the waiting area in the lobby, where she can watch for Ellen. Maybe it's a sign that this whole thing—the weekly trysts—is a bad idea. No, wait. She's a science geek who doesn't believe in signs and all that voodoo. The plumbing issue is a small complication, that's all. And even if Ellen doesn't want to wait around in the lobby until the room is ready, maybe they can get a quick drink or go for a walk—without conversation straying too far into the personal. There must be something amusing or entertaining or interesting they could talk about, because strangely enough, Amy finds herself wanting to spend more time with Ellen, and not just in bed. *Wow, that's new. Seeing Ellen outside of a bedroom?* Her palms turn clammy at the prospect, but there's something exciting about it too.

Before she can obsess over it any further, Ellen walks into the lobby, her thick, wavy hair flowing past her shoulders. Her posture is perfectly straight, her stride purposeful. Amy's gaze drifts down to her long and shapely legs, and she is instantly reminded of how they feel wrapped around her. Ellen, as usual, is dressed impeccably. Tan Capri pants and a silky, short-sleeved blouse capped at the shoulders that perfectly matches the dark mint of her eyes. She's wearing onyx earrings and a slim, white gold watch that says she's a woman who likes nice things, but isn't a showoff.

Amy drinks her lover in, basks in the vision that is Ellen. Just looking at her makes her feel good. She knows she shouldn't, but she lets herself momentarily indulge in the fantasy that Ellen is her actual girlfriend. She draws in a long, slow, deep breath and is shocked by the unexpected jumble of emotions. For a single moment, she wants to be in that place again with a woman where there are no pretensions. No pretending. That place where she can be herself, where she can let everything out—fear, joy, frustration, her dreams, her disappointments—without fear of censure or condemnation or even disinterest. That place where she can be accepted, loved, protected, understood, known. If there ever is a next time, it'll have to be with someone who's an equal, who's every bit as strong as Amy, who's happy to take her share of the load. Months of counseling after ending it with Lisa had taught her that much, except she's never been brave enough to actually look for such a woman. *Do they exist?*

Ellen sees her, smiles, and strides over. "Hi! Everything okay?"

Amy explains the situation, and Ellen's look of disappointment heartens her, because she can't bear Ellen turning around and walking out like it's no big deal. She suggests a drink in the hotel bar, and Ellen goes for it, making Amy smile for the first time in hours.

Heads turn in their direction as they take a seat in a corner booth. They're looking at Ellen, Amy knows, although she supposes her own height of almost six feet is partly the reason. In her scrubs or with a stethoscope around her neck, she's used to people looking at her. Looking *to* her. It's in a hospital that she's most comfortable, most confident, most assured of her authority and her abilities. Out in the civilian world, she's never been accustomed to being the center of attention and prefers the refuge of anonymity. She's glad Ellen is next to her. Ellen, whom the spotlight seems to so effortlessly find and to whom anonymity is probably foreign.

The server asks them what they'd like to drink. Amy orders a glass of Chablis, while Ellen says she's feeling a little adventurous and orders a cosmopolitan.

The way she says "adventurous" and the way her eyes sparkle like sunshine dancing on a mountain river make Amy's heart skip a beat. There are freckles, very faint ones, sprinkled across her nose in a random pattern. They're cute. They're *adventurous*. So is the faint scar near her eyebrow. In combination, they make Amy want to get to know this woman, really get to know her. How did she acquire that scar? And did she always have freckles? She doesn't even know Ellen's actual name. And she wants to know, but she won't risk jeopardizing what they have. Honesty is too risky for them. Honesty might lead Amy out onto that limb that so terrifies the crap out of her.

"So," Ellen says. "How was your week?"

Terrible, Amy thinks, but she shrugs and says it was okay.

Ellen shakes her head. "Mine totally sucked."

Ellen's candid answer makes Amy sit up a little straighter. "Oh? I'm sorry to hear that. Actually, mine wasn't so great either."

Okay, now what? How far should they go with this little conversation? Amy wants to tell Ellen about all of it—her fellow surgeon, Atkinson, how's he's been unraveling and now the whole department is in chaos. And then there's her young gunshot patient, Jeffrey, and how touch-and-go that situation was. He's still recovering in ICU, too fragile to be transferred to hospital in London yet, but with luck he'll be able to make the trip in a few days. Of course, his future is still bleak, and she worries for him. Underscoring everything is the constant concern for her elderly parents. Yesterday they rejected the idea—again—of trying out a retirement home. But she won't say any of this to Ellen.

"How about this?" Ellen says. "Tell me one thing that happened this week that made you smile or feel good."

You, Amy wants to say but is too chicken. "That's easy. My best friend Kate, she's, like, the DIY queen of everything. She made these fabulous CBD-infused bath bombs for me. Lavender and tangerine. I almost didn't get out of the tub last night."

"Oh, God, I think I would die for one of those right now."

"I can bring you a couple next week."

"Really?" There's a look of surprise in Ellen's eyes, as though she's amused that they're talking about something as ordinary as bath bombs.

Well, Amy thinks, *I can't quite believe it either.* "Okay, your turn. Something that made you feel good this week."

"That's easy because there was only one thing. The new book I started reading. It's soooo good. So of course I had to go and order all the other books the author's written."

Their drinks arrive and they clink glasses, engage in a little game of rapid-fire questions and answers. Favorite book, favorite author, favorite movie, favorite actor, favorite music, favorite city. They're so caught up in the conversation that when their server presents them with a note from the desk clerk saying their room is ready, they don't immediately act on it.

"How did you get that scar?" Amy bravely asks. "The one over your left eyebrow."

"Field hockey. Got clipped by the ball. Bled like crazy. Hurt like crazy too."

"You played field hockey?"

Ellen looks amused by Amy's surprise. "Many years ago. In university. It happened in the provincial championship game. Had to sit out until they stitched it up because you're not allowed on the field if you're bleeding. Boy, I was some pissed off about that."

The vision of Ellen—tough, strong, athletic, competitive—is an epiphany that leaves Amy nearly blind with desire. And admiration. "Let's go, shall we?"

Ellen smiles, stands up, and there's an instant charge in the air—the anticipation of shedding clothes, of skin sliding on skin, of lips and tongues dancing over soft, wet places. Amy knows that she'll come the instant Ellen touches her.

Ellis is so wrung out from pleasure that she doesn't want to move. Sheets are tangled around them. The smell of sex lingers in the air. Abby is on her side, curled up against her. Ellis can't see Abby's eyes, but she can feel her looking at her.

"That was so good," Ellis murmurs, thinking Abby must be staring at her because she's waiting for confirmation that the sex was, as usual, off the charts. Which it was.

"You," Abby says in a voice low and thick with wonder and want, "are so lovely." She runs her fingers through Ellis's hair in that unmistakable way that says she's in full admiration mode. In awe of *her*. The urge to grab Abby's hand and hold it nearly overwhelms Ellis, and she silently commands her thumping heart, which she is sure will betray her any minute, to settle down. Abby can't possibly be in awe of her. Can't possibly be falling for her. It's the sex talking, she tells herself, because it's impossible that this is becoming something more. Ellis isn't so good at the *something more* with women.

"And you know what else?" Abby says with a smile in her voice.

Ellis turns her head to stare into those sex-hazed eyes that are as tender as a caress, the color of a cloudy sky post-storm. She can't even remember the last time a woman looked at her like she was worthy of being worshipped. "What?"

"You're a nice person, you know that?"

Ellis almost laughs. "No."

"What do you mean, no? I'm a pretty good judge of character. And you are a lovely person. I can see it in your eyes and I can feel it in your touch. I'm glad to know you."

Ellis's voice is harder-edged than she intends. "You don't know anything about me." *You don't know how I walked out on Nancy and Mia because I didn't want to be tied down, because I valued my career more than I valued them. You've never seen me walk into a boardroom with a stack of severance checks as high as the ceiling.*

Oh, the things she's done…if Abby knew, she wouldn't be here right now, and she certainly wouldn't be looking at her like she's something special. The fact that Ellis is trying to make amends with Mia, that after the current contract she's on, she's going to look for something more stable, more noble, less transient, vicious…well, Abby doesn't know about any of that. And even if she did, it wouldn't undo the shameful things Ellis has done in her past. *We're all a product of our past, with no escape from it*, she realizes. The question she's never been able to answer is how much should she let her past define her. How much leverage she should let it have over her life now. Can she really change her future? Remake herself? Abby makes her think it's possible.

"I know enough."

"Abby…" How does she even address this when they can't intimately talk about themselves? *Ah, maybe that's the whole point,* she thinks, as a sense of foreboding begins to form a hard knot in her stomach. It's because she doesn't deserve a real relationship. Doesn't deserve anything more than this superficial hookup with someone who will never know the real her. Who will probably grow tired of her soon. The gift of Abby is meant to be a cruel and temporary one.

She thinks back to the months immediately after she left Nancy. The constant emails from Nancy, the texts, begging her for a proper explanation, imploring her to come back home. And yet Ellis so coldly ignored her. With the barest of explanations, she simply shut the door. Moved on. And now she can't bear to think what a selfish bitch she'd been. Nancy's death forever robbed her of the chance to redeem herself. Trying to help Mia is the only possible road to redemption, and even then… She wipes her cheek with the back of her hand and is surprised by the confirmation of tears. *Why the hell do I always seem to be crying in this woman's presence?*

"Hey." Abby props herself up on an elbow, carefully touches Ellis's wet cheek. "You okay?"

"Yeah, sure. I'm fine."

"You're not…thinking of ending this, are you?"

She doesn't want to, but maybe she should, before things get more complicated, more uncomfortable. "Abby, I think—"

"No. Don't." Abby pulls her against her chest, strokes her head with infinite tenderness. "I don't want this to end. I need this. I need you. Please."

Abby's kisses are urgent, and Ellis feels her self-doubt slide off her like rain on leaves. Oh, yes, she needs this too. She doesn't want it to stop any more than Abby does. A moan escapes her mouth, sending a streak of fire through her veins as Abby's fingers glide over her breasts, linger over a nipple. She might not deserve a relationship, but she can at least allow herself the joy and beauty of what they have.

After they make love, Abby slowly pulls on her clothes and shoots Ellis a grin brimming with mischief.

"What?" Ellis says. She's grinning too. Mostly because she understands now that Abby likes her. Really likes her.

"Do me a favor?"

"Hmm…maybe."

Abby bites her bottom lip, the gesture so adorable that Ellis wants to scoot over to the end of the bed where she's sitting and kiss the hell out of her. "Can I…keep your underwear?"

Ellis laughs softly at the unexpected request. "You want a souvenir?"

"Yes. To get me through until next time."

"I see. And you want me to go commando until I get home?"

Abby blushes, but it's obvious she's not at all sorry. "Commando, huh? Now I have a whole new set of fantasies for my drive home."

Ellis picks up her burgundy, bikini-cut Victoria's Secret panties and throws them at Abby, clipping her in the head.

CHAPTER EIGHT

"Come with me," Amy says to Erin Kirkland, and opens the stairwell door so they can climb to the third floor, where Amy's shoebox-sized office is located.

Erin walks stiffly ahead of her, like she's going to her own execution, and Amy has to stifle a smile. "Don't worry, kid. You're not in any trouble."

Erin's shoulders visibly relax.

Amy halts their progress in the hallway outside her office door and speaks quietly. "We're about to tell the family of our patient, Oscar Flanagan, that there's nothing more we can do for him, and I want you along."

A return to tense shoulders for Erin, but she nods gamely. Amy asks her to quickly summarize the case from memory, and she does. The man is eighty-three years old, resides in a nursing home, is wheelchair bound, and has a litany of health issues: severe arthritis, dementia, a blood clot in his leg. And three months ago he suffered a minor stroke. He's frail and weak. A

CT scan has confirmed that his colon cancer has returned, with several metastases present.

Amy presses. "Knowing when *not* to operate is as important as knowing *how* to operate. Why would it be a bad idea for me to try to operate on the tumors?"

"Because he likely wouldn't survive surgery?"

"Correct. And if he did survive, it would significantly set back his quality of life for many months, expose him to the risk of more blood clots and secondary infections like pneumonia or C. difficile, plus there's little chance I'd get all the cancer anyway. Aggressive surgical treatment in a man his age and with his health complications isn't the way to go here." She's saying it more as a rehearsal because she's expecting resistance. Oscar Flanagan's daughter has refused, twice, to sign a Do Not Resuscitate order for her father.

"Got it," Erin says, following Amy into the office, where Mr. Flanagan's daughter, a nicely dressed, grey-haired woman in her fifties, sits waiting.

Amy greets the woman, extends her hand to her. "I'm Dr. Spencer and this is Dr. Kirkland. Thank you for waiting."

"Maggie Harper." She shakes hands with Amy and Erin. "So is our family doctor right? My dad's cancer is back?" Mr. Flanagan's doctor did his due diligence by referring his patient to Amy, but Amy knows for a fact that the doctor was only following protocol; his note made it clear he shares Amy's view that there is no need for extraordinary measures.

"I'm afraid so, yes." Amy sits down behind her desk while Erin takes the remaining empty chair in the room. "He has several tumors throughout his small intestine. And there's a small shadow on his liver."

"I want you to operate. I want the cancer out of there."

"Ms. Harper, I'm afraid that's not advisable."

"Why, because he's old? Because he might only have a couple more years to live?"

"Age is not the obstacle here. Your father has several chronic health issues. In his weakened state, he most likely wouldn't survive the operation. And frankly, the odds of excising all of the cancer from his abdomen are very slim. It would be a very painful procedure without much, if any, upside."

"Ah, I get it. You're a surgeon and surgeons want the best success rate they can get. You don't want to take on someone who's going to bring your…your stats or whatever down."

"No, Ms. Harper, that's not it at all. I'm a doctor first and a surgeon second, which means I'd love to be able to help your father. I *want* to be able to help your father. But your oncologist and your family doctor can do that best right now. They can keep him comfortable for as long as possible."

"But they can't fix him! They can't cure him."

"No, but chemo, if the oncologist thinks it's advisable, might slow the progress."

"So you're giving up on him!" Maggie Harper shakes her head, unwilling to be mollified. Amy's had patients and family members of patients like this before. They want the impossible. They want herculean efforts, even when those efforts could kill the patient. "You don't know what it's like, Dr. Spencer. You can't possibly understand."

Amy has to close her eyes for a second because she does, in fact, understand.

Two months ago, in a lucid moment, her father began crying, saying he hated getting old, becoming forgetful, confused, waking up to a new ache or pain every day. "A little stiffness, a little fatigue, some forgetfulness, a few aches I can handle. But dammit, Ames, I'm losing who I am. Some days it's like I'm playing a role in a movie or something, that I'm not *me*, that I don't even know who I am anymore, like I'm watching somebody else live my life. I hate it. I hate this."

"Oh, Dad, I hate it too. I don't want to lose you."

"But you will, Amy. You already are. Jesus, I never thought this would happen to me. Nobody does, I guess."

"No, you're right. We think we're going to stay exactly as we are until, I don't know, we die in our sleep or something at a ripe old age." She's seen more than enough in her career to know that such an ending is rare.

"It almost never happens that way," her father confirms. "We both know that. This is what happens if we're *lucky* enough to grow old—a slow, downward slide that begins to pick up speed, and there's not a damned thing you can do except hold on for the goddamned ride and to hope to hell there's a soft landing."

She'd never heard her dad swear so much. "But there's things you still enjoy, right? Like your television shows, your garden, your monthly lunch with the other retired doctors in town, puttering in your workshop."

He nodded slowly, smiled eventually. "You've hit on the nail on the...what do you call it? The nail on the main thing. Joy. Enjoyment." He took his hand in hers. "I've had a lot of joy in my life. I've had a good life, Ames. A great life. Never forget that, no matter how much I complain or no matter how much I...suffer later. It's been worth it."

Recalling the conversation now, Amy is almost brought to tears, except crying in front of a patient or a patient's family member is absolutely forbidden. You don't bring your baggage into the patient's room with you, an early mentor once told her, even though she would love to ask this woman if her father's had a good life, if he would think it's all been worth it.

"I do understand," she says. "I do want to see you and your dad have more time together. Which is exactly why I won't do the surgery." If it were her own father, she'd make the same decision.

The woman looks at Erin, who covers her sudden panic well. "What do you think, Doctor..."

"Kirkland."

"Are you a surgeon too?"

"No, ma'am, I'm in family practice residency."

"Fine. What's your non-surgical opinion of all this? What would you do?"

Erin glances at Amy, who nods at her to go ahead and answer the question.

"All right, well, I completely agree with Dr. Spencer. It—"

"Because she's your boss, right?"

Erin squares her shoulders, sits up a little straighter. "No. I agree with Dr. Spencer for several reasons, Ms. Harper. Your father is almost completely unaware of his surroundings and of what's happening to him."

"But that doesn't—"

"Hold on, please. What I was going to say is this. If he survived the surgery, he wouldn't understand what was happening to him or why. The pain, remaining in the hospital instead of where he's used to living, suffering from potential complications like pneumonia or hospital-acquired infections. All of these things would worsen his dementia as well as give him significant pain. I think surgery in this case might actually hasten his decline. So from a holistic point of view, taking all of your father's other health issues into consideration, it's my opinion that keeping him as comfortable as possible in the remaining time he has left is the way to go."

Maggie Harper's shoulders slump. She stares at her hands in her lap. She's weakening but not relenting.

"Ms. Harper," Amy says, "I know how hard it is to feel like you're giving up or that you're not helping your dad. But you are helping him. And nobody's giving up on him. He deserves dignity and comfort, and that's what we want to do for him."

The woman's shoulders begin to shake. "But I can't let him go."

Amy gets up and comes around her desk to pat the woman on the shoulder. "I know. Which is why I'm going to refer you to the psychologist who helps out at the hospital with grief counseling. Would you take a card if I give you one?"

The woman closes her eyes, nods in resignation.

"Well played, Dr. Kirkland," Amy says minutes later on their way back downstairs. "Very well played. I'm impressed."

"No, it was all you, Dr. Spencer."

"You're wrong. You were great. You gave that woman a perspective I couldn't quite give her. It was exactly what I was hoping for and you nailed it. We made a good team in there, so don't shortchange yourself on the credit."

Kate appears from around the corner, almost knocking into them both. "Who's a good team? I thought you and I were the best team in this place, Doc. Have I been replaced?" She narrows playful eyes at Erin.

"No, Hendy, you haven't been replaced. But our Dr. Kirkland was my ace in the hole for a tricky discussion with a patient's family member a few minutes ago. She's a natural."

Erin's face begins to turn about three shades of pink. Shades that grow darker when Kate begins to tease her that she should consider changing from family medicine to surgery.

"Although I'm not sure there's room enough for two big egos around here." Kate laughs and nudges Amy to show she's joking.

"Careful, Hendy, we don't want to scare Dr. Kirkland away."

"True, that. Hey, listen. I want to have a little barbecue at my place next weekend. Nothing special, just a few people from here. Will you come? You too, Erin?"

Amy jumps at the invitation immediately. She's not working next Saturday, which is a miracle in itself, and she hasn't had a chance to socialize with her best friend in weeks. In fact, she's had zero social life lately, other than her time with Ellen. And the lone dinner date with her sister, but that wasn't exactly relaxing.

Erin stutters, as though she's been backed into a corner and has no idea how to escape. "I...I'd love to but..."

"Really," Kate presses. "I know you're new here and all, but we're actually nice people." She winks at Amy. "Well, most of us, anyway."

Erin squirms some more. "I really would like to, but the thing is, I'm not sure if I can get a babysitter on such short notice. My sister is away this weekend, and my—"

"Say no more." Kate clasps Erin's hand in both of hers. "Bring your daughter. Seriously. It'll be fun. I love kids. Even Dr. Spencer here has a soft spot for kids."

Amy rolls her eyes. Older kids, yes. Toddlers? Not so much.

Erin carefully surveys them both. "Really? You're sure you wouldn't mind?"

"Absolutely not," Kate says. "It would be wonderful."

"All right. Cool. I'd love to get to know more people here, and yet when I get a chance to spend some time with my daughter, I hate to miss out. So this is perfect. What can I bring?"

"Nothing. I'll text you the details later if you give me your number."

"You got it. And thank you."

After Erin departs, Kate clutches Amy's arm like a conspirator.

"What?"

Kate lowers her voice to an insistent whisper. "I hear through the grapevine that our young Dr. Kirkland is into women, did you know that? *And* she's single."

Amy gently shakes her head. "Gee, thanks for the newsflash. And what do you propose I do with that information?"

"Nothing. Except that you're single too. And into women."

"Whoa, wait a minute. Not interested, thank you. And for your information, you're single and into women too." Amy winces a little belatedly. It's the first time she's mentioned Kate and single in the same breath in the time since Kate's wife died. "Sorry, Hendy. I meant no disrespect."

Kate's eyes well up. "I know you didn't, hon. It's...hard to think of myself as single, you know?" It's no doubt why she continues to wear her wedding band on her left hand.

Amy hugs her friend. "I know. And I'm glad you're having this little barbecue. I think we could all use a little something to help us decompress."

"Ames, you're welcome to bring someone, you know."

How she would love to bring Ellen as her date, show her off to her colleagues. Hell, Kate would probably faint upon seeing how gorgeous Ellen is. And how nice she is. But it's way too soon for anything like that. In fact, it's an impossibility, but a girl can dream.

"Sorry, buddy, but I'll be on my own. As usual. And I'm not looking for a hookup, thank you very much." *Already got one of those, and I wouldn't trade her for anything.*

Kate lets out a dramatic sigh. "Fine. Some other lucky woman will have to discover Erin, I guess."

* * *

"All rise."

Ellis and Mia stand as the judge, a short, white-haired woman, enters the courtroom like a black gown-clad tornado. Ellis flanks Mia along with the lawyer she's hired for Mia. They've already had a hearing with the judge, where Mia pleaded guilty to shoplifting; she's been let off on the marijuana charge with a stern warning. Today is the sentencing portion of the proceedings.

"Good morning," the judge says.

"Good morning, Your Honor." Ellis nudges Mia until she repeats the same greeting.

The judge peers over her reading glasses at Ellis and the lawyer. "All right, anything else I should know about before I render my sentence?"

The lawyer clears her throat. "No, ma'am."

"All right then." The judge looks down at the papers on her desk and begins reading out loud. "Mia Hutton, you're hereby sentenced to eighty hours of community service, to be at your probation officer's discretion, but I want that community service to be completed in the next six months over the duration of your probation. You will also reside with Ms. Hall until school resumes in the fall, at which time you will go back to residing with your grandparents. If your grandparents aren't an option at that time, you will come back to me and we'll find a suitable living arrangement for you. Any questions?"

Ellis has already agreed to the conditions, since Mia is a minor. But now she informs the judge that she's planning to move fifty kilometers east, to be closer to work.

The judge looks intently at Mia. "This might actually be good for you to get away from your current influences and habits for a couple of months. A chance to press the reset button, if you will. Do you have any objections, Miss Hutton?"

Mia's trying to look tough, but Ellis can feel her trembling next to her. "No, ma'am."

"Good." The gavel crashes down. "And don't let me see you up on charges again, young lady. Find your path. Choose to do some good in this world. Lord knows, the world needs all the help it can get."

In the car, Ellis tells Mia it will be a big change moving away for a couple of months. She reminds her that there will be house rules and that she'll be away working a lot of hours so there's a trust factor they'll need to develop.

"You don't have to try to be friends with me, Mia, or even to like me very much. But we're going to have to figure out how to live together for a little while. And that means respecting one another. Being respectful of one another, abiding by rules. Do you think you can handle that?"

Mia nods.

Oh, no, Ellis thinks. *What am I getting myself into?* She hasn't lived with anyone in the years since she walked out on Mia and her mom. And now she's going to live with a surly teenager who really doesn't like her very much? But Ellis will find a way. If she can make three-hundred-million-dollar budgets work, she can navigate her way through this too. Plus there's the fact that Mia, like Ellis, is an only child, though little else about their circumstances are the same.

"All right, then. Next weekend you'll come with me to see the place I've put a rental deposit down on. A week after that we can move in, which is perfect timing because you'll be done with school."

Mia sulks the rest of the way home, but Ellis is beyond caring. She's too busy watching the clock on the radio display. In sixty-eight minutes, she'll be in Abby's arms.

CHAPTER NINE

Funny how it takes a couple of days to come down from her Ellen high, Amy muses as she pops a cranberry-brie bite into her mouth (her friend Kate always has the best party munchies). Her head is somewhere up in the clouds, light and floating, because her hotel hookups with Ellen are like a shot of dope in her blood. If she's to parse it out, she can't really say what makes her so happy, so replenished, following these Thursday afternoons. Sure, it's partly the sex. She's come to appreciate how regular toe-curling, skin-tingling sex is good for the soul as well as the body, to the point where she wonders why she didn't embrace regular sex years ago.

But there's more to it than that. There has to be, because she isn't the type to get this distracted, this consumed, this thrilled over sex with someone she hardly knows, almost to the point of obsession. Christ, she's even got those slinky panties of Ellen's stashed under her pillow. Yet this is definitely not about love. She's not *in love* with Ellen because she doesn't know Ellen and hasn't spent enough time out of the bedroom to be seduced by the notion of love. She's also never been one to mistake good sex for love. So what is it, exactly, that has her so enthralled?

Amy decides she's not going to solve this little mystery right now, so she might as well have another drink. And more food. A delectable-looking cheese ball is calling to her.

"Erin," she says on her way to the food table, which is underneath a canopy to keep everything from frying in the hot sun. Kate's backyard has some nice leafy trees that offer shade, as well as a garden with a water feature that looks as if it came from the pages of a gardening magazine, but nothing truly softens the heat from the late June sun in what is the southern-most part of Canada. "I haven't met your little one yet."

A dark-haired little girl stands next to Erin, holding her hand tightly. She looks up at Amy with huge blue eyes that are both curious and shy.

Erin touches her daughter's back encouragingly. "Eliana honey, this is the nice lady doctor I was telling you about, Dr. Spencer. Dr. Spencer, this is my daughter, Eliana."

"Amy, please. No titles today." She crouches down and sticks out her hand for Eliana to shake. "Hello there, Eliana. I'm very pleased to meet you. How do you do?"

The girl stares unblinking at her but dutifully shakes her hand. "Are you my mommy's boss lady?"

"Hmm, well, sort of. I'm more like your mommy's teacher right now."

The girl nods her understanding, then points at Kate, who's materialized behind Amy. "Are you my mommy's teacher too?"

Erin laughs and says to her daughter, "At this point, sweetie, everyone here is my teacher."

"Eliana," Kate says and claps her hands once. "Would you like to come and see the goldfish in the pond?"

The kid lights up like it's Christmas and eagerly takes Kate's hand, any sign of shyness having quickly evaporated. From over her shoulder Kate tosses a daring wink at Amy. *Dammit, Kate, I told you I'm not interested in Erin. Or anyone, for that matter. Anyone except, perhaps, for Ellen. But Ellen isn't here and never will be here or anywhere with me as my girlfriend.*

Without warning comes a flashback of Ellen in bed two days ago, looking at her with eyes all soft and moist with unmistakable tenderness. Ellen looked so content, so happy. And Amy was pretty sure the same look was mirrored in her own eyes. So why not, then, take the next step? What's stopping them from exploring a dating relationship? If there are practical reasons why they shouldn't, fine, but Amy's logical side would like to know what those are. She has her own reticence, thanks to her exhaustingly failed relationship years ago with Lisa, but what's holding Ellen back? Should they at least talk about this? Throw it out there like a math problem to solve?

On the spot, she decides she'll initiate a discussion next Thursday about whether they have a future that involves more than holing up in a hotel room for a couple of hours each week. She's not suggesting anything that involves a U-Haul, but couldn't they talk about the possibility of going out to a restaurant together? Even if only as a hypothetical?

"So," Erin says, and there's the smallest amount of discomfort, of bashfulness, in her tone. "Can I ask you something kind of personal?"

Crap, Amy thinks, *don't tell me Kate has said something to her about setting us up.* The thought horrifies her enough to dispel this little fallacy right now. "Look, Erin. I really like you. You're nice, you're smart, you're gorgeous. But I'm not interested in anything other than a collegial relationship, okay? And it's not you, it's me. I—"

Erin bites her bottom lip, touches Amy's arm apologetically. "I'm sorry. You thought I was going to ask you out?"

Amy wants to die on the spot. She vows to give Kate a good scolding next time she gets a chance, but in the meantime, thoughts of retribution do nothing to arrest her total humiliation. "I, ah, well, I sort of did think that. Jesus, you must think I'm a complete idiot."

"You're not. At all. In fact, you're kind of my hero."

"I am?"

"Yup. If I wanted to be a surgeon, I would want to be exactly like you. You're a good doctor. A great doctor. And an awesome teacher. But I…" Her eyes find Kate, who's at the fish pond with Eliana, bending down and explaining something that has her daughter's rapt attention. Erin smiles nervously and that's when it strikes Amy. *Holy crap.*

"Oh, I see. I… You're wondering about Kate?"

"Sort of. I mean, yes. I am. She's really nice, and has a great sense of humor, and she's a rock star at her job. I'd like to know her better. She's single, right?"

Amy gives Erin a quick rundown on Kate's history—that she's thirty-five, that indeed she is fun and nice and excellent at her job. And yes, she's single, but not by choice.

"I heard something about her wife dying a couple of years ago. How awful. And now you're going to tell me she's not ready to move on with anyone else. Am I right?"

"Yes. I think."

Disappointment falls like a curtain over Erin's face. "Okay, I understand. I won't ask her out."

"That's probably wise. But Erin?"

"Yes?"

"Be her friend. She can always use more of those."

Erin flashes a hopeful smile. "All right. I will."

Kate and Eliana return as if they've been somehow magically summoned.

"Mommy! There's fish in the water. Six of them! I got to feed them and give them all names."

Erin lovingly pats her daughter's head. "That's so awesome, sweetie. Did you thank Kate for showing you the fish?"

"Thank you, Kate!"

"You're very welcome, Eliana. And you're welcome to come visit the fish anytime you want."

Eliana clutches the hem of her mother's shorts and looks up at her with sheer joy. "Oh, can we, Mommy?"

"Yes. We'll visit Kate and her fish again sometime soon, I promise."

Amy sneaks a glance at her unwitting friend, who has no idea that she's cracked the door open to friendship with Erin and her daughter. Amy does a little fist pump behind her back because she would love to see Kate stick a toe in the dating pool. If not now, soon.

"I'm going to go get Eliana something to drink," Erin says. "And Kate? Perhaps after that, you could show me the fish pond as well?"

Ooh, this is going to be fun to watch, Amy thinks with delight. She's even more delighted to see that Erin is persistent, because without a blend of persistence and patience, she won't have a chance with Kate.

"Of course," Kate says, and she and Amy watch Erin and Eliana depart. Kate's eyes drop to Erin's ass, and while Amy is dying to call her friend on it, she won't, because then Kate will get defensive and deny it all out of embarrassment. Better to let her fall into something (or not) with Erin at her own pace, in her own way, Amy decides. But damn, it takes a lot of restraint on her part not to tease.

"Hey, I heard something a few minutes ago that could be big," Kate says, her eyes swinging back to Amy.

"Oh yeah? What?"

"That you have a girlfriend."

Amy's heart squeezes, and not in a pleasurable way. How in the hell has Kate found out about Ellen? And if she knows, does everyone know?

"Whoa," Kate says, her mouth frozen open in shock. "It was supposed to be a joke. Don't tell me I've hit on something?"

"No. You haven't. It's…the heat. I think I need something to drink."

Kate leads her toward the punch bowl that contains alcohol-free sangria. "Sorry, bad joke on my part. You're not, I mean, you don't actually have a girlfriend stashed away somewhere, do you? I mean, Jesus, Ames, you'd tell me, right?"

"Right. Yes. I'd definitely tell you if I had a girlfriend. Stashed away." But not a fuck buddy, a secret lover, a girl toy, a mistress. Because she most certainly does have one of those stashed away.

"Okay, good. Listen, there's a rumor that something's brewing at the hospital. Something big."

"Like what?"

"I don't know. Something about the mother ship wanting to do an audit of absolutely every damned thing at the hospital. If it's true, it can't be good news. You know as well as I do how vulnerable small hospitals like ours are."

It's common knowledge that small hospitals have difficulty breaking even. Births, emergency cases, even surgeries are sometimes sporadic. Serving a smaller population means the hospital can't conduct an assembly line of procedures the way larger hospitals can. The hospital corporation, a county umbrella organization that runs three other much larger hospitals, wants the most bang for its buck. It wants patients in—and out—the doors in turnstile fashion. It comes down to pretty simple math. The corporation, which is reimbursed by the government for all the salaries and all the procedures to keep the place going, even the electricity, wants the hospital run at capacity so that a constant flow of funding is coming in. Not under capacity and not over capacity, but right on the line. Whatever else health care is these days, it's big business, and funding is volume driven. Even Amy, who hates having to think of the business side of it all, understands that.

"Thanks for the heads up. I'll see if I can find anything out on Monday."

* * *

Ellis has to practically order Mia, who's more interested in sitting on the front steps than helping, to carry one of the boxes to the second floor of the house they're renting. It's a large Victorian, their unit completely remodeled inside with two gas fireplaces, granite counters, pristine wood floors, and twelve-foot ceilings. Ellis and Mia have the entire second floor, plus the loft, which Mia immediately claimed for her bedroom. What mostly drew Ellis to the place was the spectacular living room turret, which offers a clear view to Lake Erie a kilometer or so away. It's also walking distance to where she'll be working, and besides, she's never lived in a house that's more than a century old. All of this is so new to her—moving to this area of the country and now living in a town with fewer than eighteen thousand inhabitants—that she figures she might as well make the leap and try living in a very old house. The landlords, who occupy the first floor, are a sweet older couple who have adopted the habit of calling her "dear."

"Do you have a bicycle?" Ellis asks Mia while hauling yet another box upstairs. She wants them officially moved in over the next week. The movers will come in a few days; it's the smaller stuff she figures they can do themselves.

"Yes. But it's dorky."

"Dorky or not, we're bringing it with you. It's how you're going to get around when I'm working."

Mia makes a face. "It's not like there's anywhere to go in this town. It's so frigging small. There's, like, one grocery store? How pathetic."

"There's two actually, and it might be good for you here. The judge seems to think so, and I can't disagree." Fewer ways for Mia to get in trouble, she hopes.

At the mention of the judge, Mia casts her eyes down. *Good*, Ellis thinks. *At least she seems to have some remorse.* "Do you know how to cook?"

"You mean I have to cook?" Mia replies in a voice that sounds like she's being made an indentured servant.

"There will be some evenings when I'll be busy with work, so yes, you might have to cook for yourself once in a while. Your grandmother mentioned that you can cook. I'll make sure the fridge and pantry are stocked."

Mia grumbles, moves with the exaggerated, staccato gestures of someone who's angry or resentful. Ellis can't take it anymore. She sets the box in her arms down and motions for Mia toward one of the chairs at the dining room table—the only pieces of furniture in the place. Mia slumps down.

"Look," Ellis says, keeping her voice calm. "I know you don't like the idea of living here. With me." *I'm not thrilled about it either,* she wants to say, but she's the adult here. "It's the way it is, and we need to make the best of it."

Mia rolls her eyes but doesn't say anything.

"And that means house rules. We talked about that, remember?"

Another eye-roll, which Ellis ignores, because she knows it's for show. Mia has no choice, except maybe going back to the judge, which, clearly, the kid doesn't want to do. Ellis isn't her mother, isn't anybody's mother, but she knows how to take control, how to run people and budgets and corporations. How to get things done. A defiant teenager doesn't stand a chance against her.

"I will have a list of chores for you each day, which must be completed by the end of that day. You will let me know where you are when you're out. If you make new friends, I must meet them. No guests in the house without me having met them first, nor without my permission. You will do your own laundry and keep your room tidy. On weeknights you're to be home by nine o'clock in the evening and in bed by ten. You—"

"Ten! Are you serious?"

"Deadly. Weekends, you can have an extra half hour. You will not smoke pot, ever, while you're living with me, and you will not drink alcohol or smoke cigarettes. And in two weeks' time I want a list from you of places where you might do some community service. Understood?"

"But…but, this is like fucking jail!"

"And you will not, *ever*, swear like that again in my presence."

Mia visibly recoils. And why wouldn't she? Ellis has seen grown men and women sweat and shake, even cry, in her presence.

"I'm not," Ellis says with a huff of breath, "trying to be mean. I want this to work. For both our sakes. But it's going to take work and commitment to make that happen, and we're going to start with talking and acting respectfully toward one another. Because without respect, we're doomed to being miserable and doomed to this whole thing failing."

"What about you?" Mia challenges. "Am I the only one who has to have rules?"

Ellis thinks for a moment instead of lashing out, because Mia has a point. "Tell you what. I'll make sure to keep work at a minimum on weekends. And I'll cook a nice meal for us every Sunday, okay? And if at any time I'm going to be out past seven or eight at night, I'll let you know. Now, is there anything you want to ask me? Because I will always be honest with you, Mia. And I will always answer your questions."

Mia tilts her chin defiantly. She's clearly not ready to make peace yet. "Fine. Why did you even bother coming to Mom's funeral?"

It takes Ellis a moment to recover from the shock of the question. "I…I loved your mom once. She was a good woman. A good mother. I wanted to pay my respects, to remember her."

"Yeah, right. If you loved her, then why did you leave her?"

She knows what Mia's really asking is why did she leave them both. But she can see that Mia is being churlish and in no mood for the truth. Her question is meant to punish Ellis. "We will discuss this one day, Mia, I promise. But not today."

She gets up, opens the nearest window in the faint hope there's a cooling breeze. The loft and her bedroom have window air conditioners, but not the rest of the place. She makes a mental note to buy another air conditioner for the living room. Voices, laughter mostly, drift up from somewhere outside. She peers through the filmy glass (a team of cleaners is due tomorrow) and sees there's a backyard party going on in the house behind theirs. Mostly women, a few men. A barbecue that's smoking away and smelling mouth-wateringly of ribs. She peers closer at the profile of the tall woman with the short, light brown hair. She looks so familiar. Too familiar. The woman turns in Ellis's direction. *Oh, no, it can't be. Could it? Holy shit, it is!* It's Abby, standing talking to two women, one of whom has a small child with her. *What the hell is Abby doing here, an hour's drive from the city? Does she live in this town? In the house right behind me?* If that's not the weirdest coincidence ever, Ellis doesn't know what is.

She feels the blood drain from her face and swears it settles in a leaden pool right in her stomach. Their life together, such as it is for two or three hours every Thursday afternoon, does not—cannot—spill over to the rest of Ellis's life. Well, not if you count the occasional sexy dream or fantasy or that one time when they were each having dinner at that restaurant at the same time. Compartmentalizing is the way they've both planned it—clean, with boundaries, without any strings or expectations or the useless, doomed little what-ifs. This kind of close proximity, she thinks as she watches Abby gesticulate with her hands as she talks, is *not* what they signed up for. This, right here, is the little pin bursting her—their—bubble.

Goddammit, she thinks, and turns her back to the window.

CHAPTER TEN

Amy takes her place at the table in the hospital CEO's massive office. To her left is the chief of staff, beside him is the chief of human resources, then the chief financial officer. The heads of other departments—OB/GYN, emergency, medicine, nursing—fill the remaining chairs, with the CEO and her administrative assistant at the head of the table. The tension in the room makes Amy feel like they've been called to the principal's office.

"I'm sorry about the short notice," says the CEO, a woman in her mid-sixties who can't seem to entertain the idea of retiring. Janice Harrison has been at the hospital seemingly forever, back when Amy's father had privileges here. "But I'm afraid it's important."

Of course it's important, Amy thinks impatiently. They wouldn't all be here if it wasn't.

"It seems that our hospital will be undergoing a lengthy and extremely detailed review and evaluation over the coming weeks and probably months. Which means I want all of you to accumulate and have at your fingertips everything there is to know about your department—the budget line by line, numbers of procedures broken down by month and year, statistics on everything from wait times to how many boxes of Kleenex are in the storage closets, any staffing issues, anything you can think of. And commit it to memory."

So Kate was right. *Shit.* Her mind swings to her own department, because when the hospital is under siege, as it surely will be, she's got to think about protecting her department first. Don Atkinson, now there's a thorn in her backside. His absence from the surgery service is very poor timing indeed. What if the corporation decides it can do without another staff surgeon after all? She puzzles out all the angles and scenarios that might await, the hows and whys, and as she glances around, she can see that everyone else at the table is doing the same—having a dialogue in their head with a slightly panicked, faraway look in their eyes. They're all mentally calculating how bad things might get, how much they might lose.

The chief financial officer, a woman about Amy's age, pushes her glasses up her nose and tentatively raises her hand, like she's unsure she's allowed to ask a question.

"Yes, Donna?"

"Any idea what this is all about? Has it to do with next year's funding?"

They are only three months into the current budget year, with hospital budgets expiring on the last day of March of each year. It seems awfully early to start worrying about next year, though not, Amy supposes, if the audit is going to take months to complete.

Janice Harrison lifts her shoulders in a tight shrug.

Donna instantly pales. Anything to do with funding will be a massive headache for her as the overseer of the hospital's $44-million budget. "It's not about some sort of irregularities in this year's budget, is it?"

"I don't think so," Harrison replies. "At least, there's no indication there are concerns about the current budget."

"Well," grumbles Bob Lakefield, the hospital's chief of staff. "It can't be good news to have the greater corporation breathing down our necks. What the hell are they looking for, Janice?"

They're a pretty tight group, given that their hospital is the smallest one in the region. Most of the staff have worked here for years, have many times been through the nail-biting that happens each year at budget time. But this, this is an entirely different beast, and Amy can feel the hairs on the back of her neck standing up. There have been rumors for as long as she's been here, longer even, that the hospital, because of its size, is in peril. For the first time, it feels like more than a rumor, like something not quite so abstract. The boogeyman is walking up the driveway.

"I can't say for sure, Bob, but I know they're looking at everything with a fine-tooth comb. The CEO of the regional corporation as well as some sort of consultant are coming here this Thursday afternoon to meet with our board, so I'm sure the plan will become more clear at that point." She casts her eyes around the room. "I would like all of you to plan to attend the meeting so that you can hear everything straight from the horse's mouth and be prepared to answer any questions. Meantime, get yourself up to speed on every nook and cranny with your department. I want clean closets, people, no skeletons. If any of you have outstanding parking tickets, pay them. If you have unhappy patients who could be a problem, mollify them. Unhappy staff, order them to get happy. Unhappy spouse, send them on a vacation." She smiles at her last suggestion, but she's the only one in the room doing so.

Amy leans back in her chair, feels her body go a little slack as others shout out pointless questions that can't be answered. She detests this political bullshit. It's not why she practices medicine, yet she also hates leaving her fate in other peoples' hands, which is why she agreed to become chief of surgery. She wants a voice at the table; she simply doesn't want a reason to have to use it.

Amy's phone chimes softly with an incoming message. Discreetly, she removes it from her lab coat and checks the text. It's Ellen (they'd traded cell numbers a couple of weeks ago, to be used only in an emergency, which they'd defined as one of them needing to cancel). *Sorry, can't make it this Thursday*, says the message, accompanied by a sad face emoji. Amy exhales her disappointment. She was going to have to cancel as well, thanks to being ordered to attend this week's board meeting, but dammit! It's the one thing a week that's all hers (well, Ellen's too). It's her only form of self-indulgence, her only escape from the frenetic pace of her life, from the adrenaline and the responsibilities, the challenges, the disappointments, even the victories, of her job. A brief respite, too, from worrying about her parents. And now it'll be almost two weeks before she sees Ellen again.

She fingers the keypad and types back: *Turns out I can't make it either, work issue.* She adds a sad face as well. *See you next week?*

Ellen's reply is instantaneous: *You bet!*

Amy slides her phone back in her pocket. *Fuck me.*

* * *

Ellis pulls into the hospital parking lot, grateful that by the weekend she'll be living within walking distance, since this is where she'll be spending most of her time for the foreseeable future. The hospital is a three-story brick affair, a couple of wings clearly having been added over the decades, if the mismatched brick is any indication. She imagines the hospital as tired inside, of having outlived its shelf life, and she's not wrong. Small hospitals were and still are important community centerpieces, though their role has begun to shift in the past two decades. Where you once gave birth in the same hospital, maybe had a minor surgery or two, eventually died there, that practice has largely disappeared. Health care today means large, sleek, shiny hospitals with multi-million-dollar diagnostic machines and specialties in very specific areas of medicine. Most hospitals can no longer be everything to everyone, a one-stop zone for the sick. It's more fiscally prudent to offer specific types of care because it's cheaper than trying to provide the same equipment, the same training for staff, and the same level of care across the board. Plus specializing offers results with better outcomes, because staff get very good at doing the same thing over and over. You need heart bypass surgery, you go to Hospital A. You need brain surgery, you go to Hospital B. You need to give birth, you go to Hospital C. Need a colonoscopy or a minor procedure, Hospital D is your destination. Simple really, but hugely unpopular among populations that want their hospital to do everything the way they've always done it.

The front lobby looks like it's seen better days—chipped tiles, faded paint. Ellis tries not to form a snap judgment on what the final pronouncement will be on this place, but she's done these reviews enough times to make an early, educated guess. There will be big changes, of that she's sure. And it means she'll have to brace herself against the outcry from staff, from patients, from leaders in the community. Nobody likes having services altered or taken away, especially with something as sacred as health care.

But Ellis hasn't been hired to hold peoples' hands, to make them feel warm and fuzzy. She's been hired to dispose of the hospital's budget deficit by offering up major cost savings, major efficiencies that will chart a sustainable future for the hospital. Politically, it's become absolutely clear that annual funding raises for hospitals of anywhere from three to five per cent, are a thing of the past. First, though, she'll need to work with staff to identify those areas that can be trimmed or even eliminated, and then she'll need to make recommendations to the board.

Ellis glances at her watch to be sure she won't be late for the board meeting. It's exactly the hour when she should be meeting Abby at the hotel. They should be in bed right now, staring out together at the hazy Detroit skyline across the river, aglow from sex. This, she thinks, as she presses the elevator button for the second floor where the boardroom is, is as far from a sexy afternoon as she can get.

Her mind is still on Abby as her heels click down the hallway. She said she would have needed to cancel their rendezvous anyway because of a work issue. What work issue? What exactly does Abby do for a living, anyway? She's imagined everything from lawyer to business owner to professor, and now, of course, there's the added possibility that she lives right here in town, which is way too much for Ellis to consider in her crowded brain. She hasn't seen Abby in the neighboring backyard since the other day, so maybe she was only visiting someone, because one thing Ellis is sure about is that this town is way too small for both of them. Their time at the hotel each week is a place where the outside world stops at the door. Seeing each other outside of that context would be weird…though the idea isn't completely annoying. Could even be fun under the right circumstances.

She opens the door and is greeted and offered a seat between the hospital's CEO and the CEO of the entire umbrella corporation—the Essex County Regional Hospital Services Corporation. There are more than a dozen others around the table, all engaged in quiet small talk, most of them ignoring her.

"My apologies," Janice Harrison, the CEO of Erie Shores Hospital, says to Ellis. "We're still waiting on the chief of medicine and the chief of surgery. Shouldn't be much longer."

The players around the table start fidgeting. Throats are cleared, fingers drum nervously on the tabletop. Finally, a beefy, ginger-haired man in a lab coat walks in, mumbling apologies. Behind him, Ellis glimpses another white-coated figure. Slim, tall, definitely a woman. The ginger takes a seat and Ellis's eyes fall onto… *Oh my God.* Her mouth and jaw are suddenly as fixed as week-old cement because it's Abby, right here in the flesh wearing a white lab coat and looking damned fine. So she's a doctor, a surgeon. But at this hospital? *Oh no.*

She wants to lay her head on the table, opt out of being a grownup, just this once. Somehow she's going to have to forget that it's Abby. Forget it's the woman who has a souvenir of her underwear somewhere…maybe in the pocket of that crisp lab coat for all Ellis knows. *How the hell can this be happening? And how the hell can the world be* this *small?* She tells herself a mistake has been made, because she's seen the list of staff names, and there was no Abby or Abigail. And yet there's her lover's name sewn above the breast pocket of the lab coat: Dr. Amy Spencer. *Wait. Amy?*

Amy can't speak, so deep is her shock that Ellen—no, make that Ellis Hall, according to the introductions—is sitting down the table from her. And trying really hard not to look at her. *Fuck. This* is the woman who has Amy's fate and the fate of the hospital in her hands? This woman with the lush, red hair tied into a French twist down her back and wearing a cream-colored suit over a mint green shell that can't hide her familiar curves? This woman that Amy has made love to every Thursday afternoon over the course of several weeks and who's begun, whether Amy wants to admit it or not, a slow migration into her heart? Her brain processes the situation about as successfully as if there's mud churning inside her skull.

Finally Ellis begins to explain why she's here. She looks around the table as she speaks, levels those same administrative and vaguely condescending eyes on Amy as she does everyone else. But even with her cool authority cloaking her like a veil, she's still gorgeous. Still sex on heels. And Amy can't help but remember the joy she saw in those same eyes the last time they were together. Ellis's vulnerability had also been on full display in bed, whether she intended it that way or not, and Amy can't quite reconcile that with the woman she sees now. This woman who is made of steel. This woman who is all business. This woman who is supremely confident in her abilities and her authority and will not think twice before she lowers the boom on Amy and her colleagues and the patients who need this hospital. This is not her lover. This is her executioner.

Amy feels sick. Because whatever happens in the coming weeks or months at the hospital, she knows one thing for sure: Her affair with Ellis is over.

* * *

Two hours later, Ellis staggers out of the meeting like she's stepping into sunlight after weeks in the dark. She slips out a back door, wanting to avoid running into Abby—Amy—at all costs. Hiding won't last, and she'll have to see Amy eventually, sooner rather than later, because she's going to start meeting privately with each department head. What she knows for sure is she can't face Amy anymore today, because her entire facade of being in control will collapse and she'll be unveiled as… what? As not wanting to give Amy up? Of needing her? Of still wanting her so badly, it almost physically hurts? That's just the personal side of the equation. On the business side of it, she has no idea how she's going to face Amy, given their history together, without her credibility ending up in tatters. How the hell is Amy going to take her seriously after seeing her naked? After…doing amazing things to her while she was naked?

She nearly runs to her car and practically dives inside. *Oh God.* Will Amy tell anyone about them? No way will Ellis be able to work with these people, especially the corporate heads who've hired her, if word gets out that she's been sleeping with the Erie Shores Hospital's chief of surgery. Everyone will assume there's a conflict of interest, that Ellis is incapable of being objective, incapable of doing her job. Christ, what a nightmare. She might not even be able to work in the business of health care again if this gets out. Not that she's done anything technically wrong. But to the outside world, what does hooking up with a stranger for casual sex say about her judgment? About her morals? About her reliability? Ellis rests her forehead on the steering wheel, unable to decide which she feels most like doing, crying or throwing up.

And then the obvious hits her like a sledgehammer. She'll have to give Amy up permanently. Immediately. And goddammit, she doesn't want to.

CHAPTER ELEVEN

"So when's your meeting with Dragon Lady?"

Kate pops a coffee pod into the Keurig machine in the staff lounge before looking expectantly at Amy. There's no separate lounge in the hospital for doctors, since there's usually only ever three or four around at any given time and sometimes only a couple. Amy likes it this way. Doctors who only hang out with each other can get too insular in their thinking, too socially incestuous.

"Dragon Lady?" *Oh, right, Ellis.* With the name recognition comes the heat crawling furiously up her neck and into her face. She hopes Kate doesn't notice. "Monday."

Kate removes her cup and slides one in for Amy, then throws another pod into the machine. "I hope you can talk some sense into her. These bean counters don't give a shit about the patients, they're only looking at numbers."

Amy winces. She hopes Ellis isn't like that, but it's more than likely that she's exactly like that. *Ellis.* She still can't get used that being her name, nor can she get used to the idea of

Ellis determining her fate, as well as the fate of her colleagues, her patients, the hospital. "Maybe she'll be different." *Please let her be different.*

"Yeah, right. They never are."

Kate is pretty much a pessimist. Or at least she has been since her wife Anne's death. Amy wishes there was something she could say or do to make Kate happy. She's been able to cheer her up occasionally, make her smile and even laugh, though laughing is rare. But happy? Not a chance.

"Maybe they won't beat us up too bad," Amy says for her own benefit as well as Kate's. "Nobody's told us what the end game is, so until then, I don't want to think the worst." If she lets herself think the worst, she'll start thinking Ellis somehow betrayed her, duped her. She doesn't want to think that, because for as long as she can, she'd much rather hold on to the fantasy that Ellis is an incredible, lovely, sexy, gorgeous, kind, and caring woman who's a firecracker in bed and who cares for Amy and would never do anything to hurt her or cause her trouble. It might be Pollyanna bullshit, but she needs, for now, to believe it.

Kate, however, is not wearing the same rose-colored glasses. "You'll fight to keep us the way we are, won't you? To keep the staff and services we have?"

Amy retrieves her coffee mug from beneath the machine and takes a sip. Not gourmet, but definitely better than the coffee in the cafeteria. "Of course I will. I'm sure they'll look at everything equally, though OB and the ER might be in for a rough ride, if I'm being completely honest." Dozens of hospitals across the country have eliminated birthing services over the past decade.

"I know our birth numbers have been trending down the last few years. But dammit, Ames, if they start closing the ER on weekends or overnight, people will die. Look at your brain injury boy, Jeffrey. He wouldn't have made it if our ER hadn't been available."

Amy shakes her head. "I'll do my best to see that we keep what we have. We all will. But…"

Kate's not letting it go. She's getting worked up. "If they shut down our OR's, I'll have to move. I don't want to switch to another specialty. I won't do it."

"You won't have to. Our operating rooms are busy. They'd be stupid to shut them down or even to scale them back."

Kate passes her a look that says nothing would surprise her. "Hey, I've got an idea. You're single. And cute."

Amy nearly drops her cup. "Excuse me?"

"Dragon Lady. And you." Kate's laughter is conspiratorial. "Maybe you could seduce her and sweet talk her into going easy on us."

Amy sloshes coffee over the rim of her cup. "Dammit."

"Whoa, a surgeon being clumsy? I hope you don't have anything serious on your schedule today."

"Very funny, Hendy."

"So you don't like my little seduction idea? You gotta admit, Ms. Hall is pretty goddamned hot. If you're into the domineering type, that is."

Domineering? Not in bed, she isn't. Ellis is putty in her hands in the bedroom. *Crap.* She knows she's brighter than a fire truck right now. And Kate's looking at her like she's grown a second head. She swallows the dry lump in her throat. "What?"

"Aha! You think she's hot, don't you?"

"Come on, this isn't high school."

"No, but sometimes it's like *General Hospital*." Kate smiles around the rim of her cup. "Your secret's safe with me. I won't tell anyone you think Dragon Lady's attractive."

Amy rolls her eyes and tries to think of a sassy retort when Erin saunters in. "Oh-oh. Am I interrupting anything?" Erin asks.

"Not at all." Amy plucks a small ball of string from the pocket of her lab coat and tosses it at Erin, who deftly catches it. "Nice hands. Speaking of which, the string is to practice tying some different knots. We've got the basic square knot, the two-hand tie, the one-hand tie, and the instrument tie. Grab a seat and I'll show you, then you can work on them in your spare time."

"Cool!"

An idea strikes Amy. She likes having Erin around because she's upbeat, fun, sharp. She doesn't want to spend the weekend obsessing about what Ellis will ultimately conclude about the hospital. She doesn't want to spend the weekend thinking of Ellis at all, if she can help it. And then there's Monday's private meeting with Ellis that she's dreading worse than a visit to the dentist. Kate doesn't need to spend the weekend stewing about her future either. They could all use a little distraction.

"Erin, are you free Sunday?"

"My daughter's spending the weekend with her grandmothers in the city, so yes, I'm free."

"What about you, Hendy?"

"Yes, I'm free," Kate chimes in, somewhat hesitantly. "Why?"

"Let's do something fun. I've got a couple of kayaks on my property I haven't used yet this season. Hendy, bring yours over. We'll kayak on the lake for a bit, then roast something over a backyard fire. What do you guys say?"

Erin sits down and starts fussing with her ball of string. "Sounds like a plan."

"I'll bring the beer," Kate says.

A fourth would be fun, and Amy's mind wanders to Ellis. Ellis in a bikini top, paddling with sweat beading down her arms, her back. Ellis affectionately bumping shoulders with Amy as a campfire crackles and dances before them. Ellis looking at her with eyes reflecting the glow of the firelight. *Stop*, she tells herself. *Stop it right now.* Ellis is a memory. A sweet one, but a memory nonetheless. And Amy is, if nothing else, a realist.

* * *

Ellis trudges up the stairs with yet another box from the moving van. The movers have carried in all the heavy items, but standing idle watching them lug stuff in at a snail's pace is too much for her impatient nature. In the living room she sets down the last box, marked "books," then stretches her back.

"I think that's everything, ma'am," one of the movers says.

She gives them each a twenty-dollar tip before they leave. Mia has been hiding out in the yard, pretending to do…well, God knows what. Fooling around with her bike, probably. The kid needs to get her butt upstairs to help unpack this mess. Ellis glances out the window and sees Mia talking over the back fence with a blond-haired, middle-thirties woman. The woman who appeared to have been the host of last weekend's outdoor party. The party that included Abby—Amy—she corrects herself again. Huh, she thinks with the tiniest jealous streak. *Mia seems to have a lot more to say to this stranger than she does to me.*

She pokes her head out the window and asks Mia to come in and help.

"I will in a minute. Kate here wants me to help her load her kayak on her car. Says she'll pay me ten bucks."

Ellis rolls her eyes exactly at the moment Kate looks up. "I'm sorry. I promise to only borrow her for a few minutes. Actually, it would probably be easier if the three of us loaded it together. Would you mind?"

Great, like I have time for this. "Will you pay me ten bucks too?" She can't keep the sarcasm from her voice, but this Kate woman doesn't seem to notice.

"How about a bottle of wine?"

Now that's a deal she isn't going to refuse. "Be right there."

She checks her image in the window glass on her way out, knowing nothing will fix her worn-out and bedraggled look. She reties the scarf on her head that's losing the battle of keeping her hair under control.

As she closes in on the fence between the yards, the woman's face changes from open and friendly to something far more guarded.

"Oh, wait," the woman named Kate says. "You're the one who's conducting the hospital review."

Ellis waits for her heart to stop jabbing her in the ribs. Of course. It's a small town. Word's gotten around, and Kate probably works at the hospital, since Amy was at her party last weekend. Ellis can't find her voice because of the jumble of regrets bouncing around in her head. She should never have left the city. It was a mistake to think she could both live and work in this fish bowl, especially while doing something as contentious as conducting a review of the hospital. People will assume the worst. Not that she can blame them.

As calmly as she can, Ellis introduces herself and holds out a friendly hand over the fence.

"Kate Henderson." Cool, clipped. Same with the handshake.

"Ellis Hall. You, um, work at the hospital, I gather?" No sense in ignoring the obvious, especially since they're neighbors.

"I do," Kate says, narrowing her eyes enough to make it obvious she doesn't plan on being too friendly. "In the OR."

Okay, thinks Ellis, *I can do this. I can be friendly with these folks. I'm not their enemy, after all. We're all in this together, trying to make a more efficient and sustainable health care system. We don't have to be on opposite sides of the fence.* She grins at the fence analogy because it's so perfect right now.

"Something funny?" Kate asks, an edge to her voice.

"Just thinking what a small world this is."

"Not a small world. Small town, though."

"Listen…" This isn't Ellis's forte, being the chatty neighbor. Usually, she doesn't have the time, or, let's be honest, the inclination to become friendly with her neighbors, because she's rarely in one place for more than a year or two. But it's different here. It's not the big city, and it's not a monolithic hospital where you never see the same person twice. She's here for a few months, and she needs people other than Mia to talk to once in a while. Then there's the added bonus of Kate knowing Amy. Not that Ellis plans to ever tell Kate about her and Amy, but maybe, through Kate, she can at least learn a little more about Amy, keep distant tabs on her. She knows Amy won't want anything to do with her now and will resent her presence at the hospital. That part was made clear by Amy's prickliness at the board meeting. "Since we're going to be neighbors and all, I hope that we can leave hospital business at the hospital. I'd like that, if it's okay with you."

Kate's desire to argue or to put up a wall or whatever negative thing she might have been contemplating falls from her face and is replaced by a smile. "Help me with my kayak and we'll call it square."

Ellis laughs, enjoying this unexpected banter. "You mean there's no more wine in it for me?"

"Well, we'll have to see how well you do first."

* * *

It takes all of about three minutes before Kate spills the beans to Amy and Erin about Ellis Hall being her new neighbor.

"You know," Kate says as they carry the kayaks down to the shore, "I was ready to hate her. More than ready. But I might have changed my mind a little. She doesn't seem so bad."

Amy loves her property along the lake. It's about an acre, with a lovely four-bedroom Craftsman style home built in the 1920s. While she isn't home as much as she'd like to be, it's her little slice of heaven when she is. "So you spoke to her for five minutes and now you've tamed Dragon Lady?" Kate isn't usually so quick to change her mind about people. She likes to pride herself on her ability to judge others' character. A handshake, a good look in the eye is all you need, she likes to say. *I can have a little fun with this*, Amy thinks.

"Well," Kate says, slipping on her life jacket. "She *is* rather nice to look at."

"Ah, so you're ready to step a foot into the dating pool now, are you?"

Kate's eyes widen in panic. "I never said that. And certainly not with her."

"Not your type?" Erin says, and Amy catches the lilt of hope in her voice.

"I've got her pegged as the domineering type." Kate shrugs. "Like, you know, all uptight in bed. Probably has a timer on the nightstand or something. And a copy of that book about lesbian sex positions. If she's even a lesbian."

Amy almost laughs out loud, because of course Ellis is a lesbian, she's anything but uptight in bed, and there's certainly no timer or a book of instructions. But she's not about to correct her friend. "Maybe you can be the nosy neighbor and have her over for tea and get the inside scoop on how she's going to decimate our hospital."

"Ha, ha, very funny."

Amy slides her boat into the water, straddling it, then carefully folds her legs in and sits down. Erin deftly does the same, but Kate's boat wobbles perilously, until finally she tumbles sideways, ending up thigh deep in the water.

"Dammit! I swear you have to be a fucking gymnast to get into these things."

Amy laughs while Erin plays rescuer, leaping out of her boat to help Kate remount hers. The chivalry makes Amy smile, and she hopes her best friend notices it too. But Kate's a stubborn one, and she has a feeling that if Erin wants to make her intentions clear, she'll pretty much have to throw herself at Kate. While naked and holding a bouquet of flowers.

Everyone's back in their boats, paddling slowly, when Kate says, "Maybe she won't recommend they take a sledgehammer to the hospital after all. Maybe it'll be some small cuts. Things we won't even notice."

"Yeah," Amy hisses. "Like getting rid of obstetrics? That small enough for you?" Losing the birthing suite would require patients to travel nearly an hour to a larger hospital in Windsor to give birth. Furthermore, if the hospital does cut obstetrics, the local gynecologists/obstetricians will pack up and leave, because delivering babies is their bread and butter, and they'll follow the money. "Two days ago you were all doom and gloom. Five minutes of chatting with Ellis Hall and you're suddenly a new woman?"

Kate sticks her tongue out at Amy. "I know. And I'll be the first one to run Ellis Hall out of town if she suggests major cuts. But I think maybe I'll, you know, reserve judgment a little while longer."

Erin looks none too pleased with the exchange. She has no stake in the hospital, because she'll be a family physician with her own practice or she'll practice with a family health team somewhere once her residency is complete. Amy can only guess she's jealous about Kate's sudden interest in Ellis. *She's not the only one.*

"Did you know she has a stepdaughter living with her? A teenager. Mia. Nice enough but a bit on the morose side."

"Aren't all teenagers?" Erin adds helpfully.

"Good point," Kate replies, then mercifully drops Ellis as the topic of conversation while they paddle up and down the shore for an hour, not venturing into waters too deep because Erin's fairly new at kayaking and Kate's not the most experienced either, despite owning her own boat. Her wife, Anne, had been the expert kayaker in the family.

Two hours later, with the sun an orange orb behind them, the three sit around Amy's fire pit, chowing down on spaghetti. Since Amy's fire pit has a grill over half of it, she cooked the pasta in a giant pot over the fire and warmed the sauce she'd made ahead.

Erin reaches for another helping. "God, what's in this sauce?"

Amy pretty much lived on her homemade sauce with an assortment of pasta throughout medical school and residency. "Italian sausage, ground beef, green and red peppers, onion, garlic, and tomato sauce of course. Oregano. Oh and a healthy splash of red wine."

"She's famous for her sauce," Kate adds. "I'm surprised she gave up the recipe so easily. You usually have to get her drunk for that."

"Oh, I'm well on my way to that." Amy takes another sip of wine. The three of them are into a second bottle.

Kate's laughter is evil as she points at the diminishing contents of Amy's glass. "Bolstering yourself for your private meeting with Ms. Hall tomorrow?"

Amy nearly chokes on her mouthful of wine. She's been doing everything she can to avoid thinking about that damned meeting tomorrow. About seeing Ellis again. Alone. She has no idea what she's going to say to her and has half a mind to skip out on the meeting altogether. She doesn't like surprises, and Ellis has provided her with a doozy. "Please. Let's not ruin the evening by talking about her any more, shall we?" She turns to Erin, whom she knows so little about. "So tell us more about yourself, Erin."

"Yeah," Kate says, her eyes beginning to turn a little glassy from the wine and the fresh air and the smoke from the campfire. "How can we possibly gossip about you if we know almost nothing about you, huh? So spill it."

Erin laughs, gives them a quick rundown on where she did her education, about how she grew up in Windsor with a twin sister and, oh, her mothers are a lesbian couple who also happen to be family physicians.

Kate's eyeballs nearly pop out of her head. "Wow. I always thought that would be so cool, having gay parents. Is it?"

"Not really. They're parents like any other parents. They've been pretty hard on my sister and me most of our lives. You know, great expectations to follow in their footsteps and all that. But they've come around. They're pretty much human now, and I kind of credit my daughter for that. They're totally putty in her little hands."

"She's a sweetie, that one," Kate says, a faraway look in her eyes. She doesn't talk about it anymore, not since Anne's death, but the two had always planned to eventually have a child together. "Such a smart little thing and cute as a button with those blue eyes and curly dark hair." Kate gives Erin a once-over like she's making a new discovery. "Pretty much like her mom, actually. She's the spitting image of you."

"Thanks," Erin says. "She's pretty much a Kirkland through and through. When she wants something, look out."

Amy chuckles to herself, imagining an unsuspecting Kate being pursued by Erin. She adds another log to the fire as Kate, losing her defenses with each sip of wine, boldly asks, "No father in the picture?"

"No father in the picture. It was…an experiment, something that kind of organically happened, but I'm forever grateful, because I wouldn't have had Eliana otherwise." Erin's eyes spark when she talks about her daughter, whom she's clearly in love with. "The timing might not have been the best, but she's been more than worth it. I can't imagine my life without her."

"I'd love to include her in something next time," Kate offers, and Erin predictably brightens.

"Really? She won't cramp your style?"

Amy laughs. "Ha, what style? Your daughter might actually give Kate a *style*."

Erin fidgets, looking uncomfortable. "I'm so sorry, Kate. About your wife."

The words hang in the air, with the power to make or break the evening. But then Kate smiles at Erin and thanks her for mentioning it. "The worst is when people don't acknowledge Anne's death. And I know it's because they don't know what to say, but it's actually worse to ignore it than to say something, anything, no matter how awkward it might seem. Two years and it still feels like yesterday."

Erin asks how she died.

"Ovarian cancer. Stage four by the time it was discovered. She was only thirty-nine." Her chin begins a slow quiver, and Amy reaches over and tenderly squeezes her shoulder.

"So, yes," Kate continues, roughly clearing the emotion from her throat. "I would love for you and Eliana to drag me out of my miserable lonely life to do something fun."

Amy glances from Kate to Erin and feels a tug of relief because both women are smiling at one another. She raises her glass and proposes a toast. "Here's to no more loneliness."

They all clink glasses, while Amy tries to ignore the dull ache in her heart. She knows she's a phony, because she hasn't felt this lonely in years.

CHAPTER TWELVE

Ellis has been glancing at the clock in her makeshift office on the hospital's second floor at least every six minutes. She can't wait to see Amy alone—finally. Even though it's a business meeting, maybe they can clear up the awkwardness between them. Perhaps, she thinks with optimistic deliberation that's as flimsy as tissue paper, they can even work out an occasional sex date or something. That is, if they can miraculously figure out how to navigate around the ethics and discretion of such a thing. A girl can dream, and if sex is completely off the table, might they at least find a way to be friends? Ellis doesn't have many of those and none around this area. Unless you count Kate Henderson, but she's more of a wary neighbor than a friend at this point.

The moment Amy walks in, Ellis sees immediately that her little fantasy about sex or friendship is just that, a fantasy. Wordlessly but with a frown that could rival the depth of the Grand Canyon, Amy sits down opposite Ellis's desk, her back straight as a two-by-four.

So that's how it's going to be? No, Ellis decides. She won't let it.

"Amy, can we—"

"It's Dr. Spencer."

Of course it is. Ellis silently curses herself, but in the blink of an eye she's back in control. "I'm sorry, but privately, when it's just us, I can't call you Dr. Spencer. Not after...the times we've shared." She hates this, acting like they've swapped gloves or something, when she'll never rid from her memory the sensation of Amy running her fingertips over her skin, of Amy's lips gently tugging on her nipples or sucking the soft and sensitive parts of her neck. Nor can she ever forget the way her insides turn to the warmest, sweetest liquid when Amy pleasures her.

"Fine," Amy says, showing about as much emotion as a rock. "You can call me Amy. In private. And I'll call you El-Ellis. But nobody can know...about us. You do understand that?"

"Er...yes. Absolutely."

"Ellis, what happened between us has to stay in the past. I can't...we can't...revisit any of it. Ever. It...was a mistake. I hope you agree."

"No. It wasn't a mistake. We didn't know our paths would cross like this." Ellis swallows back the disappointment, no, the panic in her throat, that Amy wants to wipe their past clean as if it never happened. But it did happen, every glorious minute of it. And each of those glorious moments made Ellis *feel* again. Made her feel more of a woman than she's felt in over a decade, because Amy made her feel wanted, appreciated, desired. Made her feel important, like she was someone worth spending time with, worth loving over and over again, even if only in the physical sense. "This..." Ellis spreads her arms out to include her temporary office, the hospital. "We couldn't have known we'd be in this situation."

"On opposite sides of the table, you mean."

"It doesn't have to be on opposite sides. There's no need for us to be antagonists in this endeavor. We're on the same side, Amy."

Amy's eyes are wide and searching, as if trying to locate Ellis through a heavy mist, and then the curtain drops again and she's vigorously shaking her head. "No. We're not on the same side. Let's be clear about that. You're here to make cuts to services so the corporation can balance its budget. Cuts that will ultimately mean patients will have to travel further for certain types of care. Or wait longer."

"Not necessarily service cuts and not necessarily longer wait times. There's a long way ahead of us before we—"

"Come on. I know how this works. We'll be lucky if you don't completely shut us down by the time you're done with us. You don't care about this hospital. I mean, *this* particular hospital. This particular staff. These patients. *My* patients. You care about numbers and bottom lines. That's your priority. That's your job."

Fury pounds in Ellis's veins with every beat of her heart. "You're mistaken, Dr. Spencer. Clearly you know nothing about me and my priorities." Her face is hot and her voice shakes with anger, and for a flash there's a softening in Amy's rainwater eyes, as though she's remembering them lying in bed, staring into one another's eyes, their thighs and feet and hands touching, with neither woman having a care in the world.

But then Amy looks away and begins pulling papers out of her briefcase, unceremoniously plops them on Ellis's desk. "You wanted stats about the surgery service, well, here's a mountain of them." Amy rises as if she's done what she was summoned to do, clearly intending to leave.

"Wait." Ellis pulls her glasses off her face and tosses them grumpily onto Amy's papers. "You're not going to help me decipher these? Summarize them at least?"

Amy sits back down, even though she'd love to walk out and leave Ellis to her lovely fucking stats and numbers and bottom lines instead of continuing this charade of pretending she has any real input in this despicable process. And, oh, while she's on a roll? She'd love to push Ellis on top of the desk, on top of her precious fucking papers, and make her come like she's never come before. Because goddammit, Ellis is gorgeous, especially with her chest heaving in anger and her cheeks flushed and her eyes flashing a green so dark, they're like a deep glacier pool.

"Fine." Amy nearly spits out the word. "What do you want to know?"

Ellis picks up her glasses and puts them back on with fingers slightly trembling, and Amy is inordinately pleased that she's having this effect on her. Because, dammit, Ellis has pissed her off. Coming in here, on her territory, with the authority of a dictator or a despot, to make her life and everyone else's miserable for the next however-many months. A bean counter who's probably never had to use the services of a surgeon or an OB-GYN or perhaps even an emerg doc and has certainly never lived in a small town before. Thinking she's some kind of expert because she's got a fancy degree in business or accounting and has been working with hospital budgets for years or decades or fucking centuries. Amy can't keep her thoughts from darkening further, and then she remembers that it's her job to at least try to steer Ellis into leaving the surgery service alone. Because if she abandons her duty to protect the service, then what?

Ellis flips through the pages without speaking. "Okay, so there's supposed to be three of you, but there's only two while... let's see, Dr. Atkinson is on leave? Any idea how long that's going to be?"

"Nope." Atkinson probably isn't coming back, by the looks of things. He's still undergoing medical testing, but the chief of staff has privately told Amy that Atkinson appears to have Parkinson's. The timing couldn't be worse, because Amy can practically see Ellis's train of thoughts on the matter: that if they can manage with two surgeons, there's no reason to replace him.

"Obviously wait times for elective surgeries have increased with you and Dr. Warren being the only two remaining surgeons. Correct?"

"Yes, but we're managing." *Managing, if I don't want a life outside of this hospital.*

Amy catches the subtle rolling of eyes from Ellis. Well, what did she expect, that they'd have tea together and discuss the weather too?

"And how is the workload affecting you and Dr. Warren?"

"It's fine."

"What does that mean? Working six or seven days a week? Every other weekend?"

"So your job includes caring about my well-being?"

"Look. Let's not do this, okay?"

Amy decides to play dumb, and yes, it's childish, but too bad. "Do what?"

Ellis leans back in her chair for a moment, briefly closes her eyes. There are dark smudges beneath those eyes. "You know exactly what. I think we need to talk. About the other stuff. Why don't we meet for a drink one evening this week? Or dinner or coffee? Whatever you want, wherever you want, as long as it's away from the hospital." She holds up a hand to forestall the objection Amy is about to raise. "I think we both know that we've got to figure how to move past this…this…elephant in the room. Because if we don't, it's going to bleed into the work we need to do here, and we can't let that happen. It will only make things worse. For both of us."

Amy wants to lob more of these insidious little darts Ellis's way, but instead she takes a deep breath and tells herself to calm down. Because Ellis is right: they've got to keep things separate. They've got to be professionals about this, and they can't do that if Amy keeps acting like a petulant child.

Ellis looks at her expectantly. Nervously.

"All right. Let's see. Tomorrow night I'm off at six and not on call. We could meet for dinner I guess. There's a pub on Becker Street that's kind of out of the way. I don't think anybody from the hospital typically goes there. Seven?"

"Seven it is." Ellis turns her attention back to the pile of loose papers Amy has given her. "Let's go through these one by one. Colonoscopies…" She traces a finger—a long, sensuous finger—down a column, and somehow she's managed to make the word *colonoscopies* sound sexy.

And now I've agreed to meet her outside of work. What the hell is wrong with me? But she knows what's wrong with her: her inability to say no to Ellis, in spite of her bravado.

CHAPTER THIRTEEN

Ellis likes numbers, so she's pegged the odds of Amy actually showing up to meet her at the pub at about fifty-fifty. She understands Amy's shock and dismay that Ellis is the one conducting a review of all the hospital's services. She too had been no less shocked to discover the woman she'd been sleeping with for six weeks was, well, Dr. Amy Spencer. It's not as if she'd duped Amy or done anything wrong. Neither of them had. Yet Amy has been colder than Lake Erie frozen over in winter, and all Ellis wants to do is scream "It's not my damned fault!"

Ellis foregoes the temptation to order something strong and sticks with a glass of wine. Glancing down at her short-sleeved blouse with the peek-a-boo left shoulder, she sneaks another button loose. Because, yes, she wants Amy (if she shows up) to notice her chest, and, yes, it's shameless and a tad slutty of her, but so what? Amy's the best sex partner she's ever had, and if she's totally honest with herself, she hates that they're not having sex anymore. They managed to stop the world for a few heavenly hours every Thursday afternoon, and while it's patently clear it can't happen anymore, she at least wants Amy to realize what she's missing. Realize it and suffer a little.

The door opens and in walks Amy.

Well, well.

"Hi," she says in a neutral voice and takes a seat across from Ellis.

A server promptly materializes, but Amy declines a drink. "Early surgery tomorrow," she says to Ellis, and orders a soda and lime.

"I'm sorry, Amy."

Amy's stare is one of puzzlement. "About the early surgery?"

"Well, that too. Look, I want you to know that I never meant for things to turn out this way." What she really wants to say is that she can't stop thinking about Amy—about her smile, her touch, that almost tender way she has of looking at her after they make love…like Ellis is the only woman in the whole world. That she's someone special.

The muscles in Amy's face relax, but she doesn't smile. "Me too."

"Can we… I guess at the very least I hope we can be respectful toward one another. That we can work together without an adversarial relationship."

"It would certainly make your life easier at the hospital, hmm?"

"No, that's not…" Tears suddenly threaten. Tears, for fuck sakes! Before she met Amy, she hadn't cried in years. Oh, right, at Nancy's funeral she cried. But crying over Amy—someone she's, what, sort of dated, slept with several times—is ridiculous. Infuriating. And yet here she is, hoping like hell these damned tears don't start spilling over so that Amy can see how pathetic she is, how weak she is. Oh, the grownup part of her knows there is only going forward, not backward, and yet her inner child simply wants Amy's arms around her, wants desperately to erase this last week and a half and go back to the uncomplicated way things were.

"Ellis, hey." Amy's voice has lost its bite. "I know this isn't your fault. Neither of us knew this was going to happen."

"And if you had known all along who I was?"

Amy's eyes slide down to Ellis's exposed cleavage and linger there. It's a small victory, especially when Amy licks her lips. They still want each other. "Please don't ask me that."

The server returns, takes their food order: loaded nachos and more soda water for Amy, fish and chips and a second glass of wine for Ellis. When the server leaves, Ellis says, "No, I think we need to talk about this. Amy, those weeks we had…" Ellis has to clear her throat because her heart has decided to take up residence there. "Our Thursday afternoons. They were very special to me. I would like to think they could have gone on if not for…this. It felt almost as though we were becoming friends. And I liked that. Very much. I…miss that."

"Ellis."

For a moment, Ellis thinks Amy is going to say something heartfelt, something that will echo the way she's feeling, especially when her eyes drop to Ellis's breasts again. Eyes that look ravenous. Eyes that are shot through with the worst kind of longing. But when she meets Ellis's eyes again, her guard slips firmly back into place and they're strangers again. "It's—"

Crap. Worst timing ever as the server returns with their food. For once couldn't this place be like most restaurants and take forever to get the food out?

Amy tucks into her nachos like she hasn't eaten in a week. When she finally comes up for air, she says simply, "Ellis, what do you want from me?"

So many emotions battle for supremacy in Ellis's eyes: loneliness, regret, hope. Amy knows Ellis is judging her as an unfeeling ass. She's not. But how can she possibly go about concentrating on her job every day, knowing Ellis is in the same building? Knowing she's so damned close. Hell, she even lives a mere eight blocks away in the house behind Kate's. And yes, Amy would love to sneak into Ellis's office for a booty call or swing by her house late one night. Of course she would. The sex… Amy feels the blush blooming on her checks and throat, feels her breath catch as her eyes again follow their downward trajectory to Ellis's fabulous breasts. *Oh, God, the sex!* It was simply glorious, every second of it, and if she could go on having sex with Ellis every Thursday for the rest of their lives, well, sign her up for that tour of duty.

"What I want," Ellis enunciates slowly, "is to not be adversaries. I can't…I couldn't handle that, Amy, not after… everything."

Amy gets it, she really does. She doesn't want to be enemies either. But they'll never see things from the same side, never understand each other's position. "I understand. And I won't disrespect you in public or at work or anything. But Ellis, this review you're doing, it's too important. It—"

"I know it's important. Do you think I take my work any less seriously than you take yours?"

It takes a huge effort for Amy to refrain from saying something snarky and immature, like, "Yeah, pushing paper is the same as saving lives," but she doesn't. "I'm sure you do. But this hospital, it's a big part of this community, a defining part of this community. I grew up here. I see the same people in the grocery store as I see on my operating room table or in my waiting room. We care about each other here. We're not numbers on a spreadsheet. And I'm not sure you get that."

"I do get that. As much as I can, and I live here now, so I do plan to get to know the community better. Look, I know I'm an outsider, both at the hospital and in the community. Help me not to be, Amy."

Well, she thinks, *we've all been that person on the outside, looking in and seeing our reflection, then acting like we're surprised to see our own face staring back at us.* It's not a new revelation. "I can't wave a magic wand and make you one of us." God, why is she being so nasty to this woman? Ellis has done nothing to deserve it, and Amy can admit that she's borrowing this hostility against things Ellis might or might not do in the future. But she can't seem to help herself. She's pissed at the universe, and maybe a little at Ellis too, for taking the woman she's been sleeping with, the woman she'd begun to care about, and giving her power over the hospital's future. It's not that she thinks Ellis is incompetent or uncaring or has some axe to grind. It's that Amy simply doesn't trust anyone who hasn't been down in the trenches to play God with the hospital's future.

"I'm not asking you to wave a magic wand. I'm asking you to give me a chance…to be my friend. Not, you know, sex. I know that's crossing a line."

It wouldn't truly be crossing a line to have sex, not a real line, because Ellis isn't her superior. She's an outside consultant who's been brought in by the flagship hospital corporation to do a full service review of Amy's hospital and then to make cost-efficiency recommendations. The optics of them having a sexual relationship would be terrible, but for a fleeting moment Amy imagines bringing Ellis back to her house, undressing her, making love to her until dawn splits the dark. But it would feel too much like sleeping with the enemy. Or at least, a lot like sleeping with someone she shouldn't.

"Look." Amy tries to soften the sting. "I don't see how we can possibly be friends right now, okay? But I won't…I won't be your enemy. I won't be unfriendly."

Ellis blinks like she can't quite believe Amy is turning down her offer of friendship. After rooting around in her purse for cash to leave on the table, she juts out her jaw defiantly. "It looks like we're done here. I'm going to call myself a cab."

"No." Amy reaches out and stills Ellis's hand. "I'll drop you at home. Please don't be upset with me. I'm trying my best here, okay?"

Ellis says nothing as she follows Amy to her car. On the drive, it's up to Amy to initiate conversation.

"So, your stepdaughter. Mia is it? She's living here with you?"

"Yes. Normally she lives with her grandparents in Windsor. But she's here with me for the summer. She…needed to get away from certain influences in the city."

"I see." Exactly how is it that Ellis has acquired a stepchild, she wants to know but doesn't ask. There's so much about her she doesn't know and is dying to ask, but oh yeah, she said she didn't want to be Ellis's friend. She pulls up to the curb in front of Ellis's rental house. "Man, this is a huge place. It's gorgeous. You're renting the whole thing?"

"No, just the second and third floors."

Ellis makes a move for the door handle, but Amy reaches over and touches her arm until Ellis looks at her. That's when the urge to touch Ellis, really touch her, becomes irresistible. She raises a hand to Ellis's cheek, lightly cups it. The urge to kiss her is equally compelling, but somehow Amy manages to stop herself, even as her face inches closer to Ellis's. It's like their bodies have their own memories of one another.

"I'm sorry," Amy finally whispers. Women are such a mystery sometimes. There was a time she thought she had them figured out. Or maybe it's just that *this* woman is such a mystery. Because she wants to be with Ellis almost as much as she wants to breathe, but then her head takes over and reminds her that Ellis has the power, the authority, to ruin the very things she's worked so hard to attain at this hospital and in this community. Ellis, she has come to admit to herself, is not the woman she thought she was. Or more accurately, she's not the woman Amy has built her up to be in her fantasies.

Ellis looks at her for a long time. Then she slides out from under Amy's touch and disappears into the night.

CHAPTER FOURTEEN

Ellis closes her laptop and slips off her glasses as Mia sits down across from her at the dining room table. It's so rare for the kid to actually want any kind of conversation with her, so it must be a big deal. What strikes Ellis first is the fact that Mia looks…neat and clean for a change. Her short dark hair is combed and her clothes aren't loose and ripped and in need of laundering. The kohl eyeliner is gone too. She looks like she's trying.

"Can I hang out at the hospital with you tomorrow?"

Ellis schools her expression, deciding to play it cool. She's afraid that if she shows any sign of being suspicious or skeptical about this sudden turn of events, Mia will retreat back into her morose, sulking, lazy self. "I think that would be okay, yes. Any particular reason you want to hang out there?"

"It's not like I have anything to do here by myself all day. And…Kate will be there, right? And Erin. I mean, Dr. Kirkland. I wanna, you know, see what kind of stuff they do there."

Ah, of course! Mia's developing her first crush on an adult woman. "Okay, well, as long as you're not in the way or anything, I'm sure it'll be fine. I'll clear it with someone in admin."

"I won't get in the way. Hey, I got a job. Sort of."

"You did?" Oops. She doesn't mean to sound so shocked.

But Mia doesn't appear to notice; she's too excited about her announcement. "Kate's asked me to cut her grass once a week. She's going to pay me twenty bucks a pop. She has the lawnmower and everything. I just have to show up. Hey, do you think it could count towards my community service thing?"

"What, cutting grass? No, absolutely not. But what about at the hospital? I can ask around, see if there's some kind of volunteer work you could do there. Since you're going to be there anyway." Damn, she should have thought of it sooner. They've been here three weeks and Mia's done nothing toward her eighty hours of community service. Her probation officer has already read her the riot act.

Mia's mouth forms a perfect O. "No! I don't want anybody there to know I'm...that I got into trouble and have to do volunteer stuff. Please don't you tell anybody!"

"All right, I won't. I promise. But you need to start putting in volunteer hours somewhere. As in yesterday."

"I know." Mia gets up and makes herself a cup of coffee. "Oh, um, do you want one?"

Ellis shakes her head. "Thanks, but I've already had a bucket of coffee today." *Wow, did she actually ask me if I wanted a cup of coffee? Who is this kid?*

"Have you met Eliana yet?" Mia asks.

"No. Who's Eliana?"

Mia smiles—with actual teeth showing. "Erin...I mean, Dr. Kirkland's little girl. They were over at Kate's yesterday afternoon playing hopscotch on the patio and drinking iced tea. They saw me over the fence and asked me over. That's how I got the grass cutting job."

"I see. Good for you." She still can't believe Mia's speaking in complete sentences.

"I might even be able to do a bit of babysitting. Erin asked me if there might be an evening here or there where I could watch Eliana for a couple of hours." Mia screws up her face. "Funny though, she only asked me that when Kate went into the house for something. Like it was kind of a secret."

I need to get out more, Ellis thinks, *especially since Mia's already making more friends than I am.* "That's great, Mia. Really great." Now if she could just get her to take her community service requirement seriously. "Why don't you come over to the hospital tomorrow sometime after breakfast." Which, no doubt won't be until after ten.

"Okay."

"Good." Ellis studies Mia once more before she leaves the room. The transformation is, well, not yet remarkable, but noticeable. Right before her eyes, Mia seems to be turning into a real human being.

* * *

Amy is into her second hour of operating on a car crash victim. The injuries shouldn't have been so horrific because as far as car accidents go, it was fairly minor. But there'd been a set of loose golf clubs in the back seat, and the impact sent the shaft of a club into the patient's abdomen, piercing his vena cava. He'd only been a few blood cells away from bleeding out. It is a perfect example of why the hospital needs its ER and its surgical service. Mr. Alan Keyes would have died had the transport to hospital taken a few minutes longer.

If only Ellis could see this, Amy thinks. How easy it is to sit in an ivory tower making decisions about cutting services, when actual people will die as a result of those decisions. But Ellis will never see those people. She won't be here when the ambulance has to drive on by to a larger hospital with its sick or battered patients. *I'll make a list*, Amy vows to herself. She'll comb through all the records from the last five years to identify every single case where the patient outcome would have been drastically worse had the ER and the surgical service not been available. The way to fight back against someone like Ellis is not through emotional outbursts or anecdotes about patients, but with actual statistics, because that's the world in which Ellis operates. She should have realized it sooner. Blowing up at Ellis or constantly giving her the cold shoulder is a useless, not to mention rude, exercise. Far better to shower her with information and numbers.

Transfusions have been completed and the patient's vitals are climbing nicely. Amy's already moved his bowel out of the way and clamped off the damaged portion of his vena cava. Now she begins the task of suturing the holes caused by the broken shaft of the golf club. Erin's standing next to her, carefully observing. Amy asks her again to call out the patient's oxygen saturation, pulse, respiration, and blood pressure. Mostly because she doesn't want to take her eyes off what she's doing but also to keep Erin engaged. In a more minor case she'd let Erin throw in some sutures at this point, but not this time. This one is all hers.

"I do have a job for you later," she says to Erin. "It won't be fun, but it's important. And I'm afraid it'll mean quite a few hours in front of a computer."

"Sure thing, Dr. Spencer. Happy to."

She wonders if Erin has asked Kate out on a proper date yet, but finding a way to bring up the subject has been…awkward. She doesn't want to come across as a gossip or as a matchmaker, but she wants Kate to be happy, to find someone to have some fun with, because Kate is a people person, a coupling kind of person, and it breaks Amy's heart to see her alone. Her thoughts wander again to Ellis. Is *she* lonely? She implied as much the other night, saying she didn't know anyone in town. *Well, it's not my problem. I can't be her friend, not right now.*

The patient is completely stable, back firmly in this world again. Once she finishes repairing the wound, she washes out his abdomen with a cleansing saline solution, begins suturing him up, then allows Erin a few token sutures toward the end.

Amy's pumped from the adrenaline infusion the surgery has given her. Sometimes surgeries are like running a marathon and other times they're more like a sprint, but always, an interesting surgery is a challenge to her—a challenge she's determined to win every single time. She won this one. In search of a fresh cup of coffee, she wanders into the cafeteria. It's late in the afternoon; hardly anyone is here. Except... Is that Mia, Ellis's stepdaughter, slouched at a corner table playing with an iPad? Amy has only seen her once before, at that restaurant in Windsor, but she's sure it's her.

She pays for her coffee and strides purposefully to Mia's table, sitting down without asking permission. When Mia looks up, there's confusion and a glint of fear in her eyes. Not used to someone in scrubs seeking her out, clearly.

"Hi. I'm Amy Spencer." She sticks out her hand; Mia shakes it hesitantly.

"Mia. Mia Hutton."

"Ellis Hall's stepdaughter, right?"

Mia shrugs, glances back at her iPad as though Ellis is barely an acquaintance and hardly worth talking about. The kid has a chip on her shoulder the size of a mountain, judging by the perpetual scowl engraved on her mouth. "Something like that," she finally mumbles.

Amy tells herself she should get up and walk away. What does she know about teenagers, anyway? Nothing, really. She's not especially close to her sister's kids, and she was too busy with her nose in textbooks when she herself was a teenager. But Mia Hutton looks like she's drowning in a pool full of adults who are too busy doing their own thing to notice she's going under.

"You into video games?"

"Not really."

"Oh. So you're not playing a game on your iPad?"

"Nope. Just reading."

Facebook or Instagram or Snapchat, no doubt. "I see. And what are you reading?"

"*The Bell Jar* by Sylvia Plath."

"Whoa. Well-written book but there's some pretty heavy stuff in there."

Another shoulder shrug. "I can handle it."

"You're…okay? I mean, you're not feeling the kind of stuff the character in the book is feeling, are you?"

Mia looks at her in that condescending way that teenagers look at adults. "No. Are you a psychiatrist?" Annoyance flashes across her face. "Did Ellis send you to talk to me?"

"Nope and nope. I barely even know Ellis." Except in the carnal way of course, but Mia doesn't need to know that. "Besides, I'm a surgeon. And an avid reader. What other classics have you read?"

"Why?"

A born skeptic. Which probably means she's bright. "Just curious," Amy says.

"Virginia Woolf, F. Scott Fitzgerald, Tolstoy, Tolkien, Austen, Salinger. Some newer stuff too, like Franzen and Frey. I really like Angie Thomas, her stuff is cool."

Amy sets her half-empty cup down and stands up. "Come with me."

"Where?"

"You'll see."

She's surprised Mia follows her without protest to the hospital's library, tucked into a corner of the basement. There are a couple thousand books on shelves, a few comfortable chairs scattered around, and a computer for patients and staff to use.

"This is our library and it's for patients, staff, and visitors. It's open twenty-four-seven, but we don't have enough volunteers to staff it. Or to bring the mobile book cart around to patients. Can you start tomorrow? A couple hours a day would be amazing for us. More, if you can swing it."

"What? Me?"

"Yes, you. Got anything better to do? And clearly you know books. "

"I-I don't know. I mean…I guess I could."

"It doesn't pay, but you'd be awesome at it. I'll send an email to admin to let them know. Meet me here tomorrow morning at nine. Sharp. We'll get you squared away." She should be done with rounds by then, but Mia looks at her like nine is an ungodly hour.

"Trust me, it won't kill you. You drink coffee yet?"

Mia nods confidently, playing at being all grown up.

"I'll have a cup waiting for you. And maybe a book you haven't read." She could easily pay the kid in books and makes a mental note to bring in her copy of Michael Chabon's *The Amazing Adventures of Kavalier and Clay* for Mia to borrow.

It's another moment before Mia nods again, but she still hasn't given Amy a smile. Which is fine. Amy isn't looking for smiles. She's looking for something to get this kid's head out of her own ass before it's too late, because clearly there's a brain inside that head.

CHAPTER FIFTEEN

A soft knock on her office door startles Ellis enough to make her jump, though she's glad for a distraction. Staring at her computer for hours is giving her a mild headache.

"Come in." Ellis never firmly shuts her door when she's alone in her office because she wants to signal that she's available to hospital staff. There's nothing better to fuel fearful gossip and paranoia than closed office doors and no access.

It's Amy. Looking amazing in pale green scrubs and a starched lab coat, a bit of sun having softly bleached the tips of her short, light brown hair, lending her a more carefree veneer. Ellis aches to see her smile again and to be truly carefree. She burns to see that lustful wanting in Amy's eyes, but all she gets is a pinched look, a firm set to her jaw.

"You got a minute?"

"Of course. Have a seat. It's…good to see you again, A— Dr. Spencer."

Amy nods and, still standing, thumps an inch-thick report onto Ellis's desk.

"What's this about?" Ellis slips her glasses back on while waiting for Amy to offer an explanation. She's happy to discuss anything with staff at anytime, but Amy's confrontational attitude is beginning to grate. It's as though she is set on punishing Ellis every chance she can, simply for doing her job.

"I know stats are important to you, so that's what these are. I've culled all the serious emergency cases at this hospital over the last five years. You'll see that in numerous of these, the outcome would have been extremely poor, including morbidity, if this hospital did not have a full-time emergency department as well as a surgical service."

"I see. Aren't you being a bit presumptuous about my conclusions?"

Amy ignores Ellis's comment. "I like to presume the worst and work back from there. In my job, and probably yours, there's no room for assumptions and hoping for the best. People would have died, Ellis. *Will* die, if you cut too deep. I can guarantee it. It's all in there." She points to her report.

"I understand that, I really—"

"I'm not sure that you possibly could. Not until you've walked in my shoes. Or any of the nurses' or other doctors' shoes. Or the patients', God forbid."

"You're not going to give me the benefit of the doubt, are you?" Amy's cynicism toward her—more than that, her hostility toward Ellis—is shocking. Hadn't they sort of reached a kind of truce? How is it that Amy has such a low opinion of her? The same Amy who once told her that she was lovely? That she was a nice person? Ah, but that was in bed. Outside of the bedroom, she clearly has a different opinion. Outside of the bedroom, Ellis is nothing but an interfering interloper. Ellis can't keep her frustration from boiling over. "Dammit, do we really have to do things this way? With acrimony? I thought we actually *liked* one another. What the hell happened? I'm still the same person you met two months ago, you know."

Amy finally slumps into the chair across from Ellis, slowly rubs her face with her hand. She looks defeated. Resigned. And right when Ellis thinks maybe she's gotten through to her,

Amy's words shoot from her mouth with the velocity of bullets. "We did. But this is too important. Much more important than afternoon romps in bed. Surely you get that."

Afternoon romps? Is that what Amy thinks of her? Of them? Sure, their dalliances had started out as nothing more than casual sex, but the caring, the affection, the tenderness that had begun to weave into their time together couldn't be her imagination. That deeper dimension to their lovemaking was as real as anything Ellis has ever known. Her spirit soared in those hours she spent with Amy, but clearly Amy has an altogether different memory of their time together.

Ellis tells herself to calm down before she says something she can't take back. "All right, look. I'm sorry for bringing our personal issues into this. But Amy, er, Dr. Spencer, you need to understand that I'm trying my best here, and I intend to do my very best for all parties involved in this process. So please keep in mind that I'm not the enemy. And I haven't already made up my mind on what I intend to recommend, contrary to what you probably believe. And maybe, just maybe, having me do this review is a damned sight better than somebody else the corporation could have hired."

"You may be right, but I can't assume that little will change here by the time this review is complete. In fact, I'm quite sure things will end up drastically different. The corporation wouldn't have hired you if it expected to keep everything the same, now would it?"

Arguing is pointless. Ellis has a job to do and so does Amy. It's not unusual with these reviews for people to become very possessive of their territories, stubborn about their priorities. Change is always difficult. And Amy is right about the fact that there will indeed be changes, because the hospital's budget can't sustain itself the way things are.

Amy gets to her feet, since Ellis doesn't really have an answer to her rhetorical question. "I thought so."

"Wait," Ellis says as Amy's hand lands on the door handle. "One more thing."

Back straight as a board, Amy turns around. She looks much less youthful than she looked a few minutes ago. "Yes?" she says warily.

"About Mia. Thank you so much for introducing her to the library volunteer work. I had no idea she was so into books. She actually talks about her day now when she comes home. Something I, well, am surprised about. It's really good for her to be doing this, and I know it wouldn't have happened without your intervening. Everyone needs a purpose, and good on you for recognizing that. I'm very grateful."

The thinnest of smiles skitters across Amy's face, much to Ellis's relief. "You're welcome, and I'm glad it's working out. She's…got potential, I think. She just needed a friendly little shove, that's all."

"Again, thank you. And…I'll be sure to look at your report."

Amy nods once and slips out the door.

* * *

Janice Harrison, the hospital's CEO, ushers Amy into her office and closes the door. It can't be good that Amy's been called into a private meeting, and for a fleeting moment, panic rises in her chest as she considers that Harrison has somehow found out about her and Ellis's romantic past. Ellis would probably be pulled off the case, which might be good. Or not. Ellis had a point the other day when she said someone else doing the review might be worse. At least Ellis is the devil she knows.

"I have to tell you, Amy, I'm not pleased that you furtively compiled statistics from our emergency cases over the last five years and gave them to Ms. Hall. You should have gone through me first."

"I'm sorry, Janice. I wasn't trying to be furtive. If I gave the report to you, I worried it would have to go through all the proper channels before it ended up in Ms. Hall's hands. If it all. I was trying to expedite her…research."

Harrison makes a face of displeasure. "What about patient privacy?"

"I redacted all the names and any identifiers."

"All right. Good. But, you know…" Her eyes say something different than her words. "No more end runs, please."

"Right. Of course."

"I have a task for you. And I'm afraid it's going to take you out of town for a few days."

"I have cases lined up for the next six weeks, plus my on-call shifts." She really doesn't want to have to go out of town, no matter how important the assignment.

"I know. I'm borrowing a locum surgeon from the city who can come in for four days and take your shifts and your cases."

Amy tries to banish the insubordinate thoughts she's having. She doesn't like handing over her patients to anyone else, which is why she seldom takes more than a couple weeks' holidays each year. Nor does she like being ordered out of town, but Harrison's tone brooks no room for opposition. "I see. What's the assignment?"

"I want you to go have a look at Soldiers Hospital in Collinsworth. It's very similar to ours in size and so is the town's population. I want you to really dig in and see how it's working since they implemented all their streamlining of services last year. With a full report for my eyes only. You're my emissary, my eyes and ears there so that we can be sure to file our own research-based opinion, if necessary."

Collinsworth is a town of about sixteen thousand people a couple hours' drive north of Toronto. It's famous in Ontario for its ski hills, and Amy skied there a couple of times when she was a student. "Wait a second. Didn't they dump their OB department?"

"Yes. And moved all elective surgeries."

"I don't need to go there to tell you what I think of those changes. Or what I might conclude in a report."

"You do need to go there. Because Ms. Hall is going there to observe the changes, and you're going to accompany her."

Amy feels her stomach bottom out. She pins her superior with a glare she hopes conveys her complete distaste for the whole idea. Seriously? She's supposed to go on a road trip with

Ellis? Just the two of them? For several *days*? And then she's to stab Ellis in the back with a secretive report that Harrison will hold onto until Ellis files her report?

"Wait. Can't Lakefield go?" Bob Lakefield, chief of staff, should be the one to go if Harrison is bent on a doctor accompanying Ellis.

"His wife is due to give birth any day. I can't ask him to go in light of that."

"So, if I may get this straight, you want me to be Ms. Hall's minder?"

"No. I want you to run your own parallel research. Talk to the same people she does, but form your own opinions."

"How soon is this supposed to happen?"

"My office is making the arrangements for the middle of next week."

Fuck and double fuck. She has to find a way out of this. "Soldiers Hospital. Don't you think it's a poor comparison? I mean, Ms. Hall is going to take one look at the place and want to do the exact same thing here, make all the same service cuts. Isn't this basically leading the fox to the henhouse? Giving her a template from which to copy her own recommendations?"

Harrison gives Amy an inscrutable smile. "Perhaps your being there, working alongside her, will give her a different viewpoint to consider. And if not, then your report will at least offer counterarguments to what Ms. Hall might conclude."

How the hell am I supposed to do all of that, Amy wants to argue. But if the CEO is entrusting her to help persuade Ellis against recommending drastic cuts, then so be it. She'll have to figure out how to do that, because if she's the only thing standing in the way of this hospital being gutted, well...it's a no-brainer. She'll take one for the team.

"All right," Amy relents. "I'll do it."

CHAPTER SIXTEEN

Ellis has hardly been able to think straight since she found out Amy will be accompanying her on what was supposed to be a solo field trip. They'll be flying into Toronto, where they'll rent a car for the two-hour drive north to Collinsworth, then be in each other's pocket for three days. How the hell is she supposed to handle this new development? Is there a playbook for going on a working trip with your ex-lover who can no longer stand the sight of you? On the positive side, the only reason for Amy's coldness is because they're on opposite sides of this hospital review and not because Amy truly hates her. At least that's what she tells herself. The rejection from Amy hurts far deeper than she ever could have imagined.

What the hell did you expect, that she'd propose to you or something? Okay, well, of course not *that*. Ellis has never seriously considered marriage before, not even to Mia's mother, so she's not about to start letting that crazy notion take a foothold in her brain now. She's in her mid-forties and in the prime of her career. She's financially independent, and her little fling with Amy has at least proven that sexually she doesn't need to be a loner. There are other women out there, good-looking, intelligent women like Amy who also have priorities that don't include relationships.

Except...

Ellis takes another long drink of cabernet, reaches for the bottle on the coffee table, and refills her glass. Mia is at Kate's, looking after Erin Kirkland's little girl while Erin and Kate enjoy a movie together. Now that she's alone, she realizes that she's slowly, sliver by sliver, breaking apart. Because Amy has become the cloud over her sun, the bleeding hole in her heart. And her fucking job isn't making her happy either. Buckets of money, yes, but not happy. The number crunchers love her. Board members, the bureaucrats at the Ministry of Health (because she saves them oodles of money) love her too. But the Amys and the Kates and the Erins of the world—oh, and Mia—not so much. To them she's uncaring, one-dimensional, obsessed with an agenda diametrically opposed to their own. A Cruella de Vil in a room full of puppies.

Well, they're wrong. She does care and she's not some emotionless automaton. Health care is the biggest industry and the single most expensive government-funded service in the province, and she's doing her part to keep it sustainable so that universal health care for all can continue well into the future. Doesn't anyone get that? That she's actually trying to help?

And then there's Mia, who has every right to hold her emotionally hostage for having walked out on her and her mother years ago with barely a look back. That was a mistake. Not in ending the relationship, because she was no longer in love with Nancy, but in the way she handled it. She'd been short-sighted, selfish, and it certainly wasn't the way she'd do things now. But she'd come back for Mia; she'd taken Mia when no one else wanted her.

Before she can blink them away, tears spring from her eyes. She chokes down another swallow of wine, another sip of self pity. She's a mess, something wholly unfamiliar to her, and she hates being this weak, this pitiful. She picks up her cell phone, scrolls down to Amy's number. One press of a button and Amy would be on the other end…well, if she chose to answer. What would Ellis say to her? "Hi, Amy, yes, I'm drunk, but I called to say I miss you and I want you back in my life and most especially in my bed." *Yeah, like that'll work.*

She tosses the phone aside and picks up her laptop from the coffee table. She logs into the dating website, something she hasn't done since she met Amy there. She could find someone else. *Should* find someone else. She's single after all; single and still somewhat sexy at forty-four. What the hell does she have to lose? But first she looks to see if Amy's profile is still there. Partly to see if she's looking for someone else to hook up with, but also to check out the photo that once drew Ellis in like nectar to a honeybee. It was a black and white photo, with Amy staring out at a sunny horizon, her hair windswept, her face smooth, her eyes curious but at peace, the tiniest smile beginning to curl the edges of her lips. She loves that photo, because it shows Amy's many layers.

But the picture is nowhere to be found. Amy has deleted her profile from the site. Probably took it down once they began seeing each other. Ellis should have removed hers too, but she'd forgotten all about it, hadn't even logged into the site until now. A couple of quick taps on her keyboard and now her profile is gone too. Screw it. If she can't have Amy, and clearly she can't, then she's going to forget about the whole damned dating thing for now. Or hooking-up thing. Whatever. She doesn't have the time, nor does she have the energy for all the highs and lows, all the damned work this stuff takes, all the drama, as Amy's behavior lately has reminded her. For something that was supposed to have been uncomplicated, simple fun, it's become anything but. And Ellis has nothing but her own stupid, betraying heart to blame.

Mia breezes in, locking the door behind her for the night. When she sees Ellis, with the nearly empty wine bottle beside her, she freezes. Stares at the offending bottle, the half empty glass. "What's going on? Are you drunk? Are you *crying*?"

"No and no. Well, maybe a little of both, but I'm fine. It's been a long day. A long couple of weeks, actually."

"You used to bust my balls all the time about smoking pot, but it's okay to drink a whole bottle of wine?"

"Language, young lady." Why do teenagers think it's their job to remind adults of their every little weakness, their every tiny mistake? *Jesus!*

Mia's apology comes in the form of a shrug.

"And you've given up pot, right? Like you promised the judge? And me?"

"Yes, I've given up pot. Jeez. And I thought we were talking about you, not me."

"I didn't mean to have quite that much to drink." She dries her face with the back of her hand and remembers, a little late, that she's supposed to be a role model. "Look, Mia, sometimes adults are tough on kids because we don't want you making the same mistakes we made. Or that you at least don't make really big mistakes before you have the experience and the know-how to deal with them. It's really that simple, okay? And yes, we still screw up, no matter how old we get. But I'm asking you not to screw up too badly yet. At least wait until you're thirty, okay? Please?"

Mia looks at her like she's grown a second head, and yet to Ellis, it's the most honest thing she's ever said to the girl. Some day, they need to talk about how and why she walked out of Mia's life, but not tonight. "Anyway, we'll talk another time. I need to go to bed."

"Wait. Is it okay if…if I stay with Kate while you're out of town?"

"Kate? I thought we were going to ask your grandparents if you could stay with them?"

Mia's face darkens. "I don't want to go stay with them. Please? Kate offered when I told her you were going on a business trip."

"But you barely know her and I don't know her at all."

"It's not like she's a serial killer, you know. Or, like, a pervert. She's going to come find you at work on Monday and talk to you about it."

"Is this what you want, Mia?" She has to admit, Mia's looking and acting more like a normal human being these days. She's begun styling her hair and keeping it neat, and she's been showing up the hospital for six to eight hours a day, every day, like clockwork. She talks to Ellis now. Not a lot, but it's a drastic improvement from before.

"Yes, it's what I want. And besides, who's going to man the library if I have to go back to Windsor?"

"Woman the library." Ellis takes a final sip of wine and picks up the glass and bottle to take to the kitchen. "All right, I'll talk to Kate on Monday. But so you know, we'll need to clear this with your probation officer, because the judge said if I have to leave town, that you're to stay at your grandparents."

"What if he says no?"

"I doubt he will. Kate's a responsible person, and I have no problem with the arrangement. But I'll have to tell Kate about this."

Mia's eyebrows pop into her forehead. "No! You can't. I don't want her or anyone at the hospital to know about…you know."

Ellis sets the glass and empty bottle back down on the coffee table. "Mia, I know you're embarrassed by what happened. But it is what it is. You screwed up. And guess what? We all do. We all, even Kate, I'll bet, have done crap in our past that we're ashamed of. Times where we wish we'd been a better person. Times where we'd done things differently." Dammit, tears are at the backs of her eyes again, ambushing her.

Mia's expression softens, as though she knows exactly what Ellis is referring to in her own past.

"Kate and anybody else worth their salt won't judge you. I promise you that. Now, I'll see you in the morning."

"Okay. And Ellis?"

"Yes?"

"Thanks."

"You bet, kid."

Maybe, Ellis thinks on her way to the kitchen, *there's hope for repairing this relationship with Mia after all.*

* * *

Kate takes up a lotus position on the end of Amy's bed, watching as Amy methodically organizes her suitcase for tomorrow's trip, starting with shoes on the bottom, then toiletry kit, then socks and underwear and a spare bra, followed by dress shirts and slacks. She's as OCD about her packing as she is about her instruments, her routine, in the OR. Kate, who knows Amy better than pretty much anyone, is so used to her quirks that she doesn't comment anymore. She clearly understands that it's Amy's way of preparing, of heading off problems before they happen, of reaching the comfort zone she requires in order for her confidence to be at its zenith.

"So you and Erin have had two dates now, huh?" Amy enjoys seeing her friend squirm at the question because it means it's time to press her on it.

"I refuse to call them dates." Kate's studying her nails like they're the most fascinating things on earth.

"I see. And was there any kissing after these non-dates?"

Kate reaches behind her and pitches a pillow at Amy's head. "Ow!"

"Didn't hurt, you wimp."

"Oh, I'm a wimp? What about you, too scared to give Erin a kiss?" She makes a smooching noise.

Defiantly, Kate says, "Who said I was afraid to give her a kiss?"

Amy drops the shirt in her hand to study her friend. "Seriously? That's awesome! I'm so proud of you, girlfriend. It's about time."

Kate's face suddenly crumples, and in seconds she's crying into her hands. Amy scoots over to her side and throws an arm around her shoulders. "Hey, hey, come on, it's okay. Erin's a really wonderful woman, okay? And she sure seems to really like you."

Kate nods through her tears. "I... It might be too soon, Ames. I've never kissed anyone since...Anne."

"I know, sweetie, I know. But it's only a kiss and there's no pressure for anything more, right?"

Kate sniffles, wipes her face with a Kleenex from her pocket. "Erin's been great. It's me. I guess I'm feeling guilty. And a little lost."

"Well, if it helps, I know Anne wanted you to find happiness in your life, to keep moving forward. Remember how many times she told you that? How she made you promise you wouldn't spend too much time being miserable or lonely or wallowing in self-pity? That you needed to make sure you got out there and enjoyed life?"

It'd been heartbreaking but incredibly brave of Anne to insist that Kate not spend the rest of her life paralyzed by grief. Amy didn't know if her own spirit would be so wise or so generous under similar circumstances. "Trust me on this, she would not have a problem with you dating Erin."

After a moment's hesitation, Kate concedes, abstractedly twirling her wedding band. "I know you're right. It's a hell of a lot harder than I thought it would be, that's all."

"So go slow. Take a step back if you need to. I'm sure Erin will understand. Have you talked about this with her?"

"Not yet."

"Talk to her, Hendy. She'll understand. I'm sure of it. Whatever you do, don't shut down on her."

Kate gives her eyes a final wipe. "Fine, but enough about me. What about you? And Ellis Hall?"

Amy forgets to breathe. To stall, she goes back to packing her suitcase. "What do you mean?" She wishes she could stop thinking that everyone knows about her and Ellis's former fuck buddy relationship. She's a grown-assed woman of forty—almost—and she can damned well sleep with whomever she wants. It's nothing to be embarrassed about. She'd probably have caved and confessed to Kate by now if it weren't for the thorny fact that Ellis is the consultant heading up the hospital's service review.

"I mean, it kinda sucks that you have to go away with Dragon Lady. You don't have to share a room with her, do you?" Kate's far too interested in the answer, as she scoots closer to Amy's position.

"Of course not. What is this, a high school field trip?"

"Just checking." Kate gives her a naughty grin full of innuendo. "What happens in Collinsworth stays in Collinsworth?" She lowers her voice. "She's gay, you know. She was once in a relationship with Mia's birth mother."

"So I've heard, but believe me, there's going to be nothing fun about this trip. I'm kind of dreading it, to be honest."

"Well, look, I'm only kidding when I call her Dragon Lady. She isn't so bad, you know. I spent some time chatting with her about Mia crashing with me while she's away. She's kind of nice…when she's not trying to pull the rug out from under us, that is."

"I'll take that under advisement." Amy mimes writing in a notebook. "Dragon Lady not so scary away from her job."

"I would still advise being nice to her. It can't hurt, right?"

"You really think that being nice to her will spare us when it comes time for her to make her recommendations to the board?" If only it were that simple. After all the orgasms she's given Ellis, the hospital should most definitely be golden. But Amy's not counting on miracles or on the power of orgasms.

"Fine, but try not to kill her, at least. That might not look good."

Amy frowns playfully. "Damn. I guess you have a point."

"Hey, let's celebrate your birthday when you get back, okay? I'll cook dinner and invite Erin too."

"Sounds great."

Amy zips up her oversized suitcase. She's not looking for miracles on this trip. She's looking to survive it.

CHAPTER SEVENTEEN

Ellis isn't fooled by Amy's avoidance tactics. They were supposed to be first class seatmates on the flight from Windsor to Toronto, but Amy couldn't volunteer fast enough to switch seats with a very pregnant woman who was in coach. After landing, they arrange a car rental because there's no way they can justify the expense of renting two cars. Ellis can't wait to see how Amy's going to avoid talking to her during the two-hour drive.

"You okay to drive?" Amy asks.

Ellis agrees, so Amy tosses her the keys.

"Good. I've got a podcast I want to listen to if you don't mind." She pulls out ear buds as soon as Ellis starts the car.

All right, that does it. She refuses to let Amy treat her so rudely. "Actually, do you mind skipping your podcast? It's been a long day so far and I'm a little tired. I wouldn't mind some company to help keep me alert." *Game, set, and match!*

"Well, I guess so," Amy says, grumpily stuffing the ear buds back in her knapsack. She gets to work programming the address on the GPS unit for their hotel in Collinsworth. Ellis can see on the screen that it says it's 110 kilometers away.

"Music?" Amy asks hopefully.

"No, thanks."

Amy settles back in her seat, keeps her head angled away from Ellis and toward the passenger window. To get her talking, Ellis begins going over their itinerary for the next two days. They'll meet with hospital administrators, heads of departments, and even the town's mayor for more of a community perspective.

"It'll be like a working vacation," Ellis says hopefully, not realizing until now how badly she could use a real vacation. "Don't you think?"

Amy shrugs. "Vacation? What's that?"

"I hear you. Which is why I'm looking forward to this."

Amy glances over, her gaze as sharp as a knife. "Well, I'm not. I have patients that I've had to hand over to someone else while I'm away."

"I'm sure your patients will be fine for a few days. I mean, you must go away to medical conferences periodically, no?"

"As few as I can help. My…parents are on their own and, well, they're not doing very well. Especially my dad."

Ellis wants to smile at the sharing of this nugget of personal information, but she can see that Amy is worried. "Are they going to be okay?"

"Yeah, just, you know, issues with aging. I try to do what I can, but they're sort of resistant to outside help. Which they badly need."

For the first time since they started on this trip, Ellis notices how exhausted Amy looks. No wonder. She's got patients to worry about, her parents, this hospital review hanging over her head. She looks so different, so much more worn out, than she looked during those afternoons at the hotel. Ellis recalls how her touch seemed to unlock something in Amy, resulting in what looked an awful lot like completeness, contentedness, or maybe serenity is the word she is looking for. *God, I miss you, Amy. I want you to feel those things again when you're with me.*

Ellis doesn't realize she's sighed out loud until Amy looks at her pointedly and asks how Mia's doing.

"Hmm, yes, speaking of being resistant to help. She's doing much better, thanks to you and Kate. You two have really helped bring her out of her shell."

"Good. I'm glad she's starting to find her way. She's doing great with the library. Takes the book cart around to the patients and their visitors a couple of times a day, plus she staffs the library for anyone who wanders in. She's even been putting up posters she designed herself encouraging staff and visitors to donate their gently used books."

It's a little shocking that Mia is so passionate about books and the library. Shocking too that Ellis is finding things out about Mia secondhand. "You know, I had no idea she was so into books. She's…a bit of an enigma. At least to me."

"Kate told me she got on the wrong side of the law? I mean, I hope it's okay that Kate told me. I'm not judging. We want to help, that's all."

"I know. It's all right. She's been a bit of a handful the last couple of years for her grandparents. Since her mom died."

"Oh, I didn't know. That's gotta be rough on a kid her age."

"It is. She was acting out. And she can be pretty sullen and withdrawn, as you probably witnessed. I agreed to take her for the summer, hoping that a change of scene will be good for her. So far, it certainly seems to be."

Silence fills the car until Amy veers the conversation into a slightly different direction. "So…you and Mia's mom were together?"

"We were. For three years. Mia was very young when we got together. Not much more than a toddler."

"I see. So you weren't together when her mom died?"

"No. We'd been apart seven years. And I'm ashamed to say we didn't keep in touch very often…holidays, birthdays, that's about it." She sent a card and gift to Mia every year for her birthday, Christmas too, but Mia barely responded. *Which was not an excuse*, Ellis reminds herself. She's the adult in this equation, and she should have kept in touch more often. But she's not ready to confess all of that to Amy.

Amy's eyes survey her in that frank, interested way she has. Not unusual for doctors, but Amy's astuteness continues to surprise Ellis. "Did Mia factor into your decision to return to the Windsor area?"

"She did. I...wanted to reconnect." There. Question answered.

The rest of the trip is filled with small talk followed by periods of silence. But it's progress.

* * *

Amy flops down on the king-sized bed, having stripped down to her T-shirt and boxers. She feels like a day-old rag after the long day of travel, which is also her excuse for rejecting Ellis's offer of grabbing a late dinner together. They've already had more than enough together time today. Any more and it would be weird. The worst of it is she thought she'd successfully erected a wall around her feelings for Ellis. That she'd successfully dismissed their little affair from her mind and from the dusty corners of her heart. Decided, so she thought, that she didn't care if she spent time with Ellis again because she's done with Ellis. She's over whatever it is she had once thought they were edging toward. Over it because she has to be. There's no question that Ellis holds the match that could burn down everything important in her life—her working life, anyway, which is pretty much everything. How could she possibly live with herself if she let her personal needs take priority over something as important as the hospital? Besides, in a few months, Ellis will be gone, leaving the damage behind without another look back.

And yet...she can't get Ellis out of her head. Even when she goes out of her way to avoid seeing her, thinking about her, there she is. Ellis is the dream that won't go away the next morning. Amy keeps seeing her smile. And her eyes—the almost tender way they held Amy after making love. Keeps seeing her hands too, and the sensual, balletic way they move. She sees her body, how it would fit itself around Amy, how it would respond to Amy's touch. Amy's raw, animal need for Ellis's body is like nothing she has ever experienced before. In bed, she and Ellis are pure combustion.

Out of bed, what are they? They're not friends—an impossibility—given their work relationship. They're certainly not lovers anymore and can't be again. But maybe, like Kate says, Ellis isn't the ogre Amy's worked her up to be. Maybe she's kind of...nice. She's taken in Mia, which she didn't have to do. And she's smart, has a sense of humor, possesses a surprisingly charming authenticity for someone with her kind of power. From their conversation in the car earlier, there is much about her that Amy hasn't even begun to discover. And she wants to, because in spite of everything, she doesn't hate Ellis. Doesn't even dislike her, truthfully. And even though it can't lead to anything further, not anymore, she wants to know Ellis better. She'll stop, she vows to herself, being such a bitch to her. She'll stop throwing up so many unnecessary roadblocks to getting to know one another a little better.

But still. There's a job to be done on this trip, and she's not ready to throw Ellis a welcome-to-the-neighborhood party yet. She needs to do her damnedest to insure that Ellis doesn't conclude that the cutbacks at Soldiers Hospital could easily be applied to Erie Shores Hospital. What works here won't work at home, Amy knows, and she'll try to steer Ellis into drawing the same conclusion. Failing that, she'll have counterpoints to everything Ellis might come up with.

Amy climbs under the covers and turns out her light. Ellis is in the room next door, probably doing the same. Or not. She might be a night owl, for all Amy knows, since she knows so little about her. Well, about her mind, her heart, her past, and her daily habits, but she's most certainly an expert on Ellis's body. Ah, yes, her body. Amy hasn't forgotten any of the luscious details: the long shapely legs, the notch at her hip, the finely trimmed red hair between her legs, breasts firm and round and so eager for Amy's touch. She can see clearly in her mind's eye the tender, almost translucent skin at the base of her throat. The spray of faint freckles across her nose, lips that are full and soft and perfect, eyes that are like green jewels rippling beneath the surface of a mountain creek. Ellis Hall is one of the most beautiful women Amy has ever known, and certainly the most beautiful woman she's ever slept with, hands down.

She misses those afternoons at the hotel. Misses them like crazy. Misses, she almost can't bear to admit to herself, Ellis.

CHAPTER EIGHTEEN

The morning's tour of Soldiers Hospital fails to exhaust or bore Ellis in any way. It's exhilarating to her, seeing firsthand how things work, especially since this hospital is two years out from implementing massive streamlining to its operations. Everything is clean and new, and the staff seems to be on board, even though the transition couldn't have been easy. This afternoon there'll be more meetings for them with staff, but for now, she and Amy are lunching at a popular Thai restaurant downtown with the chief of staff and the hospital's CEO.

"So tell us how the transition out of obstetrics has gone," Ellis asks their hosts, because OB is definitely a service cut she's considering recommending. Dozens of small hospitals in the last decade or two have dropped OB because of the declining birthrate, particularly in rural areas. And most of the government's hospital funding is volume driven. Erie Shores is right on that threshold line for births.

"As you know," says the chief of staff, a good-looking forty-something woman named Margaret White, "our area was seeing a declining rate of births, since much of our population consists of either retired folks or transients from Toronto who have weekend homes here, and none of those folks are having babies here. Of course, it meant we lost our two OB-GYN docs."

To be expected, Ellis understands. Baby deliveries pay doctors more money than gynecological services, so most of those doctors will move to an area where they can practice both specialties.

"How did the local folks feel about the change?" Amy asks with an edge to her voice.

The CEO, a tall, rail-thin man with a stoop to his shoulders, concedes that there was some predictable resistance, "but our population has adjusted."

"So part of the adjustment," Amy counters, affecting a neutral tone as though she's only stating a fact, "is that the locals have a forty-minute drive now to a hospital with OB services, correct?"

"Correct," replies the CEO. "But of course, we have an emergency department if there's not time to transport the patient. Nobody falls through the cracks." His smile is aimed at Amy, but she's looking anywhere now but at him. "We've also made changes to our surgical service, as you're aware." Amy's eyes swing back to him.

"Right," she says. "You've moved out electives. Things like colonoscopies, tonsillectomies, cataract surgeries, mastectomies, inguinal hernias. How many surgeons did you lose?"

Margaret White's smile evaporates. "I'm afraid a couple of our surgeons have moved on. But the good news is we've bumped up our orthopedics load."

Amy nods. "Right. The ski hills."

Well, Ellis thinks, *we don't have ski hills anywhere near Erie Shores Hospital.* She makes a mental note to compare the stats later for orthopedic surgeries at Erie Shores.

"It's rather flat where you are," the CEO says with a slightly sardonic smile. "No crashes on ski hills."

"No," Amy agrees. "But we do have a major freeway running through our catchment area. So lots of *those* kinds of crashes."

Ellis feels herself tense up. It's clear Amy is going to have a counterpoint to every argument, every statement. And she seems to be enjoying her role as devil's advocate.

"Tell me something," Amy directs to the CEO. "Do you have many migrant workers here? Farmers?"

The CEO shakes his head. "Not really. Most of the migrant workers in the region work in apples about forty kilometers west of here. They fall into a different hospital catchment area, for the most part. May I ask why you're interested?"

"Just curious."

Just curious, my ass, Ellis thinks. Amy's got something up her sleeve. Ellis has studied the demographics back home, and while it's true that Essex County is heavily agricultural, particularly in the Erie Shores catchment area, the rate of farm accidents isn't particularly worrisome. She's unsure what Amy's getting at.

After lunch, there are more tours and more discussions with department heads and staff. As the day winds down, Margaret White glides over to Ellis. "Ms. Hall. Would you be so kind as to join me for dinner tonight? I'd really love to chat with you more. There's a great little Italian restaurant not far from here."

"That sounds nice. And please, it's Ellis."

"Ellis, then. As long as you call me Margaret." The woman's smile leaves no doubt that she's hoping for more than a simple business dinner. "Oh!" she exclaims as Amy suddenly materializes, nearly stepping on the chief of staff's foot. "And you too, Dr. Spencer. Please join us for dinner."

Amy's scowl is unmistakable. She's being incredibly rude. She doesn't ask Margaret to call her by her first name. "Thank you, Dr. White, but I'm afraid I have other plans."

"All right, another time, then."

"Perhaps." The frost from Amy is so thick it could be scraped off, and while Ellis is a little embarrassed by the behavior, she's a little thrilled too, because it means Amy is, well, jealous. *Huh. So Amy is human after all.*

"What time shall we meet for dinner?" Ellis asks, eager to twist the knife a little, because it's the most emotion Amy's directed her way since their identities were revealed.

"I'll pick you up at your hotel," Margaret says, beaming like the victor, as Amy turns and walks away with a huff. "Let's say six o'clock?"

* * *

Amy's been kicking herself for not joining Ellis and Dr. White for their cozy little dinner. It was stupid, petulant, to turn down the offer. It doesn't take a genius to see that Dr. White has the hots for Ellis. And dammit, she's jealous. She shouldn't be, because Ellis is free as a bird, but it hurts. The thought that dinner might lead to sex is too much, makes Amy want to climb the walls of her room, so she heads outside to walk things off. She doesn't actually know if Ellis is the type to have sex on a first date, but with their own history of jumping into bed together so casually, she can only guess that Ellis is exactly the type. She kicks a stone along the path she's walking, sending it arcing five meters or so before it drops into Nottawasaga Bay with a dull splash.

Two figures are meandering ahead of her. It's nearly dark, so she can't identify them until she's pretty much on their heels. It's Ellis and the doctor, deep in conversation, but not, Amy is relieved to see, touching in any way. Her jealous side conjures up all kinds of ideas on how she might ruin their little date, but in her head, she can't help hearing her mother say "You were raised better than that, Amy Spencer." So she begins to turn around, intending to head back to the hotel before they notice her, but her competitive spirit races through her blood, numbing her brain and ripping her mother's voice to shreds. She turns back in their direction.

"Good evening," she announces to the backs of the two women.

They both turn around at the same time. Ellis smiles right away, while her companion looks a little paralyzed. She recovers quickly though.

"Dr. Spencer, hello. I was about to ask Ellis here, and yourself of course, if you would care to join me for a sunset boat ride on the bay tomorrow evening."

"Thank you, but are you sure? I wouldn't want to get in the way of anything." She wants to put them both on notice that she's fully cognizant of what's developing here.

Ellis shoots a couple of well-aimed invisible daggers right through Amy's forehead, her smile resembling something more sinister.

Margaret White tilts her head in confusion. "It'll be very informal. A handful of us from the hospital, mostly department heads, but I promise it'll be very laid-back. A chance for all of us to get to know each other a little better."

I'll bet, Amy thinks. "Well, in that case I'd be happy to join the crowd."

"Good. Great." Margaret shuffles in place, looks from Amy to Ellis like she's waiting for a signal that isn't coming. Finally she begins to back away. "Well, I'll call it a night then. I'll see you both at six tomorrow night down at the marina."

When she's gone, Ellis's fury is like a powerful gust of wind ready to mow Amy down. "You can take your jealousy, or whatever this is, and stick it where the sun don't shine. Understand?"

"Whoa. Who said I was jealous? And of *her*? Please. She probably went to medical school in Grenada or something."

Ellis's withering look is enough to make Amy dial things down a notch. "All right, all right. But don't pretend that Dr. White isn't all hot and bothered over you. Couldn't be more obvious."

"So what if she is? I mean, what's it to you? Seriously. You don't even want to be friends with me, so I don't understand what business of yours it could possibly be."

They begin walking back toward the hotel, their strides infused with anger. Amy doesn't have an answer for Ellis. And Ellis is entirely right. What business is it of hers if she wants to sleep with Margaret White or anybody else? The problem is she can't bring herself to admit that she still wants Ellis, that she cares for her...plus there's any number of other unnamed, complicated feelings gumming up her emotions. It's a mistake, but she decides to go on the offensive anyway.

"She's trying to soften you up, you know, charm the crap out of you, and not only because she's attracted to you. She wants you to think everything at her hospital is perfect and wonderful."

"Honestly, why would she care if I think things at Soldiers are wonderful and perfect? It's not like she's trying to sell me something."

Ah, but that's where you're wrong, Amy thinks, *because Margaret White is trying to sell you on her.* But she can't exactly say that to Ellis, not without igniting a war. She's fully backed herself into a corner, and she predictably flails around. "I don't know. Maybe she thinks you have some sort of pull with the Ministry or something. She's obviously trying to impress you. I mean, dinner? A boat ride? Really?"

"I think a boat ride would be amazing. Do you know how infrequently I get to enjoy something like that?"

Amy opens the door to the hotel for Ellis without thinking. "Please try to be objective, all right? That's all I'm saying."

"Oh, I think you're saying a lot more than that."

They don't speak in the elevator because two other people have joined them. But in the hallway in front of their rooms, where they're alone, Ellis lets her have it with both barrels.

"Dammit, Amy, what do you want from me? I'm trying to do my best here, with my job *and* with you, all right? Stop putting your foot out to trip me up every damned time I walk by. Jesus." Her face is as tight as an elastic band, and all Amy wants to do is hold her, soothe her, make her smile again. She hates all this anger between them, and yet she has no idea how to fix things.

"I..." What can she say? What *should* she say? That she misses Ellis? That she wants her more than ever? That she might be falling in love with her? Her throat tightens and she clears it roughly. *Falling in love? Is that what this is really about?* The jealousy, the constant thoughts of Ellis, the little ache in her chest every time she tries to breathe when she's around her, when she looks at her? No, she reasons, she can't be falling in love. They had spectacular sex, they had a great time together those few weeks, but love? Amy refuses to accept she's falling in love with Ellis, and all the complications such a ridiculous thing would mean. "I'm sorry, Ellis," she finally says. "I don't…mean to be such an ass. Well, mostly I don't."

Ellis shakes her head lightly, steps closer. "What am I going to do with you, Dr. Spencer?"

Amy's heart is a jackhammer in her chest. Oh, she knows what she wants Ellis to do with her, all right. That part has never changed. "Kiss me," she says without thinking, because she's desperate for Ellis to kiss her.

Ellis does. Without hesitation. The touch of her lips heats Amy from the inside, spreading through her limbs, leaving her numb and liquefied and wanting more. She melts into Ellis, kisses her back with a singular focus. Ellis's mouth is so perfect at expressing her desire for Amy, and Amy knows it wouldn't take much at all to move this little show into one of their rooms.

Breathless and unsure of what comes next, Amy manages to pull away, stares at Ellis, and is stunned by the soulfulness in her eyes. God, how she wants to take this woman to bed. It would be so easy to go with it, but then she remembers why they're here, and it's like cold water on her libido.

"I…think I better get some sleep," she says lamely. "I've set us up for a breakfast meeting tomorrow morning. Meet me in the lobby at eight?"

Ellis's mouth opens in confusion, but she nods shortly and gives Amy a smirk to show she knows perfectly well that this is about cowardice and not about having an early morning. "All right, Amy. We'll do it your way."

"Huh?"

Ellis fishes her room key from her pocket. "See you in the morning."

CHAPTER NINETEEN

The more the conversation around her intensifies, the more Ellis feels like Amy has ambushed her. The breakfast meeting also includes the mayor of the town, the general practitioner in charge of the local family health team, and the head of a patient advocacy group that fought the changes to the hospital. For thirty minutes, their three guests have been making it clear that it's not been as smooth a ride as Ellis and Amy have been led to believe and that many in the community continue to be unhappy about the changes.

Amy has shown no signs of regret or excitement about their surprise kiss last night. She greeted Ellis earlier this morning with a nonchalance bordering on rudeness, and now she's single-mindedly throwing herself into the conversation, raining questions on their guests, stopping occasionally to write something down in a little leather notebook. Ellis could have easily slapped her last night instead of kissed her for all the reaction Amy has shown since. It was Amy who asked to be kissed. It's Amy who keeps changing the damned rules.

It's not that Ellis disagrees with meeting folks who hold an unflattering view of the changes at the hospital. What rankles is that Amy refuses to trust that she might come to her own conclusions in a fair and thorough way, that she's incapable of considering all the angles. She thought they'd reached a certain level of trust with one another. Apparently, it didn't go further than the bedroom.

"How much of a hardship," Amy says to the family physician, "has removing the birthing suite and delivery services been for local women?"

Dr. Jennifer Glassman purses her lips before she speaks, making it obvious which side she's on. "As you probably know from our demographics, most of our population consists of seniors and people from the Greater Toronto Area who own vacation properties here. So those folks aren't having babies in our town. And that's what drove the decision to remove OB from the hospital. But for local women who are having babies, it is indeed a hardship to have to drive forty minutes away, especially with the winters we get."

"The demographics for our area are quite different," Amy replies, glancing at Ellis to drive home her point. "We have a much younger population. We have a massive amount of agriculture, which means we have migrant workers who spend months at a time with us. Many of those people don't have the means to drive to a distant hospital, and paying ambulance fees would be a hardship for them. Many of them deliver their babies at home, but if we lose OB, we won't have obstetricians to help them out."

Ah, Ellis thinks, *so that's where Amy's going with the agricultural theme.*

"The medical community around here isn't happy with losing OB," Glassman continues. "The two obstetricians we had moved away, of course, so now family docs are having to pick up the slack with pregnant women who can't always travel the distance for their checkups and follow-ups. And with gynecology too, so I more than get your point. There's no one here at the moment who practices gynecology or OB. It's a real gap in medical services."

The mayor, a woman who's mostly been sitting back observing, says, "This is the kind of thing that really hurts us from attracting young people and young families to our town. Don't get me wrong, it's fine to have the transient folks from the city, because they do spend a lot of their money here. But we also need permanent members of the community. The people who work at the ski hills and the restaurants and the stores that all the weekenders and seniors frequent—those are the people who keep things running in this town, and we can't forget about them. These changes have been hard on those people, there's no doubt."

"What's tough too," says the patient advocate, an impeccably dressed middle-aged man, "is that our citizens now have to travel that same forty minutes away for their elective surgeries. A lot of seniors aren't capable of driving that distance for their cataract surgeries, their colonoscopies." He shakes his head, sneaking a recriminating glance at Ellis. "I wish we could go back to the way things were, but they tell us it wasn't *efficient*. Like that's all anyone cares about these days." He raises his eyebrows at Ellis as if to challenge her. "It's not working to model rural hospitals after urban hospitals. Our needs are completely different than, say, Toronto's."

Ellis wants to scream out that she's not the enemy here, wants to remind them that she had nothing to do with implementing the changes in Collinsworth. This afternoon she's going to meet with the hospital's chief financial officer to take a look at the books. She has no doubt that all the changes are keeping the hospital in the black. Which is something these folks don't seem to want to acknowledge, because without remaining in the black, they're at risk of losing their hospital altogether. If that happens, everyone loses.

Ellis snaps to attention. "Tell me how things were working at the hospital, from your perspective, of course, before the changes."

The mayor smiles. "It was a great little hospital. People could give birth here, have their broken bone set here, or their gall bladder taken out, and they could die here too. A hospital is one of the most important pillars of a community. Now…we have to tell people that we can't do everything here."

"Tell me if I'm wrong," Ellis points out, "but you never could do everything here, right? There's no MRI, no oncology department, things like heart surgery or brain surgery have always been done elsewhere."

"True," the mayor says. "But for more common things, like babies and elective surgery—things that affect more people than those who need brain or heart surgery—it hurts that you can't do that here anymore."

The patient advocate pulls a sour face. "It's like they decided to cater to the ski hills and the wealthy people who come here to play on weekends, and screw the actual people who live here."

"Now, Fred," says the mayor. "It's not quite that drastic, although you make a good point."

"From the reports I've looked at," Ellis says, directing her comment to the family physician, "births at the hospital had been decreasing annually, to the point where there were only thirty-two of them in the final year of obstetrics here."

"That's true," Glassman concedes. "In fact—"

The patient advocate cuts her off. "So we say to hell with those thirty-two people? And what is it really costing the hospital to keep a birthing suite anyway? I mean, it sat empty when it wasn't being used, but so what? An empty room isn't costing anything."

"Ah, but it is," Ellis says and watches him squirm a little. "Empty spaces in hospitals may not be costing much money, but they're also not bringing in revenue. You have specially trained staff too who aren't using their skills, so that's costing money. The ministry today wants every corner of a hospital in use and it wants staff resources put to where they're most needed. Centralizing services, as this hospital has done and many others have done, accomplishes all that."

Ellis feels Amy stiffen beside her.

"A cookie-cutter approach," Amy says with a slight edge to her voice, "can't possibly work everywhere. Every hospital and every geographic area has its differences, its idiosyncrasies, which means they all require a unique approach."

"I couldn't agree more. Each hospital and each community needs its own unique methods of delivering health care services." It's why Ellis was hired, to specifically tailor a plan for Erie Shores Hospital and nowhere else. She digs into her boiled egg. She doesn't need to look around the table to know that the others aren't exactly jumping on her bandwagon. "Look," she finally adds. "I know you all want what's best for your community. But trust me when I say we *all* want hospitals to survive in this world of ever-increasing budgets and ever-increasing demands. Changes are a reality, and the trick is finding the right balance to keep patients happy and to keep the people who write the checks happy. And that's what we all need to strive for if we want a sustainable future for our universal health care system."

The mayor mumbles, "Good luck with that, Ms. Hall."

* * *

The water is like glass, leaving it an unblemished mirror for reflecting the setting sun. Conditions couldn't be more perfect for a boat ride, and this boat is a luxurious ride. It's a twenty-eight-foot wooden Chris-Craft cabin cruiser, a refurbished beauty from the late 1930s, Margaret White has been only too happy to explain to those on board. *More like brag*, Amy thinks, then reminds herself to quit holding it against the woman that she's attracted to Ellis because, well, who wouldn't be. It really is a beautiful boat, its wood polished to a fine gleam, and it slices through the water like a hot knife through butter. There's seating at the bow and the stern, plus a cabin below. Besides Amy, Ellis, and Dr. White, there are six others on board, all of them staffers at the hospital. There's a nice steel tub full of ice containing champagne (not the cheap stuff), wine coolers, and beer, and there are plates of cheese and fruit to nibble on.

To laughter, somebody starts singing the theme song from *Gilligan's Island* as Margaret unspools the anchor. The shore is about a kilometer away, and there's no one else out here, save for gulls and the occasional loon with its tranquil trill. *I could get used to this*, Amy thinks. The peacefulness, the beauty of the rocky shore and the hills beyond it, which are so unlike the flat lake her house sits on. Lake Erie has none of the rough edges, the rustic beauty, of Georgian Bay.

Amy has wandered to the stern, where she can be alone. The rest are at the bow or in the cabin below, where the food and beverages are. She can't keep her eyes off the sun as it slowly sinks into the water, painting the sky above it various shades of pink and orange and purple. She deeply inhales the fresh air, made cooler out here by the water. Even in the height of summer, the bay remains chilly because of its deep, rocky bottom. The tranquility reminds her that she should do this sort of thing more often—take time to be alone with her thoughts, to commune with nature. She loves her work, it's like the constant purring of a motor in her soul, but she knows it can't be everything. There's her family, but that's not exactly smooth sailing these days. Her parents are fast declining, and her sister, well, she has a full plate and a complicated life so far removed from Amy's.

It's been a long time since she's reflected seriously about her love life. Lisa ruined her dreams of finding a soul mate, a life mate. For a long time, anyway. Drained her heart and her energy dry, as only people with addictions and mental health issues can do. But Amy survived by throwing herself into her work, moving back home to be near family, having her friend Kate to distract her. And it worked until Ellis came along. Now there's a new force inside her, a force that demands more, that wants a full life that includes love, and it grips her now, making her stagger a little as though she's seasick.

"Whoa, you okay?"

She hadn't noticed Ellis, a half-filled champagne glass in her hand, making her way to the stern.

"Fine, yes." Amy sneaks a hand onto the railing for support.

Worry lines crease Ellis's forehead. "Are you seasick?"

"No, especially not when the water is like glass. Probably a little hypoglycemic, that's all."

"Come downstairs and get some food."

"Ellis…"

"Yes?"

Food. And company, that's what she needs. Ellis's company, to be specific, and without Margaret White and her bedroom eyes and her love of beautiful things. "Would you like to have dinner with me once we dock?"

Ellis's expression is annoyingly blank, and right when Amy thinks she'll say no, Ellis surprises her with a yes. "Did you know the restaurant at our hotel has daily fresh-caught fish on the menu? I wouldn't mind the whitefish. Being on the water is making me hungry, and these hor d'oeuvres aren't quite cutting it."

Amy plays along. "Good. I'm famished too." *Yes, that's it, make it all about the food, then we can pretend I don't want Ellis's company. We can pretend I'm not missing the hell out of her. We can pretend this means nothing more than a couple of colleagues sharing a meal, and not about two women who can't quite banish one another from their thoughts, from their hearts.* "Are you sure you don't have other plans?" An image of dumping Margaret over the side of the boat flashes through Amy's mind.

"I don't, though I was already asked to dinner." Ellis chuckles. "I turned it down."

Of course. Margaret White strikes again. And strikes out.

At the dock, Amy thanks Margaret for the cruise, catches her eyes and says, "You have good taste." She enjoys the mild look of confusion on the doctor's face before she and Ellis head to their rental car for the drive back to the hotel.

CHAPTER TWENTY

They agree not to talk about anything work-related over dinner. Initially, Ellis was worried Amy would clam up once that topic was off the table, but Amy has been surprisingly good company. The bottle of wine they've already gone through has certainly helped play the role of peacemaker, and Ellis orders a second one, something a little sweeter this time.

"Hey, dessert!" Amy says with a new twinkle in her eye. "We can't have wine without sharing a piece of cake."

Ellis raises her eyebrows but says nothing. Her hips don't need cake, but the thought of watching Amy eat cake from a fork makes her mouth water. Amy does everything not only with precision, but with intense spirit and passion. Like the way she makes love, withholding nothing. *Jesus*, Ellis tells herself, *stop thinking about sex!* There's nothing worse than thinking about what you can't have, and last night's kiss was a painful reminder of that. For Ellis, anyway. Amy hasn't shown the least indication that she enjoyed it. Or that she has an opinion about it one way or another.

A slice of cake is ordered—the chocolate, decadent kind with cherries and blueberries nesting in butter cream frosting. And Amy, with Ellis's blessing, has changed the wine order to a bottle of champagne. Not, she points out triumphantly, the same brand of champagne that Margaret White served on her boat.

"So," Amy says casually. "Siblings? Parents? Where'd you grow up?"

It hadn't occurred to Ellis before that she knows far more about Amy's background than Amy knows about hers. "Only child. Grew up in Halifax. My parents were both professors at Dalhousie."

"Sounds pretty idyllic."

"It was in a lot of ways. Except I lost them both when I was in my early thirties. Cancer took them two years apart." It wasn't fair, losing them so close together. But it was how they would have preferred it, having rarely been apart in their years together. Ellis often felt like the third wheel, that more often than not they preferred each other's company to hers. It's a comfort to her now rather than an irritation.

"I'm sorry. So...was Mia's mom your last serious relationship?"

The sudden veer in the conversation takes Ellis by surprise, but it's a fair question, especially now that Amy is getting to know Mia better. "My last and my only serious relationship, to be exact. Nancy was an accountant. We met through work."

"Was it love at first sight?"

"Not really. I was attracted to her. She was smart and had a great sense of humor." Ellis remembers how Nancy would drizzle hot sauce on their eggs to make funny faces. She bought Ellis fuzzy moose slippers one Christmas, after they'd almost hit a moose while driving through Northern Ontario on a camping trip. "She was fun and I needed that in my life. The fact that she had a young child complicated things a bit. I never really aspired to become a parent."

"I get that. I never did either. Which doesn't mean I don't like kids. I just didn't want the pressure of raising them."

"Makes sense, what with your career and all. I always felt the same. My career came first. And that's ultimately what destroyed my relationship with Nancy. That and…" Her hesitation draws the hard inquiry of Amy's eyes, but Ellis clams up. She doesn't owe Amy the explanation of how she literally woke up one day and simply couldn't do it anymore—couldn't play the role of partner and stepmom, not when those roles had become a burden against which she began to rebel and rebel hard. She started staying later and later at work, began volunteering to attend more conferences, to go on more business trips. A few times she snuck out on her own to catch a movie or to have a solitary dinner at a nice restaurant. She lost herself in that relationship or more like got buried beneath the avalanche of responsibilities and expectations. She's no longer the same person who walked out on Nancy and Mia with barely a look back, but how can she explain all that to Amy in sixty seconds or less? "Well, it's enough to say that it didn't fit who I was at the time."

"Any regrets?"

"Only in the way it ended. I never really apologized, you see. Never made up for what was definitely not my finest moment. And now it's…too late."

"But it's not too late with Mia, right?"

"I hope not, but…we'll see, I guess." Mia is a complicated kid. And one who, with her little digs at Ellis and her rebellious attitude, still hasn't forgiven her for walking out all those years ago.

"No." Amy shakes her head but says nothing more as the champagne arrives, their server pouring for them while announcing their slice of cake is coming right up.

Ellis sips the frothy perfection. "What do you mean 'no'?"

"I mean, there's no guessing involved. You're fighting for Mia, I can see that. You're all in, and Mia knows it. I think that's why her tough exterior is starting to chip away."

Ellis lets Amy's kind words sink in. She'd underestimated her powers of observation. "You really think so?"

"Absolutely. You two are going in the right direction, and that's what matters now. Last I heard, you can't change the past."

Ellis smiles, clinks her glass against Amy's. "Thank you for that. Your turn now. What's your big regret in the love department?"

* * *

Oh, God, Amy thinks, *why did I open this can of worms?* As if she's an expert on relationships and making amends. And now she's supposed to spill her guts about Lisa? No. No way. Because confessing all of that means confessing her own flaws, not to mention dredging up a painful period in her life that still has the power to hurt her. Like when you think an injury has healed until you suddenly move a certain way, and there it is again. Not as sharp as it once was, but there in the form of a dull ache.

She'd intended to make small talk during dinner, mostly succeeding until the wine began loosening her up. She has no one to blame for straying into personal territory, and now Ellis is looking at her expectantly. Because fair is fair. But now, luckily, she's saved by the cake's arrival. It's placed between them on a plate that nearly disappears beneath the mound of chocolate goodness, two forks perched on the side.

Amy downs half her glass of champagne and thanks the universe for sending the cake at this exact moment. "I think eating this cake takes precedence over discussing ancient relationships, don't you?"

"Well, since you put it that way."

Ellis's gaze—sexy, interested, engaged—nearly undoes her, and she dives into the cake to avoid looking into those viridescent eyes. How had she honestly thought she could avoid succumbing to her attraction for Ellis? Worse, how had she managed to convince herself she was the boss of her own feelings? Because in spite of the mountain-sized obstacles between them, the familiar tingle between her legs and the heat radiating inside her is enough to make her forget why she ever decided in the first place to try to keep Ellis at arm's length. She feels not a speck of the strength she felt last night when she'd ended their kiss. And it scares her.

"Ellis, I really think…" She looks up right as Ellis is licking frosting from her fork. Not just licking it, but luxuriating in it. Melting from the ecstasy of it. And it's so not fair. For the life of her, Amy can't remember what she was about to say, because every thought except for one has been sucked from her brain. *Jesus, I want to be the one to give her that kind of pleasure.*

After another bite, Ellis says, "Yes? You were about to ask me something?"

Amy mentally scrambles, finally remembers there is a question to which she's dying to know the answer. "Why *did* you turn Margaret White down tonight?"

"That's easy. I don't want Margaret White."

"You don't?"

Ellis's smile is playful if a bit sadistic. So is the way she's absently stroking the stem of her wineglass with a long, elegant finger. And then there's the heat ascending in her eyes, and Amy has no more defenses.

"Nope. She's not the one I want."

Amy swallows hard. She wants to hear the answer, *needs* to hear the answer, because she can't possibly be out on this limb all by herself. "Who, then?"

They look at each other, the truth catching up to Amy at the speed of her galloping heart.

"I want," Ellis whispers, leaning closer, "you. Only you, Amy, don't you know that by now?"

Ellis, with her sexy fork licking and flashing eyes and honey-thick voice is driving Amy crazy. So is the copious amount of wine she's drunk tonight, and yet, she's the most sober she's ever felt when she says, "Come up to my room with me."

They barely make it inside Amy's room. As soon as she closes and locks the door, she's pressing Ellis against it, kissing her as though she's trying to make up for the weeks of, well, not kissing her. Even in the elevator, they couldn't stop kissing, couldn't keep their hands from roaming. Desire cuts through Ellis, building to an explosive force. They're instantly transported back to that hotel in Windsor, it's Thursday afternoon all over again. They know so much more about each other now, but none if it has lessened Ellis's desire for Amy.

"You," Amy says, her voice thick and scratchy. "I want you so much, Ellis Hall. I can't stop thinking about you. Can't stop wanting you no matter how hard I try not to." Her words are exclamation points to the things her hands are doing…caressing Ellis's breasts through her blouse, gliding down to her ass and squeezing lightly, tenderly, then back up her hip to her abdomen, where her fingertips skitter lightly over the silk material, trailing up to the buttons of her blouse. Ellis moans as Amy gently licks her neck, her throat. She's so hot for this woman, she's already soaking her panties, the muscles in her legs like guitar strings about to snap. She throws her head back when Amy relieves the final button on her shirt and unclasps her bra.

"Bed," Ellis grinds out from behind clenched teeth.

Amy has other ideas. "Not yet."

Her hand is under Ellis's skirt, while her other hand fondles Ellis's breast. It's torture of the sweetest kind, the kind Ellis has been dreaming about and fantasizing about for the last six weeks. She's never stopped wanting Amy, but she's not naïve enough to believe that sex is all she wants from this woman. For right now, though, it's enough. *God, is it enough!*

"I want to touch you," Amy says, her voice so hoarse that Ellis barely recognizes it.

"Please."

Her hand finds Ellis's panties, skims an abstract pattern over them, driving her wild. She's hard and throbbing and wants Amy with an urgency that's more powerful than anything she's ever known.

"What do you want me to do to you?" Amy says. "Tell me."

Her brain has gone to mush, but Ellis pushes out the words. "I want your mouth on me. And…I want you inside me."

They manage to part long enough to strip down and fall onto the bed, Amy on top of Ellis, sliding slowly down the length of her body. She's kissing her way down, until she reaches her destination. Then she stares at her prize, licks her lips, and Ellis silently urges her on. She knows she'll come quickly; Amy does that to her.

The first touch of Amy's tongue sends hot liquid through Ellis's veins. She begins moving her hips in a quest to beg for more, and Amy obliges. Ellis squeezes her eyes shut, concentrates on every stroke, fascinated by how Amy switches up the speed and intensity of her lovemaking. Right when Ellis is on the very edge, when she thinks she can't take it anymore, Amy enters her. Slowly. She adds another finger, increases the pace until she's thrusting inside even as her lips begin slowly sucking Ellis into heavenly oblivion. Ellis swears she's going to break under the relentless salvos of such pleasure, but instead her body hungrily laps it up, absorbing every delicious blow until her orgasm rushes through her with a force that nearly levitates her off the bed. Her nails dig into Amy's back as she draws every last tendril of pleasure from her lover. Then softly, she cradles Amy's head in her hands, urges her up.

"Do you know," she says, her breath coming in hard rasps, "no one's ever made love to me the way you do?" It's more than that. No one's ever made her *feel* the way Amy makes her feel in bed, but she doesn't want to spook her. It's too soon for the kind of vulnerability that comes with complete honesty.

"Do *you* know," Amy says with a smile in her voice, "that no one's ever made me want to make love to them like that before?"

Ellis kisses her, tasting herself on Amy's lips, and it makes her want to do all those wonderful things to Amy that Amy's done to her. "I want to taste you," she moans into Amy's ear. "So badly."

The sight alone of all that wavy, red hair cascading over her thighs nearly makes Amy come. Ellis is like a starving woman, her tongue laving over Amy's sensitive flesh, sending fire streaking through her. Her fingers are dancing at her entrance, teasing, until Amy reaches down and pushes them inside her. She rides Ellis's face and hand, thrashing her head against the pillow. Being in bed with Ellis turns her instantly into a wild animal. And it's never been like this with anyone because she could never really let herself go, could never fully trust herself or her lover enough to let her own body take the wheel. It didn't happen with Lisa all those years ago, nor with the few transient lovers she's had in her life. Some day she'll analyze why that is, but not right now. Right now she needs to come. And she does, with a force that leaves her shaking and wrung out, even as Ellis climbs up and cradles her against her chest.

"It's okay," Ellis murmurs. "I've got you."

The simple declaration leaves Amy's eyes stinging with unshed tears, and her heart, well, she doesn't know what the hell is happening to her heart, except that it feels like it's going to explode. She's dying and being born at the same time, but she can't—won't—verbalize any of this to Ellis. She needs to figure out exactly what is happening to her first, and then she needs to weigh her options on what she's going to do about it all. *If* she's going to do anything.

"Stay here tonight?" she says to Ellis. She knows the invitation is a potential minefield for later, but for now, she wants to feel Ellis's body against hers all night long.

"Absolutely."

The next morning, Amy's head is throbbing a little from all the wine last night, but the rest of her is happily tingling from the sex. They'd woken and made love again some time in the middle of the night. Ellis has retreated to her own room for a shower and to pack, because they're hitting the road for home today. They've overslept a bit, so they grab breakfast sandwiches from the fast food joint down the street, then point the car in the direction of the Toronto airport for their flight home.

"Are you okay?" Ellis says to her once Collinsworth is in the rearview mirror.

They haven't talked yet. Had sex, lots of it, and ate their breakfast from their laps in the car, but they haven't talked about what this new development means or where they're going with it. Amy needs to be alone to think it all through before she plucks her heart out of her chest and places it on her sleeve for

Ellis to see. "I'm fine," she says, wincing at the inadequacy of the words.

Ellis, as is her nature, presses. "Amy, I can't make love to you and then have you ignore me or hate me or whatever. I want to see you. I mean, actually *see* you when we get back home. I want us to figure this out. I need us to figure this out."

Amy nods. "I'm not going to ignore you or hate you. But being together—it's a massive conflict of interest. For both of us." And just like that, her hesitation dies. Her excuses too. She wants to continue seeing Ellis. She wants to spend time with her, get to know her, be a part of her life, because with one match at a time, Ellis has gone and relit the lamps in the darkest, loneliest corners of her heart. "Christ, Ellis. Maybe I'm crazy. But I don't want to keep fighting this. Us. Not after last night. I can't."

Ellis reaches over and intertwines her fingers with Amy's. "Then let's not fight it. Entirely."

"What do you mean?" The hospital and the town they live in have eyes. And ears. And a boatload of judgment.

"We certainly can't be open about seeing each other, and as much as it kills me to say this, we can't sleep together again until I wrap up my work at the hospital. I'm only four months in, and I've got at least another three months of groundwork to do before I start preparing my report. I don't want to get pulled off this assignment by muddying the professional waters with—"

"Sex? Like we did last night? Twice?"

Ellis's cheeks are aflame, but she's grinning. "Right. Like that."

"But how the hell am I going to keep my hands off you?"

Ellis throws her head back against the headrest and laughs. "I'll dress like a nun. And maybe stop showering. Oh, and every other word will be the f-bomb. I could start smoking too, would that help?"

Amy laughs too, until it hits her that spending time alone together like this will be almost impossible. She stares bleakly ahead, through the drops of rain beginning to blur the windshield. "So we have three months where we sort of quietly see each other but don't have sex?"

Ellis nods, bites her bottom lip. "We can't risk officially dating. But I don't think I can handle pretending we don't mean something to one another."

Jesus, Amy thinks. *How the hell can this possibly work?*

CHAPTER TWENTY-ONE

"Ellis?"

Mia has had little to say since Ellis's return from her field trip. Not that she's ever been one to walk around like a talking doll with its string constantly pulled, but she's been more introspective than usual. She swore she enjoyed her stay at Kate's, so it can't be that.

"Yes?"

"What happens when you die? Like, to you as a person, do you think?"

Ellis's heart skips a beat. Is it an innocent question, or is there more behind Mia's words? One can never be sure with teenagers, and Ellis is by no means an expert.

"Why do you ask?" Ellis feels like she's picking her way through a minefield.

Mia shrugs. "Being around the hospital. Being around people like Kate and Erin and A— Dr. Spencer. And, you know, seeing people in the hospital that look like they're not going to make it out of there."

Ellis exhales her relief. Ok, simple curiosity, nothing to be alarmed about. "Well, I guess nobody knows for sure. Maybe it's one of those things that we get to create our own idea of how it's going to be, of how we want it to be."

"I'm asking what do *you* think."

They're having dinner out, something they haven't done in about a month. In the past, they would share a meal with minimal discussion because Mia is typically absent while present. As in, not interested in talking with Ellis. Until lately. It's a nice change, but one Ellis hasn't fully adapted to yet. She thought teenagers enjoyed talking about movies, celebrities, their friends, current events—not the kind of stuff you need a PhD in philosophy to answer.

"Okay. Well, I like to think that it's peaceful. That you're surrounded by the people and things you love and only by good memories, because you've shed all the negative stuff. And that you feel all that love while you kind of close your eyes and let everything go. After that, I have no idea what awaits. Hopefully good things. Hopefully some other place for your soul to go."

Mia chews thoughtfully for a while. "I think it was like that for my mom. The passing part."

"I sure hope it was. I'm sure it was."

"Did you know that…my mom stopped being mad at you a long time ago?"

"She did?" The food Ellis is eating sits like a rock in her stomach. "I'm so glad to hear that. Thank you for telling me."

Mia goes back to her burger and fries, the subject seemingly dropped, but to Ellis, it's an opening for something she's needed to address for months.

"Mia, I need to apologize for walking out on you and your mother. I'm sorry I failed you. And her."

Mia looks surprised. "You don't have to."

"No. I do. I handled it like I was walking away from a purchase I no longer wanted. Like the two of you didn't mean anything to me. Because you did. You *do*. I hate the way I handled leaving. Or didn't handle it, more accurately. I'm ashamed, Mia, deeply ashamed. I'm sorry." It's the regret that won't go away…

not from the passage of time, not from confessing her shame. But it's a start, she hopes.

Silence stretches out until Mia simply says, "Okay."

Okay? That's it? Ellis wants to press Mia to define what she means by okay, what she really feels about it all. Instead, she relaxes against the back of the booth and decides to let Mia process the apology in her own way, in her own time. "If you ever want to talk about it some more, please, I'm willing to answer anything you want to ask me."

Mia thinks for a long moment, smiles. "How come you don't date someone like Dr. Spencer?"

"Sorry?"

"She's really nice and super smart. And pretty good looking too."

Ellis clears her throat in a lame effort to buy some time. And to hide her shock. Apparently, Mia has been observing everything while pretending to hide behind that wall she's erected around herself. "Yes, I suppose she is all of those things."

Mia leans over the table a little and drops her voice. "I think she likes you."

"You do, eh? How do you figure that?" Around the hospital, Amy has been, if anything, cool toward her. Intentionally aloof, so as not to draw attention. It's nothing short of amazing that Mia has picked up on their feelings for one another.

"I can tell."

Jesus, when did this kid get so smart?

"Well, I'm afraid I—"

"Do you like her?"

Warmth suffuses Ellis's cheeks, not so much because Amy is the subject of their conversation, but because she hates the idea of lying to Mia. Betrayals start with lies hidden in the shadows of silence. And yet, she can't risk telling her the truth. Not yet. If she gets pulled off this hospital service review, someone else, someone far less fair-minded and competent might end up doing it. Maybe it's her ego talking, but she doesn't think anyone else can do the job better than she can.

"Look, Amy is all those things you say. Plus a really good doctor, from what I hear. But I can't date anyone right now who works at the hospital. It would be a conflict of interest."

Mia looks disappointed, but then she starts chatting about Kate and Erin, how they seem to be dating, and the subject of Amy, thankfully, is forgotten. If only, Ellis thinks, she could back up to the day she first met Amy Spencer and clairvoyantly end things before they ever started. A pointless exercise though, because Amy is a yearning Ellis can't exorcise. And if she's honest, she doesn't want to. There's too much substance that keeps her coming back, keeps her wanting more. Amy might be the best thing to come out of this job she's been hired to do.

* * *

Amy's mother greets her with her customary kiss on both cheeks.

"Where's Dad?"

"Puttering in his workshop."

It's code for sitting in a lawn chair in the garage, which used to be William Spencer's workshop, one where he made beautiful carvings and woodworking. A year ago, with his reluctant consent, the family had most of the power tools removed and sold off, because it wasn't safe for him, what with his declining cognitive abilities. He can still hand carve little pieces of wood though—wine bottle stoppers, figurines, key chains. He likes to sit out in his workshop and sketch things he might make, dream about what he might still accomplish.

"How was your trip north last week?"

Amy helps her mother pour some iced tea. "Fine. Productive, I guess, though no surprises." She's talked to her parents about the hospital review, though her father acts like it's news every time the subject comes up.

Amy and her mother take their glasses to the rear screened-in patio, where it's shaded and somewhat cool. Her mom moves slowly, eases herself down in her chair.

"Arthritis acting up today?"

"A little." That was her mom, always downplaying her aches and pains.

"Mom, when are you going to let me arrange more help for you both?"

"Please, not that old subject again. Your father and I are fine."

"You're not." The housekeeping is noticeably declining. The house isn't dirty, but it's dusty, untidy. The same old figurines and framed photos, decades old now, litter almost every surface, collecting dust, the photos becoming faded, the frames now chipped or scratched. Her mother never would have allowed such a state of shabbiness a few years ago. "I've got someone who can come in and clean for you once a week. They're prepared to start next week."

"Oh, dear, you know we can't afford that."

They're always complaining they're poor (they're not). "I'm paying for it, don't worry."

"No. Absolutely not."

"Okay, then you can pay for it. But it's happening." Enough negotiating. Begging, more like. Amy decided during her trip to Collinsworth that she would bring in extra help for her parents with or without their blessing, though getting them to buy in is preferable. She's been more than patient with them. "And I've got another idea. There's a young girl I've gotten to know who does volunteer work at the hospital, a teenager. What if she came for an afternoon a week? She could do whatever odd jobs you wanted. Yard work, groceries, laundry, or even just to provide company to sit with." She has yet to discuss the idea with Mia, but she'll be halfway there if her mother would agree to it.

She can see her mother's frustration and sense of helplessness beneath the veneer of cheeriness. It's a struggle to stay in their own home, and her parents hate the idea of being a burden. But there comes a time, Amy understands, where pride and ego and independence must take a back seat to reality. Her mother needs to come to that conclusion too.

"She needs the work," Amy hastens to add. "You'd be doing her a favor. She's also trying to find her way a little bit after some hard times, and I know you guys would be a great influence."

Her mother has always been a sucker for a good cause. "Well. Do you really think it could work? I mean, are you sure she even wants to do this?"

"I'll talk to her. And I'll set up a meeting. How's that?"

Her mother stares at the sky for a minute. "What's her name?"

"Mia."

"I like that name."

"Me too. So it's a deal?"

"If you think it's a good idea. For her, I mean."

"Oh, I absolutely do."

"Then I guess it'd be okay."

"Good. Great." She might need to enlist Ellis's help to get Mia to agree, and the thought that she'll have to chat with Ellis, alone, makes her smile. They've only seen each other lately in hallways or in the cafeteria at the hospital. It's too risky to text or email, though they've shared a handful of dirty late night phone calls.

"How's Dad, any changes?"

"Not really. Why don't you go sit with him for a bit?"

"I will. I'll bring him some iced tea."

In the garage, Amy hands her father a plastic cup of iced tea and unfolds a lawn chair next to his. "How's it going, Dad?"

"Hi-ya, Amiable." It's his pet name for her when she was a kid, and she's surprised he's remembered it. "So, how many knees have you replaced lately?"

Amy's heart sinks. He's forgotten she's a general surgeon, but there's no use in correcting him. She smiles through the disappointment she has to hide. "You know how it is, always lots of work available for a surgeon these days."

"Bah, surgeons. They're such a humorless bunch."

Amy wants to laugh but doesn't. She finds it best to go along with whatever direction his thoughts take him. "You're right. I should have become a family physician like you, Dad."

"Na, no money in that, my girl."

True, but then, her father never cared much about money.

"Dad, do you remember when I was about five and we were in the city, and you took me on my first escalator ride at the department store?" She can remember how scary those moving metal steps looked, their razor-sharp teeth poking out, how they could swallow up your feet and maybe your whole body if you didn't time your steps properly. He'd taken her hand, and at exactly the right moment, effortlessly swung her up and onto the first step. He was always there to rescue her anytime she thought something might go drastically wrong. Now he's the one who needs rescuing.

"Escalator? What's an escalator?"

She explains it to him, but confusion stares out at her from his glazed eyes. Probably shouldn't have brought it up, but sometimes he remembers the weirdest things. They drink their iced tea in companionable silence until he says, "They say it might snow this weekend."

"Rain, Dad. We shouldn't have any snow for a few months yet."

"Ah. Rain. Isn't that what I said?"

"Right. Yes. My mistake."

Amy tightens her grip around her glass. It's the only thing she can think to do to keep from bursting into tears.

CHAPTER TWENTY-TWO

The smell of coffee, real coffee, greets Ellis before she hears the knock on her office door, which is open a crack. She doesn't care who's there. With coffee smelling that divine, she's willing to invite in the Grim Reaper himself.

"Come in, whoever you are, as long as that manna from heaven is for me."

It's Amy, a cardboard cup in each hand. Coffee forgotten, Ellis smiles and peels off her glasses. "You're a sight for sore eyes." She keeps her voice low in case anyone else is wandering the hall. She hasn't seen Amy alone in days, and it's like Christmas and her birthday all rolled into one.

"Thought you might like a real coffee. It's from the café down the street."

Ellis gratefully accepts her cup, her fingers intentionally brushing Amy's, and the brief contact is almost like sticking her finger into an electrical socket. Amy gently nudges the door shut behind her, then perches on the window ledge a few feet from Ellis's desk. Sitting there sipping her coffee like that, she reminds Ellis of a cowgirl, minus the hat and the blade of grass hanging from her mouth. She's cocky yet humble, gorgeous yet accessible.

"Mmm," Ellis says as she savors her first sip of coffee. It's the good stuff, arabica beans with a hint of cinnamon. "Thank you, this is delicious. But first things first."

"Yes?" Amy's voice is low and sexy, and a swoop of her hair falls rebelliously over her forehead, kissing her eyebrow. The definition of muscles in her shoulders and thighs can be plainly seen through the thin cotton of her scrubs, and it occurs to Ellis that Amy's totally clueless about how sexy she truly is.

Amy Spencer, what am I going to do with you? Well, she has a few ideas, and can't dismiss the little fantasy of kneeling before Amy right now and making her a very happy woman. "Do you have any idea how sexy you are in scrubs?"

"What, these old things?" Her grin is playful, teasing.

"Yes, those old things. But you'd look hot in anything."

"Says the woman who's itching for a booty call?"

"Guilty as charged. And how are you managing this little exercise in carnal deprivation?"

Amy's grin disappears. "Not so well." She hops off the window ledge, setting her coffee aside, and places her arms on either side of Ellis's chair, her face inches away from Ellis's. Oh, such sweet torture. And such sweet surrender. They kiss, and Ellis closes her eyes, luxuriating in those impossibly soft lips and the promise they hold. While it's a promise they can't act on, it's there, and Ellis is instantly reassured that Amy wants her every bit as much as she always has.

"Now that we've got that out of the way," Amy says, chasing her words with a small growl from deep in her throat. "God, you look and smell so good. Remind me why we agreed to this celibacy thing again?"

"Oh, you know." Ellis points to her laptop. "Something about our jobs, I believe."

"Oh. Right." Amy expels an exasperated sigh and goes back to the window ledge. "How many more months? Or can we measure it in weeks now?"

Ellis softly shakes her head. "Don't."

"I can't help it. I hate this. I want to be with you." She's keeping her voice low, but Ellis glances at the door, which does not have a lock.

"I know, believe me." Her voice cracks. She needs to keep it together. "Anyway, I assume you're here on some kind of pretense? Other than bringing me this delicious coffee."

"I am. I finally got my parents to agree to have someone come every week for housecleaning. Also a meal service that will bring them a hot meal five days a week. My mom has even given me permission to have someone stop in for an afternoon a week to help with the odd chore, like laundry or lawn raking or just to keep them company if they need it."

"That's great." Amy has mentioned that her father has dementia that's been progressing and her mother has arthritis, but that they're resistant to giving up their own home in favor of assisted living.

"Trust me, this is a major victory. The thing is…I'm wondering about approaching Mia to do the weekly afternoon thing. And what you think of the idea."

"Wow." Good for Mia that Amy trusts her enough to ask her to help out her parents. "I'm so glad you think Mia is up to a task like that."

"She is. But I wanted to get your take on it before I ask her. I'd pay her twenty-five dollars an hour."

"I'm sure she'd love it. But the thing is, she's only with me another month."

"What? I thought she was, I don't know, sort of yours now."

"No. Her grandparents in Windsor have legal custody of her. She's supposed to resume living with them as soon as school starts the second week in September."

"Crap."

"I'm sure she can help out your folks until she has to leave, though."

"Sure. That'd be great. But Ellis, if I ask you something, will you answer me honestly?"

"Of course."

"What's going to happen to her when she moves back there? I know she got into some trouble back in June, but she seems to be doing so well here. I don't want to see—"

"I know, I don't want to either." Ellis has lain awake at night worrying about what's going to become of Mia when she has to return to the city. "And you're right, she's a different person since she came to live here with me. I know it's a vulnerable age, an impressionable age, but I have no legal claim on her."

The fact that Amy cares about Mia touches Ellis. Amy is a good woman: strong, caring, moral, patient. She rates much higher on the good-person scale than Ellis does, and Ellis vows to herself as she falls into the grey oceans of Amy's eyes that she'll do better, that she'll *be* a better person. She doesn't simply want Amy; she wants to deserve Amy.

"I'll talk to Mia about what she wants to do when school starts. It ultimately comes down to her grandparents, but I don't want that kid to fall through the cracks either. She's come too far for that to happen. I won't let it happen."

"Good. Should I ask her about working for my parents?"

"Absolutely."

"And…if I can help with the other. I mean, if my recommendation, or vouching for her or whatever, would help with her grandparents or with her probation officer, please let me know."

"I will. Thank you, Amy."

Amy hops off the window ledge, zero enthusiasm in her body language as she says, "I guess I better go. Wouldn't want to kick the rumor mill into high gear for being in here too long."

Ellis walks her to the door. "Hey, what about, I don't know, going for a drive after dark one evening, out to the lake or someplace…private." Ellis hasn't had a make-out session in a car since she was a teenager, and she swears it's the best idea she's had in months. Maybe years.

There's a massive twinkle in Amy's eyes when she says, "You're not just a pretty face, do you know that?"

"Um, yeah, I kind of did know that."

"Good. What about this Saturday night? I'm going to be at Kate's for a little barbecue with her and Erin, but I won't be there more than two or three hours."

Ellis bites the inside of her cheek to keep from giving anything away. Kate's hosting a surprise fortieth birthday party for Amy, and she and Mia have been invited. "All right. I'm already looking forward to that late night car ride."

Before she slips out the door, Amy gives her a look that feels like a caress.

* * *

Amy tightens her hold on the two bottles of wine—one red, one white—as she rings Kate's doorbell again. *Where the hell is she?*

Kate finally appears from along the side of the house. "Hey, buddy, come on around to the back."

"All right." She follows her friend around the side of the house, where she swears she can hear whispers and shushing noises. "Everything all right?"

"Of course. I'll take the wine from you and put it in the house," Kate says, accepting the bottles, "while you go hang out on the patio."

By the time they enter the backyard through the gate, a chorus of voices yell out, "Happy birthday, Amy!"

There are more than a dozen people gathered, and they're all grinning, all looking at her expectantly. Her parents are even here, along with her elusive sister, Natalie. So is Mia and…Ellis. *Oh, no.* How are they going to pretend in front of all of these people? Amy is a planet and Ellis is the sun, and all she wants to do is be next to her. They'll have to behave toward one another exactly as they do at the hospital these days, polite but not too friendly. "Are you serious? A surprise party?" she says to Kate in a scolding tone, but she's not upset. It's the nicest thing anyone's done for her in a long time.

"Well, it is your fortieth, after all."

"Can you say that a little louder?" she teases. It doesn't bother her that she's forty, because it means she's now officially entered the prime of her career. A recent study concluded that the best surgeons are in their forties and early fifties because they're still at their physical and mental peak and have accumulated a suitable amount of experience to accompany their training, which remains relevant and fresh.

Amy dutifully goes around the patio and greets everyone. She hugs and kisses her parents and congratulates them on not letting the cat out of the bag when she was at their house a few days ago. She hugs Natalie, inquires after her husband and kids. She fist bumps Mia, and when she gets to Ellis, she can barely breathe. Her hair is pulled back in a ponytail, and she looks incredibly youthful in bright yellow, knee-length shorts and a white cotton shirt that's short-sleeved but with peek-a-boo shoulders and a low neckline.

"Hello, Ellis. Thanks for coming." They shake hands, and Amy prays that they look neither awkward together nor too familiar. It's a fine line that she's not sure she'll handle deftly.

"My pleasure. Happy birthday." Ellis's eyes sparkle, giving voice to a hundred things that her mouth can't. Amy gives her hand an extra squeeze, fights the urge to run her thumb along Ellis's palm and up to her wrist. Torture. Sweet torture, touching but not touching.

There's a smattering of coworkers to greet, plus Erin, who's glued to two other women, one of whom looks exactly like her. Ah, the twin sister. At last.

"You must be Ellie," Amy says to the woman who's so clearly Erin's identical twin.

Ellie laughs, and instead of shaking Amy's hand, she wraps her in a big hug. "My sister idolizes you, which makes me an automatic fan too. You know, since we share the same brain and all."

"I highly doubt that," Amy says. "Your sister thinks you're pretty fantastic, in case she's forgotten to tell you lately. She talks about you a lot."

Ellie beams and clutches the hand of the woman next to her. That's when Amy notices the small tummy bulge Ellie is sporting. "Amy, this is my wife, Claire."

"Hi, Claire." Amy shakes the woman's hand, taking note of the fact that Claire is quite a bit older than Ellie, something Erin failed to mention. Probably because nobody cares, including Amy. "It's nice to meet you. And thanks for coming."

"Thank you for letting a stranger help you enjoy your special day. Erin has been talking nonstop about you, so you really don't feel like a stranger at all."

"Thanks, Claire. I'm glad you could come."

Eliana appears from behind her mother, then points to her aunt's stomach. "Aunt Ellie's having a baby. I'm going to be a big cousin!"

Amy scoops the little girl up in her arms. "I see that. Tell me, Eliana, are you hoping for a boy cousin or a girl cousin?"

"A girl! Girls are more fun than boys."

That draws a huge wave of laughter. "Can't disagree with you there, kid." Amy sets her down next to her mother, congratulates Ellie and Claire, and urges them to make themselves at home. "Be sure to save room for cake."

"Amy," Kate says. "Come into the kitchen with me and help me with the salads?"

"Sheesh, does the birthday girl have to do everything around here?"

"She does." Kate goes up on her toes to whisper into Amy's ear. "Especially when I need to talk to my best friend."

"Your wish is my command. Lead on, then."

On the counter, Kate sets down the bottles of wine Amy brought. "Grab yourself a glass, kiddo. And don't pour lightly. It's your birthday. You can walk home if you need to. Or catch a ride with somebody."

Amy does as she's told and pours herself a glass of red. "Or crash on your couch?"

Kate's cheeks are suddenly bright red.

"Um…oh, unless you're entertaining an overnight guest tonight?"

"I am. I think. Mia and Ellis are taking Eliana to their house tonight for a sleepover so Erin and I... Oh Christ, Amy, what the fuck am I doing?"

"Well, I'd say you're getting lai—"

"Stop!" Kate swats at her. "I'm serious."

"So am I. It's about time, Hendy. It's called living your life, and Erin's a wonderful woman. I'm so pleased. I think it's awesome. You two seem perfect for one another."

"But I feel..."

"Don't. Don't feel anything except happiness, okay? Or you're going to blow this chance. Look, it's going to feel weird whether this happens now or a year from now or ten years from now. Accept it. And understand that it won't feel so weird the second time. Or the third time, or the fourth time."

Kate busies herself removing large, plastic covered bowls of various salads from the fridge, while Amy retrieves spoons and salad tongs from a drawer. When she looks at Kate again and her busy hands, she notices something missing.

"Holy shit, you've put your wedding ring away. Oh, Kate. That's a huge step for you, but I'm so happy you're moving forward. Are you okay?"

"Do I look like I'm okay?"

"No, but you do look happy. The okay part will follow, trust me."

"I don't know, hon. It's all so new and so...weird." She reflexively touches the part on her finger where her ring used to reside. Amy can imagine it feels like when your tongue keeps searching for a missing tooth, finding only the gap.

"Answer me one thing," Amy says. "Does Erin make you happy?"

Kate stops what she's doing. Grins. "Yes. She does."

"Well, look at you."

"What?"

"You're in love. And I couldn't be happier for you." Amy gives her friend a quick hug, feeling Kate's shoulders relax against her.

"Thanks," she says, "for talking me off the ledge."

"No problem. But as payment, I expect to hear all about it tomorrow."

"Ha, you wish. What about you? I don't like you being lonely."

"Who says I'm lonely?"

"Come on, cut out the 'I'm happier on my own' crap. You're talking to a pro here who wore out that line a long time ago. And for the record, your dry spell is a hell of a lot longer than mine."

Hmm, not exactly. But to Kate, she puts on her single-for-life act. "I'm too busy to get involved with anyone right now. I'm covering for Atkinson, remember? And this review is hanging over all our heads. I'd be miserable company for anybody else." Not exactly lying.

"Not buying it," Kate murmurs, barely above a whisper.

"What?"

Kate glances out the kitchen window to where everyone is mingling on the patio. "Do you know who would be absolutely perfect for you? You even look good together. And I swear there were sparks coming off the two of you out there."

Oh, God, don't say it, don't say it.

"Ellis Hall."

Crap. She said it. Amy has to really work at mustering up a look of incredulity. She brushes her sweaty palms against her shorts, pretending she's picking off lint.

"I'm serious. And she's not nearly the big meanie I thought she was. She's terrific with Eliana. Mia too. I mean, it's obvious she really cares about that girl, even though they've had their issues. Mia told me a bit about their background together, and I'm impressed Ellis is stepping up to the plate, you know?"

Amy clams up, afraid she'll put her foot in her mouth and give everything away. Afraid too that even without speaking, Kate will figure everything out in about two more minutes. Either way she's a dead woman. "Hey, how about I start taking these salads out? People look like they're about to start eating their arms. And besides, you don't want everyone staying all evening."

Kate looks aghast. "Shit, you're right. Let's get these people eating, now!"

Amy laughs. "They'll eat so fast, they'll get indigestion."

Kate points to a giant bottle of Tums on the counter. "Got it covered, buddy."

Ellis isn't surprised by how attentive Amy is with her parents. She pulls out chairs for them, dishes up food and takes it to them, makes sure they're comfortable. Her eyes rarely leave them. Except for when they find Ellis. And then Ellis feels the most pleasant of aches in her throat. Even when her back is to Amy, she can feel when her eyes land on her. Is this, she wonders, how it feels to be in love? To be so perfectly in sync with someone else, that you know exactly when they're looking at you? Or what they're going to say? *Wait*, she silently commands herself. *It's way too soon to be thinking about love.* They're so far from being able to have a public relationship, a *real* relationship, it's not funny. And what if they truly end up on opposite sides of this hospital review? What if Amy can't abide by any of her recommendations and, worse, takes it personally? What if Amy hates her by the end of all this? That, she reminds herself, is why she needs to emotionally protect herself. At least a little.

"Ellis?" Amy has snuck up behind her, her mere proximity setting off a wave of goose bumps along Ellis's arms.

"Yes?" Ellis turns and is looking at not only Amy, but at Mia and Amy's parents, and Amy's sister Natalie. She feels the tug of emptiness at having no family of her own, but only a little, because she'd rather smile at what's before her. She supposes these people could be her family—someday—if she so chooses. And if they let her. But she's getting way ahead of herself.

"We've been getting to know your daughter," Amy's mom, Rose, says. Ellis doesn't correct her on calling Mia her daughter. "And she's a lovely young woman."

She is? Oh, right, she is. At least, this new Mia certainly is. "She is. I'm very proud of her."

Mia shrinks at the compliment, which secretly pleases Ellis.

"What do you think," Rose says, "of Mia coming to our place one afternoon a week?"

"I think it's a great idea, as long as Mia agrees."

"I'm going to get twenty-five bucks an hour," Mia says with excitement. "I've never made that much money before. Not even doing Kate's lawn."

"Ah, an entrepreneur," Amy's dad, William, says. "Nothing wrong with that. But if you really want to go where the money is, go into orthopedics. Like Amy here."

Amy discreetly rolls her eyes. "Forget medicine, Mia. Go into business, like Ellis, if you want to go where the real money is. Right, Ellis?"

Ellis playfully narrows her eyes at Amy. "I'm not the one driving the Audi Q5."

Amy laughs. "Guilty as charged."

Natalie thanks Mia for agreeing to help her parents. "I wish my own kids…well…never mind." She turns to Ellis and begins to fangirl. "Gosh, has anyone ever told you you're a dead ringer for Rayna James on the show *Nashville*? You could be, like, her stunt double or something. It's uncanny."

"I've heard that a time or two, but I don't watch much television, I'm afraid."

"So you've known my sister awhile, then?"

With her eyes, Ellis sends out an SOS to Amy, but they're saved by the racket Kate and Erin are making as they haul out a big birthday cake onto the patio, one with about a million candles on it. The crowd joins in on serenading Amy, who enlists Eliana to help her blow out the candles before they drip all over the frosting.

"Thank you, everyone." Amy can't escape giving a little speech, because the crowd starts chanting, "Speech, speech," and they're not letting her off the hook. "All right, all right, I get the hint. Wow, you guys. You really did manage to surprise me, especially since I was hoping nobody noticed I was turning forty today. I kind of figured I'd drink away my sorrows over hitting the big four-oh, so thank you for not letting me do that alone."

She glances at her watch for effect. "Although there is still time for that. Okay, everybody, out!"

They all laugh, and Amy raises her palms to show she's kidding. "Seriously, thank you. And let's not wait for somebody's birthday again to do this. Kate? You outdid yourself, my friend, so thank you. All of you made today very special." Her eyes flick to Ellis for an instant, and the butterflies fire up again in Ellis's stomach. There's no mistaking the heat in that look. Ellis has seen it many times before when they were alone together, but never in a crowd. This is definitely new. And sort of wonderful.

"Mia," Ellis says, "why don't you take Eliana to our place? I'm sure it's almost her bedtime." The sun is quickly setting and the child has begun yawning now that the excitement of the party is drawing to a close. "I'll be along in a few minutes."

"All right." Mia takes Eliana by the hand and they wander off to say their goodbyes and to collect Eliana's overnight bag.

Amy steps up to Ellis, keeping a respectable distance between them. "That's really nice of you to take Eliana for the night. I know Kate and Erin really appreciate it."

"Hey, I know what it's like to crave some alone time with your lover. God, do I ever." She moans so quietly, she doesn't think Amy hears her until Amy grins slyly at her, steps a little closer. Ellis can feel the warmth radiating off her skin.

"Since you're helping babysit, I guess our car-ride date for tonight is out of the question."

"Dammit, I'm sorry."

"Walk you home instead?"

"Yes, please. Though it's only around the corner."

"Take the long way?"

"How did you get so good at reading my mind?"

Amy laughs, dares to give Ellis's wrist a quick squeeze. "Let me make sure my parents get into a cab and I need to say a few goodbyes first."

"Of course."

Ellis watches Amy depart, her mind imagining some ingenious ways of sneaking her into the house later. Into her bedroom, to be exact. Then she remembers how nothing gets past Mia. As in, zero. The kid could be a professional spy.

A walk will have to suffice.

It's almost dark, so Amy slips her hand into Ellis's once they're away from Kate's house. If a car comes along they'll separate in a hurry. All this sneaking around, it reminds Amy of her first girlfriend, a classmate in her Grade Nine gym class who was super religious and didn't want anyone finding out about them. "You know, it feels like we're cheating on somebody."

"I know. I'm so sorry about that," Ellis says it with such sadness that it nearly breaks Amy's heart. "At least it's temporary."

Amy doesn't respond because she can't. What is their future? Do they even have one? The better question is, does she want a future with Ellis? She's not sure, because if she's completely honest, she's still holding back the biggest part of herself—her heart. Because even if she takes Ellis's job out of the equation, she can't be sure her heart knows how to love again, to trust again. There's no question it can't endure another heartbreak. But what if the old excuses are just that, old? And worthless? What is she really afraid of?

"Amy? How come you never talk about her?"

The question comes as a shock. Amy knows damned well who Ellis is talking about, but she makes her spell it out. "What? Who?"

"The woman who so badly hurt you."

"How do you know there's a woman who's hurt me?"

Ellis slows their pace so she can look into Amy's eyes. "Because it's there. In your eyes. A shadow of something devastating. Your heart has a ten-pound weight attached to it."

Amy shrugs because she doesn't want to deal with this, not now, but she can't help but be impressed by Ellis's astuteness. What else has she figured out about her? "Most of us have a past relationship that didn't end particularly well. Yourself included. Right? I'm no different. It was a long time ago."

Ellis has that tenacious look in her eyes, the one that says she'll keep pestering her about Lisa until she gets an answer.

And she's right to want to know. Amy might be stubborn but she's not stupid. She knows she will need to talk about Lisa if things go further with Ellis, but it's not going to be tonight. She clutches Ellis's hand tighter and twirls her around until her back is up against a thick tree trunk. She brushes her lips against Ellis's mouth, lingers there until Ellis responds. They kiss deeply, Amy losing herself in the citrus and mint of Ellis's hair, in the warmth of her body pressed against her, in her lips that are so soft and perfectly moist. She drops a kiss onto Ellis's bare shoulder, then another and another. If her body and her heart ever truly align over this woman, Amy knows she'll be a goner.

"Aren't you afraid someone might see us?" Ellis's breath is ragged, her chest beginning to heave slightly, but the hungry look in her eyes says she cares only about more kisses.

"Not really. Some things are more important."

They kiss again, and Amy longs to run her finger the length of Ellis's thigh. The little PDA was supposed to be a diversionary tactic to keep Ellis from asking questions, but damn, she's so turned on! What she really wants to do is unzip Ellis's shorts, right here against the tree in the murky light, and fuck her senseless with her fingers.

"Wait." Ellis pulls away. Clearly she's read Amy's mind. "We can't, not here."

"I know. Damn it, I want you so badly."

"I want you too. But I want more of you than…sex, Amy."

"I know." It sucks, sneaking around for a few quick feels and kisses that leave them both wanting more. It's not enough, same as their Thursday afternoons in the hotel weren't enough either. It took only a couple of afternoons with Ellis in that hotel room before Amy could think of nothing else, no one else, but Ellis. Her mistake was in thinking that she could handle wanting more. Actually, her mistake was failing to consider how complicated things would become for them. She'd been too busy enjoying the ride to wonder about its destination.

"I've got an idea," Amy says. "Let's have a real dinner date." She needs more than a few cheap thrills up against a tree on a dark street if she's ever going to know if her heart is strong enough for this.

"How?"

"Do you have an evening free next week? I mean, one where Mia's busy doing her own thing?"

"Yes, I think Tuesday night she'll be at Erin's babysitting."

"Good. I'm free then too. Meet me at that Becker Street pub again. I'll get there first. Walk in like it's a last minute decision, like you're there to eat alone, but then you see me and we're simply two…" Amy's tongue gets twisted because what she really wants to say is *lovers* instead of *strangers*.

"Work colleagues who happen to be at the same place for dinner?"

"Exactly."

Ellis's agreeable smile is all the answer Amy needs.

CHAPTER TWENTY-THREE

Like clockwork, Amy sits alone at a table exactly when she said she'd be there. That Amy is so reliable, so responsible, edges Ellis's respect for her up a few more notches. She's a keeper, she truly is, but there's so much distance yet between whatever this tepid dance is they're doing now and being a real couple. They're a long way from having anything worth counting on. So much so that it makes Ellis's heart sink. Alone at night with her glass of wine, it's too easy to tell herself Amy will never be hers.

"Good evening, Dr. Spencer. Mind if I join you?" She says it loudly in case anyone is eavesdropping.

Amy smiles up at her, leaps to her feet like a gentlewoman until Ellis sits. "Absolutely. No sense in both of us eating alone. Nice to see you again, Ms. Hall."

"By the way." Ellis sits down, lowers her voice so only Amy can hear. "I meant to tell you, your parents are lovely. I was so glad to meet them at Kate's. Mia's really looking forward to—"

"Her name was Lisa."

"Oh."

"We met in first year at med school and became inseparable. McMaster U. She was fun. Smart. Pretty." The look on Amy's face is not fond or wistful, but pained. "We moved in together within six months. We were never apart. She wanted to go into gynecology."

"Okay." Ellis doesn't want to spook Amy; she wants her to continue. "What happened?"

Amy gives her head a little shake, as though she's swamped by memories too painful to share. It's another minute before she speaks. "She…began to fall apart by second year. From the pressure. She fell behind in her studies. Couldn't sleep, didn't eat properly, eventually wouldn't leave the apartment. Began self-medicating with drugs and alcohol because she was afraid that if she sought help, she'd be kicked out of her studies. She had to drop out anyway by the end of third year."

"Oh no. You tried to save her, didn't you?" Of course Amy did, it's her nature.

She only nods, but the heaviness in her brow makes Ellis's stomach tighten into a hard knot. It's easy to imagine Amy trying to help her girlfriend study, bringing her notes from classes, desperately urging her to seek help, maybe even lining up appointments for her. Because those are exactly the things Amy would do for someone in need. "I couldn't help her, ultimately. It was hell." She chokes out the last bit.

Neither woman speaks for a while, and their server interprets the silence as a good time to approach. They order a giant, fully loaded pizza to share along with a glass of red wine each, which Ellis hopes is a mood lifter. Seeing Amy so vulnerable is breaking Ellis's heart.

"I almost didn't survive it."

So it was worse than Ellis imagined. "But you did. You saved yourself. You did the right thing."

Amy shrugs one shoulder. "I know. But…"

You're too good for your own good, Ellis thinks. "No, Amy. You saved yourself instead of becoming a second casualty. It was the only reasonable choice you were left with. How long were you together?"

"Almost five years."

"Almost *five years*? Of hell?"

"Not all five years were hell. Just the last three and a half. I don't take commitments lightly."

Was that a dig at her own past, at walking out on Nancy and Mia? She searches Amy's face for evidence of an intentional insult but can find none. "No, I can see that you don't. But I think it's more about your habit of putting other peoples' needs ahead of your own." Ellis smiles to soften her judgment. "A wild guess on my part."

"I've been accused of it before." Amy smiles too for the first time since Ellis sat down.

"So…what happened to Lisa?"

"Her parents took her back to Vancouver. I heard she was eventually diagnosed with bipolar disorder, but we haven't kept in touch. I have no idea how she's doing. I mean, I hope she's doing well, but I…can't be friends with her. I can't go back to being emotionally invested in how she's doing."

"I understand. And so your experience with Lisa has left you…"—*relationship-phobic comes to mind*—"hesitant to get too serious with anyone again?"

"I guess I'm not much of a mystery, am I?"

"Nope. So no serious girlfriends since?"

"Nothing past three or four dates." Amy shifts uncomfortably in her seat.

Ellis can relate. After Nancy, she stayed away from serious entanglements because, for a long time, she worried she would break someone's heart again. But she's not the person she was in her late twenties and early thirties, and neither is Amy. She feels she's speaking for her own benefit as much as Amy's, because they could both use a little pep talk. "You're not that person anymore. You're strong, you're smart, you're so good in here." She taps the center of her chest. "It would be a real loss for you and for…the woman in your future…if you forever close yourself off because of your past. Don't let it define your future, Amy. Don't let yourself keep being a victim."

Amy's gaze sharpens. "Is that what you think I am? A victim?"

"I think you have been a victim, yes. But now I think you let your feelings of guilt, of fear, paralyze you from taking a chance again. You're victimizing yourself. You won't allow yourself to be happy because somehow you think you don't deserve it. Or else you're an eternal pessimist and think nothing will ever work out for you."

Amy looks like she's going to bite Ellis's head off, but then her shoulders relax and her anger vanishes. "I did ask, didn't I?"

Ellis badly wants to reach out and hold Amy's hand; she practically has to sit on her hands so that she won't. "I meant it when I said I want to be your friend. I'm not trying to hurt you. I want you to be happy. I want you to be okay. And not just because I want to date you, but because you deserve to be happy. You deserve to be okay, Amy."

Amy looks away, like she's weighing something in her mind. When her eyes drift back to Ellis's, it's as though a storm has been swept away. "Thank you."

"You're a survivor, Amy. You *survived*."

Amy tucks into the pizza, the weight that's been removed from her shoulders leaving her suddenly famished. *We're all survivors of something*, she supposes. Oh, she's not naïve enough to think she'll never be completely out from under the specter of Lisa, from those years of being in the trenches of mental illness with her. There are still scars, but the word *survivor* resonates in her mind. She pulls her phone from her back pocket, apologizes to Ellis, types for a few seconds.

"Survivor," she says, quoting an online dictionary. "A person who continues to live, especially after a dangerous event." She says the word *live* like it's an epiphany. Which it sort of is. Kate, during many of their mutual pep talks, has been telling her to get on with her life, but Amy never had a reason to until Ellis walked into it. Ellis makes her want to *live*. Ellis makes her want to jump on the carousel instead of standing there watching it go around and around.

"My point exactly." A smug smile tugs on Ellis's lips, but she's being joyful, not rubbing it in. "You're *alive*, and that means *living* life, not just enduring it."

"I'm not sure I know how to be in a relationship without waiting for the other shoe to drop." Which is exactly why this off-and-on, sort-of-but-not-sort-of-dating Ellis thing is ripping her in two. But she doesn't want to be sad anymore. She wants to laugh with Ellis. She wants to feel normal, whatever that is. "And do you have some ideas on how I might enjoy my life more fully?"

"Oh, I most certainly do."

A young woman, late teens or early twenties, shyly approaches their table. "I'm so sorry to interrupt. Dr. Spencer? I just want to thank you for everything you did for my mom last winter."

Amy recognizes the girl but can't remember her name or the patient she's talking about.

"Sorry," the young woman says, including Ellis when she casts her eyes around their table. "Emergency appendectomy. Martha Thompson."

"Right!" The woman's appendix had burst on the operating table. Her outcome would have been much worse had her surgery been delayed even a few more minutes. She was one of the redacted cases on the files she'd prepared for Ellis. "How's she doing?"

"Fantastic. Back to golfing almost every day, thanks to you. She's very lucky. I mean, we're very lucky to have you, Dr. Spencer."

"Thank you, er…?"

"Autumn Thompson."

"Autumn, I'm so glad she's doing well. Thanks for letting me know."

Autumn slips away with another apology and more words of gratitude. Ellis quirks her head at Amy. "You could practice surgery anywhere. Be a star at a big-name hospital in a world class city. So why practice here?"

"Why not here?" Amy takes another sip of wine. "This hospital has everything—well, we don't have MRI and we don't have specialized surgical equipment for brain and heart procedures—but I have a lot of latitude here to do all kinds of surgeries. And our staff is second to none."

"Growing up here, having your parents here. I'm sure that's part of it?"

"Sure, absolutely. I enjoy my work, and if I can do it anywhere, I'd rather do it where I'm comfortable. Where I have roots. Where I know everyone."

"It doesn't bother you, having strangers come up to you at a restaurant like that?"

Amy laughs, explains how there's no such thing as anonymity for doctors in a town of eighteen thousand people. "That's part of the appeal. Seeing or hearing how patients you've operated on are doing once they're off your roster. I get to see firsthand, outside of the hospital, my patients as people. They check me out at the grocery store, deliver my mail, fix my car. It's a community here and I love being part of that." She shrugs lightly because to her, it's no big deal, but Ellis studies her like she's pulling back the curtain on something mysterious.

"Hmm. Being part of the community. Is that why the hospital staff seems to go the extra mile? I mean, I've noticed some of them staying well past their shift. And not putting in for overtime." Ellis's cheeks begin to pink. "I checked."

God, could she be any more adorable? Amy grins at her. "We're not much of a mystery, us small town people. Well, except for when we meet strange women in hotel rooms in the big city."

Ellis laughs, blushes. "Do you have any idea how nervous I was that first time?"

"Probably about as nervous as I was. I felt like we were doing something illegal. Like masterminding a bank job or something."

"And that at any moment the cops were going to bust down the door?"

"Exactly."

"So why did you, er, want to hook up with a stranger for sex? What made you do it?"

Amy still can't believe she had the guts to go through with meeting Ellis that first time. It was so contrary to anything she'd ever done before. "I'm not sure. I guess part of me was trying to bust out of this...this little prison my fears have kept me in. I guess I was desperate to do something that I didn't really have to answer to anyone for, including myself. No guilt, no commitments, no responsibility. All I had to do was show up and have a good time." It sounds shallow, but Ellis is nodding.

"I felt the same. Plus I was in a new city and didn't know a soul. And now here we are, living in the same small town. On an actual date together."

"Except we're pretending we're not."

"There is that. But...Amy? There's nothing fake about how much I want to be with you."

Amy looks at Ellis for a long moment. She'd give anything to be able to discard every last fear about being with this woman. Her heart is resilient. There's room for Ellis there. What she can't reconcile is if Ellis plays wrecking ball to the hospital, because that would take a permanent chunk out of her soul. "In the mood for dessert?"

"Not unless it's a piece of cake."

Amy nearly moans out loud, remembering their shared slice of cake in Collinsworth and how Ellis seductively relieved the fork of its crumbs and frosting. She sweeps her eyes over the scooped-neck blouse that shows off the smooth skin of Ellis's cleavage with its fine spray of freckles. She appreciates how Ellis always wears clothing on the alluring side when she knows she's going to be seeing Amy. "On second thought..." She casts around to see if anyone's watching them. "I think cake might be trouble."

"Can't disagree with that."

"Did you drive here?"

"Cab."

"Would you like a ride home?"

Ellis's smile is one of pure innuendo. "Thought you'd never ask."

A pleasant swarm of butterflies invades Ellis's stomach when Amy turns her Audi SUV down a dead-end road not far from her house. She knows what's coming, and a hot make-out session is exactly the kind of dessert she craves. She misses Amy's body. Misses the intimacy of lying together, of holding one another, of shutting out the rest of the world. But Amy, as much as she tries to hide it with a sexy comment or a ravenous kiss, continues to keep her heart tightly under wraps. Amy is the shadow Ellis chases and can't quite catch up to. Ellis gets it, she really does, but she worries she'll lose Amy, that Amy won't have the guts to take a chance on them when the time comes.

"Do you know," Ellis says in a voice thick with emotion, "when I realized I'd started caring for you?"

"When?"

"It was after we'd been together a couple of times and I saw you with your sister at that restaurant. I realized I was jealous. That I wanted it to be me sitting across from you."

Amy laughs softly. "And I saw you there with your former in-laws and Mia. I was afraid I was the only one who was jealous. It kind of felt like we were a couple, and yet it made me realize I knew nothing about you. That you were a complete mystery. And I didn't want you to be."

"I know. Seeing you out of context like that was jarring. It made me want to know you."

Amy pulls the car over on a deserted section of the road. It's dark now. She turns off the headlights, cuts the engine. She looks at Ellis with a searing heat that goes straight to Ellis's crotch. God, she wants this woman so badly. How on earth will they be able to control themselves?

Amy reaches for her hand, twines her fingers with Ellis's. It's such a sweet and unexpected gesture. "I want to make love to you as much as I want to breathe. More, if I'm honest."

"I know. Me too. It drives me crazy every time I see you."

Amy raises their joined hands and kisses the back of Ellis's hand. "So I'm only going to kiss you and only for a few minutes, because I won't be able to stop if it goes on for long. Or if I let my hands wander."

"All right. I understand. But…Jesus, I want you too, Amy." Ellis runs a finger from her free hand down the length of Amy's cottoned thigh, feels the immediate tensing of muscles beneath. She trails her finger back up, this time along the inside of Amy's thigh.

Amy darts her hand out to capture Ellis's. "I can't," she says hoarsely. "Seriously. I won't be able to stop."

"Kiss me, at least." *And dammit, I wish you* wouldn't *stop.*

Amy's eyes grow dark and hazy as she leans in and presses her lips to Ellis's. Her lips are soft, delicious. Kissing Amy is both familiar and new every time. The kiss grows deeper, greedier, until it becomes oxygen to the fire raging inside Ellis's belly. What Ellis really wants to do is crawl into Amy's lap, sit astride her, press herself into her, guide Amy's fingers down into her waistband until they find her wetness. She can barely endure the torture.

Amy doesn't want to stop kissing Ellis. She wants to haul her into the back seat and fuck her and be fucked by her until their screams echo through the compartment of the car and out into the night air. What is this insanity that's taken over her? Is it because she and Ellis started their relationship (if that's what this is) with sex first? Has it always been the forbidden, naughty aspect of their togetherness that holds her so captive and smitten? She breaks from the kiss, closes her eyes against the headrest. No. This isn't about the sex or the sneaking around. It's their chemistry, both in bed and out, but it's also Ellis: a woman who's so strong, smart, independent, incredibly capable and confident, and yet who's also soft and kind and vulnerable when she chooses to expose that side of herself. She loves how soft Ellis's eyes can be in that surprising, amazing way that only women who are supposed to be hard and invulnerable can do. It both breaks her heart and fills it.

"Penny for your thoughts?" Ellis's question pulls Amy from her introspection.

"You really want to know?"

"Of course I do. I don't ask questions if I'm not interested in the answers."

That's certainly true. "Sorry. You're right. I'm trying really hard not to be a downer…about us."

"Talk to me, Amy. I'm not going to cry or run away no matter what you say."

"All right. What's going to happen to us when this review is over? Once you've submitted your recommendations?"

"What you really mean is, are we going to survive it as a couple?"

It's remarkable how well Ellis already knows her after only a few months, and Amy wonders if she's that predictable or whether it's because Ellis really understands her. Either way, it feels weird. It's been so long since she's cared about someone else's thoughts and feelings. It'd be easy to give in. All she has to do is give Ellis a promise, even a hint of a promise. The kind of answer Ellis wants, which is, "Yes, I'll wait for you no matter how the review turns out." But Amy can't do it. The hospital, her heart, they're two sides of the same coin because the hospital takes up so much of her heart. This review is like tree roots hidden beneath a carpet of leaves, waiting to trip them up. No matter how much they try to avoid talking about it, it's still there.

Ellis doesn't wait for her to answer. "We can survive it if we want to. If we trust one another. I guess that's the big stumbling block, isn't it? Do you trust me, Amy?"

Amy doesn't honestly know the answer, but the pause has Ellis huffing out a frustrated breath.

"Look," Amy finally says. "What happens to this hospital means everything. I could get a job anywhere, I know that, but I want my job to be here, in this community. And every single person in this community cares about that hospital and needs that hospital."

"I know that. Which is why I'm trying to help save it."

It's Amy's turn to huff in frustration. "I think we have different definitions of what's required to save it. If it even needs saving. And we have far different visions of what it might or should look like when all this is over."

"Fair enough. But please. Let me do my job. Trust me to do my job and to do it well. Okay? Because if you can't…"

She doesn't need to finish. They both understand that they're hanging on to each other by a thread.

Amy starts the car. "I'll take you home now."

At the curb in front of Ellis's place, Ellis turns in her seat to face Amy. "Do I mean something to you?"

"You do, Ellis. A great deal."

"Do I mean as much to you as the hospital?"

"That's hardly a fair question."

"Maybe not. But if I don't, then the answer is no, we may not survive this review."

Shit. "Ellis…" She doesn't know what else to say, except she doesn't want this to end.

Ellis pulls on the door handle. "I want you, Amy. All of you. And I'm still going to want you after this review is done. But I have to do my job, if that's all right with you."

"Yes, of course it is." Is it, though? If some outsider tried to influence Amy on how to perform a particular surgery, would she react any differently? Not likely. "Ellis, I'm sorry, okay? And I don't want this to be goodbye. I do *not* want to say goodbye to you."

"You aren't." Ellis hops out, then leans back in. "But I think maybe we should cool things down for a little while. Let us both concentrate on our work, okay?"

Amy nods because she can see that arguing will do no good; Ellis closes the car door and walks away.

"I adore you, Ellis Hall," Amy whispers into the emptiness.

CHAPTER TWENTY-FOUR

Ellis has noticed the downturn in Mia's mood lately. Not anti-social and snarky like she once was, but something is definitely up with her, given how much she's been moping around. Ellis has taken the cowardly route of trying to keep her distance the last couple of days, hoping Mia's mood improves on its own, but the waiting game isn't working. They need to talk about her living arrangements with school starting in little more than a week, and waiting for Mia's mood to change might take forever.

Over Mia's favorite take-out pizza for dinner, Ellis asks her how she likes working an afternoon a week for the Spencers.

"It's fine. Good. They're nice."

The clock from the stove ticks as they chew their food.

"And your volunteer work at the hospital is going well too?"

"Yup."

Oh, boy. "You've more than met all your volunteer requirements now as part of your probation. Do you think you'll keep your work at the hospital going for now?"

"Definitely."

"Great." Ellis pushes her plate aside, waits for Mia to meet her eyes. "But we need to talk about what's going to happen once school starts."

Mia's gaze sinks back to her plate, where a half-eaten slice of pizza awaits. "I guess. If you really want to."

"I think we need to."

Mia's voice cracks as she says, "You're going to send me back to Windsor, aren't you?"

"No. I didn't say that." No wonder she's been waiting for the other shoe to drop. "You get a voice in all this, you know. What do you want to do?"

"Stay here. With you." Mia looks like she's miraculously shed a huge burden as she tries to swallow down a sob. She's suddenly the little girl that Ellis remembers, learning how to ride a bike.

"You do?"

Mia nods. It's a relief that she finally accepts Ellis's contrition, Ellis's attempts to make things right, but this is a big deal. "We need to talk this out so we're both sure. You don't want to go back to living with your grandparents?"

"No."

"Can I ask why?"

"They don't really want me. And they're old and boring and I know I get in their way."

"They care about you, you know."

"Yeah. But it's not the same as wanting me."

No, it's not. "I can't disagree with that. What is it that you like about staying here?"

Mia looks hopeful for the first time. "I really like this town. And the friends I've made…Kate, Erin, Dr. Spencer. And you're, well, a lot nicer to be with than I thought you would be. I like it here. With you."

Not a huge vote of confidence, but Ellis will take it. "I do care about you, Mia, a great deal. And I'm so glad to see you doing well here. You're bright, you're caring, and you're a hard worker. The sky is the limit with your potential, do you know that? What about the high school here, do you think you would like it?"

"You mean I can stay?" The look of surprise on Mia's face would be almost comical if the subject weren't so serious.

"I think I can more than handle you staying here. But. And it's a big but. You're not sixteen until October, so until then, we would need your grandparents to sign off on you continuing to live with me. And we need the judge to sign off on it as well, since returning to Windsor is part of your probation order."

Mia's mood plummets again. "Do you think we can actually make all that happen?"

"I think there's a good chance. I'll start making some calls tomorrow, okay? And if all goes well, we'll get you registered for school as soon as we can."

Mia leaps out of her chair, races around the table, and throws her arms around Ellis's neck. "Thank you, Ellis. I mean it. Thank you so much! I was so scared you were going to send me back."

"I know we still have our issues, Mia, but I'm not sending you someplace you don't want to go, okay? I'll never do that to you. And one more thing. I don't want you to lose your connection with your grandparents, so how about we talk to them about you spending one weekend a month with them."

Mia pauses. "Do I have to?"

"Yes, you have to."

"Okay."

Well, that wasn't so bad. "Good." Ellis hugs her back. It's the most affection they've shown each other in years. "Remember, kiddo, that you deserve to be happy. Always."

"I will. Ellis? Do you think my mom would be okay with this?"

"I do. I think she would be more than okay with this."

Mia grins. "I'm going to go text Kate that I'm going to be staying here!"

"Okay, but hold on for another second. You need to know that, after Christmas, I'm not sure what my plans are. I mean, technically I'll be pretty much done with my work on this project by then or shortly after."

Mia's face falls. "You mean we're going to have to move?"

There was a time when Ellis loved the thrill of moving on to another project, another city. It was always like reinventing herself, where she'd fall in love all over again with her work. But it also reinforced old habits, like running away from relationships, from responsibilities. Now the idea of moving away holds little appeal. It's nice here. The people she's gotten to know are friendly, and they're good. Plus she's serious about giving Mia a home, because somebody's got to, and she owes that much to Mia and to Nancy. She also can't ignore the Amy factor. Amy, who's in her thoughts every night before she falls asleep and every morning when she wakes up. She wants to be here, close to Amy. But Amy and the rest of the folks in town aren't going to be very happy with her once her report comes out. Because as much as folks don't want things to change at the hospital, they're going to have to change, and Ellis will be the architect of what those changes will look like. Unless the board rejects her report, which almost never happens. She will probably lose Amy over this, and the thought steals whatever appetite she had. "Let's not worry about January," she says to Mia. "We'll figure it out later. Let's get you settled in at the school here and get that first semester under your belt. I promise I'm not going to leave you high and dry, Mia. I'm afraid you're stuck with me for as long as you want, and any future decisions, we'll make them together."

"Really?"

"Really. You have a home with me any time."

The relief on Mia's face melts Ellis's heart. *It's all been worth it, these crazy last few months, for this moment right here,* Ellis thinks.

* * *

Amy is on her way to a private meeting with Janice Harrison, the hospital's CEO, when she rounds a corner and smacks square, chest to chest, into Ellis. A folder of papers goes flying. Papers from Ellis. Amy's folder of papers is intact, and she squeezes it tighter to her body before helping Ellis retrieve her scattered papers.

"Thanks," Ellis murmurs, averting her eyes.

"Sorry, my fault." Their fingers brush for a moment, and the memories of every time she's ever touched Ellis come bubbling to the surface. There's so much she wants to say since their parting more than a week ago, and no amount of cursory touching can convey all she feels. She wants to know exactly how long they're supposed to cool things down. And how much cooling, because this feels more like the Ice Age than a cooling down. "Are you...doing okay?"

"Yes, thank you. How about you?"

Not good at all, Amy wants to say, but that's not a conversation for a hallway in the hospital. "I'm okay. Hey, I hear Mia is staying with you permanently now. That's fantastic. I'm really happy for you both."

"Thanks. She's really turned a corner over the summer, you know? And I want her to keep with that momentum. I want her to keep doing all the right things. She's happy here."

"Funny that you never planned on being a parent and, well, here you are." Amy is smiling as she says it, and Ellis smiles back.

"It's...interesting, to say the least. But, ah, I don't know how permanent things are yet."

"What do you mean?"

"She can stay with me as long as she likes but...I'm not sure how much past Christmas we'll continue to live here. Once my...work here is done."

"Oh." Disappointment, regret, sadness all fight for supremacy in Amy's heart. And then panic decimates all of it as she considers that right when she's found someone worth falling for, right when she's on the brink of happiness, it's being snatched away. Her throat tightens; she clears it roughly. "Can we talk more about this?"

"Yes. But not here, not now."

"I know." She whispers, "I miss you."

Ellis's smile teeters, breaks. Her voice is equally strained. "I miss you too."

"I have to go. But...we *will* talk, right?" Amy is already moving away from Ellis because she's a minute, maybe seconds, away from blubbering like the scared, heartbroken fool she is.

"We will," Ellis says before turning and continuing down the hall.

Minutes later, when Amy is sitting in front of Janice Harrison, she scrambles to pull herself together. She can't think about losing Ellis, and yet it's the outcome with the highest probability and one that is completely predictable. *And yet I went and fell for her anyway, goddammit.*

Harrison takes a few minutes to scan the twenty-page, confidential report Amy has handed her. It's the report of her observations and conclusions from her three days in Collinsworth. With Ellis. The memory of tasting Ellis again, of being inside her, assails Amy, nearly sucking the air from her lungs. Their lovemaking had been exquisite, beyond exciting. One minute frantic, as if they were unable to get enough of one another, the next tender and sensual, like they had all the time in the world. She wonders, not for the first time, if they will ever enjoy each other that way again, but it's too sad to think too long about. Amy is not optimistic, and Ellis has done nothing to prove her pessimism wrong.

Harrison pulls off her reading glasses, sets the report down. "Very thorough, Amy. Thank you for this."

"For background only, correct?" She wants to make sure the report is for Harrison's eyes alone, exactly as they agreed.

"Of course. You paint a pretty dismal picture of the changes their hospital has undergone. But nice job of explaining exactly where the gaps are and how each change only benefits a portion of the population. We want to do everything we can to avoid the same cookie cutter approach here. As your report points out, our demographics, our community needs here, are completely different."

"I hope it will be enough to convince the mother ship that those same changes would be a disaster here. Even one of those changes, like losing obstetrics, would be devastating. Especially for all our migrant workers."

"Losing our emergency department, or cutting back on it, would be equally terrible. I'm very glad to have your earlier report on that, too." She referred to the report Amy had given Ellis awhile back, outlining all the emergency cases and surgical cases that would have had poor outcomes, even morbidity, had this hospital not had a full-time, fully functioning emergency department and a staff of surgeons. "Your work certainly gives us a lot of ammunition. Thank you."

"Any time." Amy rises from her chair, but Harrison motions for her to wait.

"One more thing. It's about Dr. Atkinson. He's been confirmed as having Parkinson's."

"Oh no." It explains a lot, but the diagnosis also means the man's career as a surgeon is over.

"I'm going to submit a request to take on another general surgeon. But I have to warn you, I don't think we'll be granted permission from the board until we know which way this review is going. I'm sorry."

"I'm sorry too. Mostly for Dr. Atkinson." Also for herself and the other surgeon, Dr. Warren, because it means they'll have to continue to be on call every other weekend and there will be no respite from long days. Taking a vacation is folly. On the upside, the more she works, the less time she has to stew about her situation with Ellis.

"Thank you, Amy. That'll be all."

Amy takes her time heading back downstairs, hoping to run into Ellis again. No such luck. *I should just tell her that I'm in love with her and that I'll do whatever it takes, whatever she needs, for this to work between us.* It would mean abandoning her concern for the hospital's future and resigning herself to letting whatever happens, happen. She could work anywhere, follow Ellis anywhere. *Maybe it's time to grow up, move away from home,* she thinks with a sick feeling in her stomach.

She sags against the stairwell wall. No matter how much her heart bleeds for Ellis, it's an impossible situation. She knows she can't, won't, abandon the hospital, her colleagues, her patients, her elderly parents. She simply can't let go of all the things that matter to her, not without a fight.

CHAPTER TWENTY-FIVE

Ellis opens her laptop and clicks on the minutes from last night's board meeting. She didn't attend because it was a meeting of the Erie Shores Hospital board, and she's not a member of the board nor was she invited to attend as a guest. She answers to the CEO of the Essex County Regional Hospital Services and its board, but she likes to go over the monthly reports from Erie Shore's board to keep tabs on what's happening at the hospital.

It takes her several minutes to click through the various reports attached to the minutes, and the board actions resulting from the reports. She stalls over a report by Dr. Amy Spencer, titled "Observations from Service Changes at Collinsworth Soldiers Hospital." She clicks on it, opens it, begins reading it. Several pages into it, she can't disagree with anything Amy's reported on. Mostly it's statistics and summaries about the hospital's services, the demographics there. Then the report lays out the services and demographics at Erie Shores for a comparison. Again, Ellis sees nothing amiss. It's all the same information she's obtained as well. But then Amy lists her conclusions. Conclusions that are damning toward the changes at the Collinsworth hospital. Amy states that almost none of the service changes at Soldiers Hospital would work here and explains why (younger population, lots of migrant workers, much more blue collar, a massive provincial highway nearby that sees serious crashes on a monthly and sometimes weekly basis). She's laid out her case that any changes at Erie Shores should be little more than minor tweaks (though of course she doesn't say what those are).

Ellis throws her reading glasses down in disgust. Minor tweaks aren't going to cut it. Hasn't Amy looked at the budget lately? Doesn't she know there's a deficit and that provincial funding for hospitals is decreasing? Who's going to pay for the services Amy so dearly wants to maintain in this universal health care system? Staff salaries go up each year, in accordance with strict contracts; diagnostics get more and more expensive as technology continues to evolve; procedures too. Taxpayers won't stand for a gigantic tax hike in order to pay for hospitals ballooning budgets. *Goddammit!* Amy's gone and done an end run to try to state her case, on the record, before Ellis's report is complete.

Ellis slams her laptop shut, grabs her sweater, and heads up to Amy's office. She has no idea if she's there, but she'll be around somewhere. Ellis is pretty sure Amy works a minimum of ten hours a day, probably more like twelve, not to mention that she's in almost every weekend, either on call or checking on her post-op patients.

Amy's office door is half open; she's at her desk, working on her computer, probably patient reports, if Ellis has to guess. Ellis knocks twice. When Amy looks up to see who's there, her face lights up before she rearranges her expression into something neutral.

"Can I talk to you?"

"All right." Amy stands up, yawns, tosses her lab coat onto her chair, then pulls a windbreaker from a hook on the wall. She seems to be taking no notice of Ellis's mood. "Let's go for a walk. I need some fresh air."

Ellis isn't pleased with the suggestion; she has work to do, and unloading on Amy shouldn't take long. She huffs her displeasure, but Amy ignores her. "Fine."

It's late September now, the time of year Ellis always thinks about school. Because while autumn represents the slowing down, the ending of many things, school is a new beginning, and she wants to hold onto that feeling of new things, of fresh starts. A chill has begun to creep into the air, a trace of color edging into the leaves, and Ellis is reminded of the first line of the "To Autumn" poem by Keats: "Season of mists and mellow fruitfulness." Autumn is so much more than about the end of summer; it's about bounty and harvests too—fruitfulness. Her spirits lift. Amy is beside her and they're alone, away from the ears and eyes of the hospital, and it's a little bit glorious. She almost forgets her annoyance with Amy.

"You're upset with me," Amy states plainly.

"Yes." Ellis dredges up her anger, though it's like pulling something hard by the roots to extract it from the ground. "I don't appreciate your end run to the board with that report you did from Collinsworth."

Amy curses but doesn't deny anything. "That was supposed to be confidential, for Janice Harrison only. Her admin assistant screwed up and accidentally included it in the board report. Believe me, I was not happy when I found out this morning. It was not intended to be an end run. It was background only. For my boss."

Ellis is used to her outsider status when she conducts hospital reviews. The territorial, suspicious, uncooperative behavior from staffers and others, well, it's to be expected. But Amy is supposed to be different. Amy is not supposed to be an adversary, but someone who, Ellis has hoped, can see both sides. She's smart and she's a realist, traits that should allow her to eventually come to the same conclusions as Ellis. But Amy is blinded by how much the community means to her, and Ellis simply can't compete with that.

"First off, it makes it look like you're setting the table for some kind of uprising later on when my report comes out. And secondly, it shows bad faith. It shows you and this hospital have zero confidence in me to make the right decisions, to come to the proper conclusions. It shows an irrefutable level of suspicion and lack of cooperation."

They've walked around the block and start a second lap.

"Whoa. Ellis, I think you're reading too much into this."

"How can I not?"

"Look, why do you think Janice Harrison sent me with you to Collinsworth?"

A sick feeling descends on Ellis. "I see. It was to keep an eye on me."

"Not exactly. She wanted someone there seeing and hearing everything you saw and heard, in case you…skewed your findings. She wanted more information to help refute conclusions of yours that my hospital might not agree with. It's…a second opinion, that's all. A second opinion based on the same evidence you're seeing."

"And did your assignment from your CEO include sleeping with me? Was that part of the deal to keep an eye on me?" It's an outrageous allegation, but goddammit. *Doesn't Amy have any loyalty to me at all? Doesn't what we have mean anything to her? Doesn't it mean* something? *Or is there nothing more important to her than this hospital?*

Amy halts their momentum by softly touching Ellis's wrist. As always, her touch is electrifying, and Ellis wonders if it will always be so. This time, the thrill of her touch feels like punishment for not being able to let her go.

"I'm going to pretend you didn't just accuse me of sleeping with you for any reason other than that I'm insanely attracted to you and I…" Amy's emotions pinball from anger to disbelief to desperation. "How dare you, Ellis? How fucking dare you?"

Ellis pales. "I'm sorry, Amy. I didn't mean it the way it came out. I'm frustrated. And I'm sad, because I don't like being…at odds with you or whatever the hell this is. I hate all of this. I hate not seeing you smile, and I hate not spending time with you, talking with you, being with you. And…other things."

Her words are like darts that sting, because Amy feels the same way. Is it ego that's keeping them apart? Fear? Pride? Whatever it is, it sucks.

"I miss all of those things too. I miss you, Ellis. God, why can't we get past this? It's not like they're going to close the hospital." Amy's emotions are as erratic as a stone skipping across water. "Are they?"

"No, absolutely not. That's not in the cards, Amy. Not if I have anything to say about it, and I've never heard a whiff of that kind of talk."

"That's some comfort, I guess. So what can we do to align our views? Or to put our views aside and pretend…oh hell, I can't pretend this isn't important to me. But you're important to me, too." An understatement, but Amy doesn't want to risk too much.

Ellis steps closer. It would be so easy to kiss her right now. A mere tilting down of her head and her lips would be on Ellis's. They've got to find a way to stop being adversaries, because this tangle of feelings is a daily torture.

"Mia is away at her grandparents this weekend. She spends a weekend a month with them now. Why don't I cook us dinner and we'll talk some more? See if we can't figure a few things out."

Amy jumps at the life ring Ellis has tossed her. "All right. Thank you." She doesn't want to think about what it might lead to, in case it doesn't. But there's a new spring in her step as they walk back to the hospital.

Kate is waiting outside the main doors, frantically waving her arms at Amy. *Aw shit.* But they didn't page her, so what can possibly be so urgent?

"Oh, good, there you are! Hurry, there's someone here to see you." She's beaming but no more forthcoming about what's going on.

"All right." Amy's discovered from experience not to fight Kate when she's excited about something, and clearly she is.

In the front lobby are a man and a woman, and between them a young boy in a wheelchair. Amy looks closer. "Jeffrey?"

The boy smiles and so do his parents. Amy produces her hand for a handshake, but instead the couple instantly wraps her in a hug. Jeffrey's mom and dad are both crying as they thank Amy over and over again for all she did to help Jeffrey back in late spring, when he'd been brought in unconscious and suffering a grave head wound from an accidental, self-inflicted gunshot wound. She'd never performed brain surgery before, but without it, the seven-year-old would surely have died. He wasn't stable enough, nor was there time, to transport him to University Hospital in London and put its neuro team to work on him. Ten days after her life-saving surgery on the boy and while he was still in an induced coma, he was transported to London. But Amy never expected to see him again and certainly never expected to see him functioning to this level. Once she makes a decision to operate on someone, there's no room for pessimism, but in her heart, she was truly doubtful the kid would survive. When he did survive, she grew doubtful he would ever recover much physically and cognitively. But this! This is the best surprise she's ever had.

"Wow, Jeffrey!" She bends over the wheelchair to examine him more closely. Barely a scar visible now on his head. He's smiling and his eyes are alert. "You're doing so well. It's so wonderful to see you."

"Th-thank you," he says haltingly.

"You're welcome, but the only thanks I need is seeing you doing so well."

She feels Ellis next to her, taking it all in, probably bursting with questions. Amy explains to her that Jeffrey suffered a grievous head injury and that she was pressed into doing "a little brain surgery" to help him out.

"She's a magician," Jeffrey's father cuts in. "She is the miracle that saved our son. He wouldn't be here now if not for Dr. Spencer." His eyes begin to tear up.

Amy lets herself enjoy the praise, but only for a moment. It does help her forget the patients she couldn't save, helps remind her of why she went into this business in the first place, but she doesn't want to get too hung up on the past. Doesn't want to drown in her own ego, either. "Your son is a strong little boy. A real fighter, and I'm so glad things have worked out. How are you feeling, Jeffrey?"

"I...I can walk. Kind of." With his mother's help he pushes himself slowly out of the small wheelchair. He takes a gingerly step, then another and another. He's limping, but he's on both feet.

Amy claps her hands together while fighting back tears, and for a moment she can't speak. She feels Ellis quietly rub her elbow from beside her.

Jeffrey's dad explains how his son spent a month in neuro intensive care in London, then moved to a rehabilitation center. It's only in the last week, he says, that Jeffrey began to walk and talk again. It won't be a complete recovery, he says, "but it'll be close enough. And the best part is that he's home now, with us."

Amy hugs Jeffrey before he climbs back into his wheelchair, lets his parents hug her again too. "Thank you for coming in," she says.

"Thank *you*," Jeffrey's mom says.

After they've gone, Kate shakes her head at Ellis and Amy, but she's grinning. "Ellis, don't ever let Amy deny that saving that kid was the best work she's ever done. I mean, freakin' brain surgery! Ames, you're a bloody rock star, and don't you forget it."

"Yes, mom." Rock star? Nope. But yeah, she's a pretty damned good surgeon, and she's going to remember this boy for the rest of her life.

"I want," Ellis whispers pointedly, "to hear a lot more about this."

CHAPTER TWENTY-SIX

Ellis opens the oven to check the chicken-spaghetti casserole for about the sixth time in the last twenty minutes. It still has awhile to go, but she needs something to do with her nervous energy. Amy will be here any minute. She knows instinctively tonight will be a watershed moment for them, because they're going to talk—about everything. She has no idea how Amy's going to react. She doesn't even know what she's going to say to Amy any more, because everything has changed. It was seeing that little boy and his parents. Ellis can't explain why the current of her thoughts has shifted so drastically.

She's always understood that severe changes to the services a hospital offers result not only in inconveniences to patients, but sometimes death or at least less desirable outcomes. It's a tough reality of such decisions. Removing or cutting back on emergency department hours almost certainly leads to patient deaths—that one's a no-brainer. But the less headline-grabbing changes, like removing obstetrics or certain surgical procedures, can lead to an exodus of doctors and nurses who no longer want to work in that environment, prompting patients to lose confidence in the hospital too. It's a vicious circle.

Ellis opens a bottle of red wine to let it breathe. She can't get that little boy Jeffrey out of her mind—his sweetness, his gratitude. And to see him push himself out of that wheelchair and walk a few steps was nothing short of amazing. She didn't miss the emotion in Amy's voice and in her eyes either. Without Amy, without the hospital's ER and its staff, without well-trained surgical staff too, that boy would surely be dead, and Ellis can't pry that thought from her mind. Jeffrey is not a statistic, he's a little boy with his entire future in front of him, and Ellis isn't cold enough to offer up cuts to the board that will decimate the hospital and kill a kid like him. She doesn't want blood on her hands. But if she doesn't offer up something, the county hospital board is going to start arbitrarily chopping things because there is no other choice. The hospital has a deficit and the government has made it clear that it will not throw more money at hospitals. Which isn't fair, because fixed costs like heating and electricity and salaries all go up. Find a way to make do with what you've got is the common mantra.

Ideas have begun germinating in Ellis's mind, but she has days, maybe weeks of research, before she can hammer and chisel them into something worth putting down on paper. It's a long shot, what she has in mind, but it's her duty to look at everything, to put as many options on the table as possible. For the first time since she began this review, she feels like solutions are at her fingertips—real solutions that everyone can live with.

The doorbell rings and her stomach does a pleasant little flip. She smiles as instinctively as taking a breath because it's Amy at the door. "Hi, Amy. Thanks for coming," she says, because if she doesn't say something, she's going to rush into Amy's arms and kiss her.

"Hi." Amy's eyes rake over her, leaving Ellis light-headed. "You look great, Ellis."

"Thanks. You're a sight for sore eyes yourself. Come in."

Amy hands her a bottle of red wine. "Wow, something smells delicious. I guess you probably have figured out by now that I don't have a lot of time to cook."

Ellis laughs. "In other words, you'd like anything I cook for you?"

Amy's eyes do that top-to-bottom sweep of her body again, and it's all Ellis can do not to throw herself at her. "My mouth is watering, if that's any indication."

Watering for what, Ellis wants to say but doesn't, in case Amy doesn't want to take the flirtation further. She can't decide from hour to hour these days whether Amy wants to rip her clothes off and jump her bones or throw her on a raft and cast her out to sea. "Glass of wine?"

"Love one."

They stand around the kitchen island as Ellis pours them each a glass. She has never fallen for someone before who is so closely aligned with the work she does, and she's doing a shitty job of handling it. She knows she should demand that she and Amy put their relationship above anything that might happen at the hospital, that they separate the two things. But rarely do ultimatums work. It's obvious that neither of them is going to give in, is going to volunteer to put their work second, but she's hopeful they can find a way because of Amy's words the other day—that she misses her and cares for her. It's something to build on, and dammit, she's going to grab onto it with both hands.

Ellis fusses with the garlic bread while they make small talk about Mia, about Amy's parents, about Kate and Erin, until it's time to plate up. Amy tucks into the casserole like she hasn't eaten in a week.

"You like?" Ellis asks.

"I love. I'm a huge pasta freak."

"Good. So am I. Hey, that boy, Jeffrey. The brain injury kid? I can't get him out of my mind. Would you tell me what happened?"

Amy walks Ellis through that day, admits her lack of confidence almost paralyzed her until she decided that Jeffrey had nothing to lose and everything to gain, that she would be letting him down if she didn't try. "It's like this. If I didn't go for the home run swing, the game would have for sure been lost. It actually made the decision simple."

"And did you expect him to recover so well?"

"No. I figured his best outcome would probably be non-verbal with the cognitive abilities of a three-year-old. And I certainly never expected him to walk again."

"Seeing him and his parents, how grateful they were, boy, it's humbling. How does it make you feel, knowing you not only saved his life, but saved who he *is*? And that you saved his family from the worst kind of heartbreak?"

Amy twitches, clearly uncomfortable talking about herself this way. "I don't know. Thrilled, of course. Surprised but thrilled. And…happy that it worked out."

"Amy…" Ellis shakes her head. And here she thought surgeons were supposed to be a bunch of arrogant prima donnas. "If you hadn't been there—"

"I did my job. And I happened to do it well that day, with lots of help. But mostly it's because the hospital was there. Because we have an ER and surgeons and surgical staff and nurses and—"

"I know, Amy."

"Then why can't this be easy? Why can't we find a way to keep the things we do well here?"

Ellis swallows her doubts and states boldly, "I think we can."

"What do you mean?" Amy can't possibly have heard correctly, because until now, Ellis has made it clear that drastic changes to the hospital are needed. Which, in Amy's experience, is always code for major service cuts.

"Come on, let's go sit in the living room."

The anticipation is killing her, but Amy follows Ellis into the living room, sits on the sofa while careful to leave space between them. She places her glass of wine on the coffee table and waits for Ellis to continue.

"I think I've been going about this all wrong."

What? Is she talking about us or the hospital? And that's the problem in a nutshell right there, Amy decides. She never knows where the lines are with Ellis, because sometimes they're drawn in sand that quickly shifts or washes away and sometimes they're as thick as the Great Wall of China.

"In my line of work," Ellis continues, "it's almost always about cutting services, because let's face it, funding has been static now for a few years while costs keep going up. I mean, of course we can nickel-and-dime things, like adding more self-check-in kiosks or increasing parking fees, charging a patient a dollar or two every time an ER doc has to write them a prescription. But we both know that's not going to be enough here. It's poking a hole where we need to dig a trench."

"You're scaring the hell out of me."

"Sorry, I know. And you had a right to be scared."

"Had? Past tense?"

"Hopefully."

"You want to tell me what's going on in that big, sexy brain of yours?"

"It's actually quite simple. I'd been so fixated on the expenditure column that I ignored the revenue column. I mean, that's oversimplifying things, but I know what the revenue column looks like, and it's pretty flat with very little flexibility. We have government funding, and then we have things like parking fees the hospital can charge, community fundraising for equipment, a few small nickels and dimes here and there, but that's it."

"Okay. So what are we missing?"

"That's exactly what I'm talking about. I was missing a key part of the solution. Or what could be the solution to this whole problem. And it requires an entirely new approach."

Amy takes a sip of wine for something to occupy her hands. She's going to go crazy if Ellis doesn't spit it out.

"What I was missing was this: Your hospital could keep everything it has if only it can bring in enough revenue to help offset its costs."

"We don't allow for-profit care. That's—"

"I know. I'm talking about adding instead of subtracting."

"You've lost me. You already said that things like parking fees aren't enough." Amy's hopes for a solution are perilously close to crashing again.

"Sorry. I'm talking about adding programs that will bring in government revenue. I've got about a million ideas, none of which I've worked out all the nuts and bolts for yet, but here's a few. The way the hospital pairs with training family physicians such as Erin Kirkland could be the tip of the iceberg. More medical schools, nursing schools, pharmacy schools, social work programs, and so forth could pair up with the hospital, providing not only bodies, but much needed money in return for teaching their students. Even paramedic programs. Become a teaching center, because those are tremendous streams of revenue. And there's more. Did you know there's more than three thousand square feet of unused space in the hospital? Why not rent that out to a physiotherapy provider or even a dentistry business? The hospital would get monthly rent and it would bring hundreds more people into the facility each week, with all those people having to pay for parking." Ellis is practically vibrating, and she's talking with such conviction that Amy has no choice but to be swept along with her. "Then there are programs, a whole host of publicly funded programs the hospital could apply for. Again, it would bring in money that would help pay for staff, help pay for the electricity that keeps the lights on."

Amy keeps her voice neutral. She's afraid to get too excited. "What kind of programs?"

"There's a two-year pilot project on offer right now for hospitals that want to take on a cardiac rehab program. Patients recovering from heart attacks come in a couple of times a week for a checkup, plus an exercise program, they learn about nutrition, talk to a social worker and so on. Staff are usually contracted out for this part—nutritionists, physiotherapists, social workers—but my research shows that the nutritionist you already have on staff could easily absorb this into her workload. Same with the physio assistants. Social workers could be students doing a co-op placement here. This would all be extra money in the hospital's pocket, and the cardiac rehab program pays $250,000 a year."

Amy whistles. "That's enough to pay the annual salaries of three nurses."

"Exactly. There are other possibilities too. What's to say this hospital can't become a regional center for colonoscopies? Right now, four hours a week of OR time is devoted to colonoscopies. Suppose all the hospitals under this regional umbrella could be convinced to hand over their colonoscopies to Erie Shores, increasing the OR hours from four a week to, say, twenty. Bingo, you've brought in enough revenue to hire another surgeon and probably another OR nurse."

"Holy crap, Ellis, you're right. Our operating rooms are idle thirty-six percent of the time. If we could keep them going five or even six days a week, twelve hours a day..."

Ellis's grin is the most beautiful thing Amy has ever seen. "Wait, I'm not done yet. There are a dozen extra beds in the hospital that haven't been used in years, since a previous round of cutbacks. The county badly needs more palliative care beds. Voila. Turning four of those beds into palliative care beds would bring in another half a million dollars a year in funding."

Amy's nodding, unable to contain her enthusiasm. "So you're saying maximize our space, maximize our staff to bring on board programs that the government is happy to shell out money for, turn this hospital into a money generator instead of a money loser."

"Absolutely. I'm also thinking of suggesting an IT consultant be hired to introduce new software programs that could scale down the workload in administration, meaning downsizing a body or two in that department. For instance, the average proportion of costs devoted to administration in Canadian hospitals is 12.4 per cent. At this hospital, it's 13.5, so we need to get that figure down."

Amy's stunned into silence.

"I think we could do these changes quite easily here," Ellis says. "It's going to take a few more weeks of research for me to get everything down on paper, but I know there's money out there for hospitals. It's a matter of doing the right things, doing the things the government of the day decides is a priority, and then being flexible enough to adapt. We can't keep doing things the way they've always been done and expect the money to keep rolling in. It's about—"

Amy leaps across the space between them and kisses Ellis on the mouth. "You're brilliant, do you know that?"

"Well, I don't know about brilliant. But will you give me genius?"

Amy laughs and kisses Ellis again. "I love you, Ellis Hall."

Ellis's eyes widen almost comically, but so be it. Amy's said the three magic words and she's not going to take them back no matter what Ellis says next, because you know what? If Ellis feels differently, well, it does nothing to change how Amy feels. It's done, she's put her heart on a silver platter for Ellis. And she will survive it.

CHAPTER TWENTY-SEVEN

"Amy, are you sure?"

They're still sitting on the sofa, but closer so that the lengths of their bodies are touching.

"Sure of what?"

"That you...love me?" The urge to touch Amy is irresistible, and Ellis raises a hand to her cheek, cups it lightly, hopes it conveys the tenderness she feels toward this woman.

"I am. And I do."

"Oh, sweetheart." Ellis chokes on the sob rising in her throat. "I love you too. I've been in love with you ever since those Thursday afternoons at the hotel."

Amy holds her tightly; they're both choking back tears.

"I didn't dare to hope that...you would be able to love someone again," Ellis says. She hadn't expected the declaration, not yet. "It's...thank you for being so brave."

Amy pulls back to look Ellis in the eyes. "It's not bravery. It's being smart for a change. And it's about growing up and getting over myself. People get hurt all the time in relationships. Mine didn't work out. And yeah, the things Lisa and I went through sucked, especially for her, but when I see a kid like Jeffrey and his parents pushing on, moving forward, having hope, how can I not do the same thing in my own life? I'd be stupid to let you go. And I'd regret it for the rest of my life."

Ellis places both hands on Amy's face, pulls her into her, and kisses her again. Tenderly. She's so in love with this fabulous woman, it shocks her. Shocks her because she's never felt this way about anyone before, never thought she was capable of it, never thought she'd find someone worthy of her love. The stuff in movies and romance books? She always swore it was a bunch of drivel fabricated by the entertainment industry, a fantasy completely unattainable for all but the very lucky. It was never truly something she thought would be in her future, because she wasn't a sucker like everyone else. *Well*, she thinks with satisfaction, *who's the sucker now?*

Amy looks at her funny. "What are you chuckling at?"

"Myself. I never thought I'd be a mere mortal who actually fell in love."

"And now?"

Ellis grows serious. "Now I think falling for you is the best thing I've ever done in my life."

Amy kisses Ellis again, slowly, then trails her mouth along her jawline, planting soft kisses with a touch that's featherlight. Ellis tingles everywhere, so exquisite is Amy's touch. "I want you so much it hurts."

Ellis has to work at finding her voice. "There's...so much we still need to talk about."

"Not now. Oh, *so* not now."

Ellis laughs, takes her cue, and jumps up from the sofa. She holds out her hand to Amy. She wants to worship her lover's body, and damn, it's been far too long. The rule they made about not sleeping together until her report's finished...well, she can't *not* make love to Amy after all this. She's throbbing and wet and her voice is a low rumble when she says, "The bedroom's this way."

Amy takes her hand and lets herself be led. "I thought you'd never ask, darling. But are you sure?"

"More than sure. I'm going to die if we don't."

"You do know I possess advanced lifesaving skills?"

"Come here, you." Ellis stops, turns, and kisses Amy hard on the mouth.

In the bedroom, Ellis is impatient, but she lets Amy undress her. It's killing her that Amy is unwrapping her like a long-awaited gift, but she's delighted to see Amy's face light up with each article of clothing removed.

They're on the bed, both of them naked now. Amy is circling Ellis's nipple with a fingertip, and Ellis feels her gaze every bit as much as she feels her touch. She runs her hands through Amy's hair, pulls gently when Amy's tongue traces the same pattern on her nipple. She alternates to the other nipple, and something dislodges in Ellis. Something so much bigger than any of her inhibitions or fears or imagined obstacles. She wants a life with this woman, and if they have to wait a few more months until she completes her report, then she'll do it. She'll do whatever it takes, because her work means nothing compared to what's filling her heart. Putting something ahead of her career, putting love ahead of her career, is brand new territory for her, but Ellis is going to let her heart lead her for once. And oh, what a ride it's going to be.

Amy's finger glides down her belly, to her thigh and back up until it finds her pulsing need. She moves it around the wetness. Slick now, her finger traces patterns around Ellis's clit, down to her opening, back up again. Ellis's gasp is followed by an urgent moan, and she gently pushes Amy's head down, lower lower lower. She *needs* Amy's mouth on her, and Amy doesn't waste time getting the message. She slides down her body, her hot breath warming Ellis's skin. She loses herself completely when Amy's mouth finds her. Expertly Amy licks and sucks, changing up the pace, her finger doing a dance inside her. Ellis can't hold it in anymore. She is in full surrender, and she has never felt so complete with this exquisite coming together of everything— her heart, her mind, her body. She arches her hips into Amy one last time, for one last capture of her mouth and her finger before the explosion obliterates everything. Trembling, she rides it for as long as she can, wanting to hold onto every last strand of pleasure for as long as she can.

"Sweetheart," she urges. "Come here. Let me hold you."

Desire echoes in every cell of Amy's body as Ellis makes love to her. Each touch sends a tiny jolt of electricity skittering along her skin, and Amy embraces it. All she wants is to love this woman, to be loved by her. She's trusting Ellis not to break her heart, and while the thought of something going wrong between them terrifies her, it terrifies her more to think of her life without Ellis. Because without Ellis, her life is little more than work and helping out her parents when she can. She sees now how detached from her own feelings she'd become. She let the damage from her failed relationship with Lisa hollow her out for way too long.

Ellis is teasing her with her fingers, thrusting them in and out, and the sheer ecstasy blinds her. She rises to meet each thrust, groans from deep in her throat to urge Ellis on. When Ellis's mouth finds her, Amy can't hold on. She clutches the bedsheet like a lifeline, bracing herself as her orgasm washes over her, leaving her boneless. Leaving her more in love with Ellis than ever.

"You're a wonderful lover," she whispers to Ellis as she nestles against her.

"Not half as good as you, my love. Did you miss me these last few weeks?"

"Miss you? Jesus, I was so miserable. I couldn't stand us being apart like that. That was a very bad idea you had, that cooling-off thing."

"I know. Not the smartest decision I've ever made. I promise, no more bad ideas again where you're concerned."

"Ooh, now I feel spoiled."

"Good. Because I want to spoil you like crazy." Ellis turns her back to Amy so they can spoon together. Her skin is warm, and Amy plants a kiss on her shoulder. She feels sheltered with her whole body touching Ellis's. How long has she craved a lover's touch like this? Never, it occurs to her.

"Well, I'm not going to say no to that. But please tell me we don't have to keep sneaking around forever."

Ellis sighs. "We won't, but we shouldn't be obvious around each other until I wrap up the rest of my research. No PDAs, no announcements. We're just friends."

"Ha. Friends with benefits who secretly confess their love to one another. And exactly how long is this charade supposed to take?"

"A couple more months, now that I'm switching gears with my approach."

"In that case, take all the time you need."

"Really?" Ellis purrs, teasing.

"Wait, no! I can't go on with hardly ever seeing you, with barely touching you. It's torture."

"Well, I do recall that you have a pair of my underwear stashed somewhere. Perhaps it can keep you company on the lonely nights."

"Believe me, it already has."

Ellis laughs, her voice like melted honey. "A few more weeks of torture, sweetheart, then I'll be able to finish my report at home before I hand it in after Christmas."

"And what about Mia? What is she going to think of…us?"

"Are you kidding? Mia thinks we should be a couple. She's baffled that we're not dating."

"I always knew that kid was smart. Are you going to tell her?"

"Yes, but not yet. I think we should tell her together."

"All right. But I have to warn you, I have very little experience at this parenting thing."

"And you think I do?"

"Good point." Amy kisses Ellis's shoulder again. "Hey, her birthday is in a couple more weeks, right?"

"Yup. Sweet sixteen. At which point she won't technically need a guardian. Or she can petition the court to be emancipated.

I don't expect her grandparents to give her a hassle if she wants to keep living with me."

"Does she? Want to keep living with you?"

"She does. And I'm happy to have her. I think we've made some real strides in reconciling. I was such a jerk, Amy, all those years ago when—"

"Hey, shhh. Let's make a promise right now not to beat ourselves up anymore about the past, okay? I want a fresh start, Ellis. For both of us, right now. Deal?"

Ellis moans in pleasure. "Deal."

"Hey, I have one more suggestion. Well, a couple. Why don't you let me host Mia's birthday party at my place? I mean, you haven't even been to my place yet and this would be a perfect excuse for a visit."

"I'd love to see your place. And yes, I think Mia would be thrilled to have the party at your house."

"All right. That's what we'll do, then."

"Wait, you said you had a couple of suggestions."

"Oh, right." Amy's desire for Ellis rampages through her again, turning her blood into fire. She strokes Ellis's hip before reaching around and cupping her between her legs.

Ellis grins. "You read my mind."

CHAPTER TWENTY-EIGHT

Ellis falls immediately in love with Amy's house. It's a large, older Craftsman that's been completely updated inside and out, with an open concept kitchen, two gas fireplaces, refinished oak floors. The front porch is to die for with its antique loveseat swing, and so is the property. It encompasses an acre, stretching out across ninety meters of waterfront. There are trees on the property, plenty of room for flower gardens and vegetable gardens or even a pool, though she imagines Amy has no time for gardens and pools. There's a big patio with a built-in fire pit that the birthday guests have gathered around to keep the chill at bay. Ellis loves late autumn, with its scent of dying leaves and the clean crispness of winter in the air.

Ed and Marjorie are here and they're showing none of the stress and worry about their granddaughter that was wearing them down months ago. Amy's parents are here too, and so are Kate and Erin and Erin's little girl. Mia's new friend, a girl named Susie, has shyly joined the celebration, and Mia sticks to her like she's afraid she'll bolt at the least goofy thing that might happen.

"You doing okay?" Ellis asks in the kitchen as she pours coffee into cups for Mia to take outside for the guests.

"Sure." She shrugs as if to ask why wouldn't she be okay.

"And Susie's doing okay?"

Mia blushes furiously. "She's fine."

"Good. I'm glad you have a friend you really like."

Mia smiles but doesn't say more. She hoists the loaded tray of coffee cups and carries it outside with expert precision, another surprising thing that impresses Ellis. Every day she's discovering new things about Mia. Or perhaps, she thinks, it's really Mia who's discovering new things about herself—new talents, new abilities, new confidence. Mia is turning into a woman right before Ellis's eyes.

Amy scoots past Mia at the door, gives her a pretend high-five, but Mia, with her hands full, doesn't fall for it.

"I can't believe how different she is since you guys moved here," Amy says.

"Me too. Honestly, if she hadn't matured, I don't think I would have offered for her to keep living with me. She was a handful before. Sullen, rebellious. I'm so pleased that little phase seems to be over for good now. Jeez, I better knock on wood or something."

"She'll be fine. She's got you." Amy puts her arms around Ellis's waist, pulls her in for a kiss that's more mischievous than tender. "And I've got you too, babe."

Ellis kisses her back with her own brand of playfulness.

"Whoa!" It's Mia, staring at them with her mouth wide open. They didn't hear her return. "Cool!"

"Oh, um, we ah…" Ellis extricates herself from Amy as quickly as she can, tries really hard not to show that this isn't how she wanted Mia to find out about them.

Amy gently nudges Ellis with her elbow. "I think Mia is okay with this."

"Like, yeah! I thought you two were never going to get together."

"I'm sorry we didn't tell you sooner," Ellis says. She and Amy planned to take Mia out to dinner this week and tell her. Except Amy can't keep her hands or her lips to herself. But then again, Ellis doesn't want her keeping her lips and her hands to herself. It's killing her that they have to sneak kisses behind closed doors, chance a few gropes here and there. They haven't made love in almost two weeks, and if that carries on much longer, Ellis is going to march Amy into her bedroom no matter how many people they're entertaining, and have her way with her. "We were going to tell you this week. It's…we're trying to keep it on the down low for now."

"Sure, but how come? Why can't we tell everyone? You're not ashamed, are you?"

"No," Amy says forcefully. "Never. It's because of work. Ellis, in case you haven't figured it out, is a bloody genius and she's working on saving all our butts at the hospital right now. We don't want anyone thinking I've been, er, influencing her in any way. Or forcing her to do something she doesn't want to do."

"That sucks. Why would anybody think that?"

Ellis rolls her eyes. "Trust me, kiddo, there's a lot of politics involved. If my final report is to be viewed as credible and objective, we can't have people thinking that my relationship with Amy has factored into any of my work and made me, well, less objective than I might otherwise have been."

"Well, I'm glad you're saving the hospital, Mo—" Mia's hand flies to her mouth and her eyes threaten to swallow her face.

Ellis doesn't dare move. "Did you…were you going to call me Mom?"

Mia nods, an expression of surprise frozen on her face. "Sorry."

"No! Don't be. I'd…really like it if you called me Mom. I mean, if you want to. It's not like I'm trying to take the place of…" Amy's hand slips into hers, and her rapidly beating heart settles. "Your real mom."

"You won't be, but I think I'd like to call you Mom. It kinda feels like I should, weirdly enough."

Amy goes to Mia and hugs her, whispers, "You've made Ellis a very happy woman. Thank you, Mia."

Mia brushes off the compliment, lets Ellis hug her too before she quips, "If we're done all this mushy stuff, I need to bring some cream and sugar outside."

"All right," Ellis says. "Operation Mushy is complete for now." After Mia departs, she says to Amy, "What the hell just happened?"

"I think you became a mom."

"Well, if I became a mom, you became a...stepmom?"

Amy gathers Ellis into her arms again. "I think we can tackle anything together, including raising a teenager." She leans her forehead against Ellis's and laughs. "Wait. What did I just get us into?"

Outside Amy gives a tiny fist bump to Erin's daughter, who's come to the party in her witch's costume because she simply can't contain her enthusiasm for Halloween, which is two days away. "How's our very scary little witch doing?"

"Fine. Can I come to your house for candy on Halloween?"

"I'll be extremely disappointed if you don't."

"Hey, stranger!" Kate slips her arm through Amy's. "Care to walk down to the water with me?"

"Sure. That'll take us all of about three minutes."

"We'll take our time."

Away from the warmth of the large fire pit, Amy zips up her jacket. "Everything okay?"

"More than okay." Kate's grin hasn't left her face all afternoon, and Amy has a funny feeling in her stomach that her best friend is about to confess something important.

"Hmm, why do I have a feeling a certain woman and her young daughter might have something to do with you dragging me away?"

"Because you have good instincts."

"I'm so happy for you, Kate. I've been waiting for this day to come."

"You're not going to get all sappy on me, are you?"

"I might."

They stop at the lake's edge and stare at the muddy water churned up from yesterday's rainstorm. The tang of rain remains in the air but thankfully has held off for Mia's party.

"So," Amy says. "What's up?"

"I'm in love with her, Ames. I want to be with her. And Eliana is such a great kid. I want them in my life…" She glances hesitantly at Amy, waiting for her reaction. "For the duration."

"Wow. That's fantastic!" She reaches an arm around her best friend and gives her shoulders a squeeze. She'd always wanted this for Kate, but the rapid pace at which it's happened still shocks her a little.

"Is it?" Kate looks uncertain, as though she doesn't quite believe Amy. "I mean, do you think it's rushing things? That… Anne would be okay with this? Because it's a hell of a lot more than dating."

"Are you kidding me right now?"

Kate's chin is trembling, the telltale sign that she's close to tears.

"If it's right, it's right, no matter what the timing is. And to hell with anybody who doesn't agree, don't listen to them. Erin's a great gal and I can see how happy she makes you. And as for Anne, how can you even ask that? She loved you more than anything, and when you love someone, you want nothing more than for them to be happy. She would want this for you. Trust me."

"You think so?"

"I know so, so stop worrying about it. And I'm going to be brutally honest with you." They've been friends too long to hold anything back. "It's time to start leaving Anne out of the conversation and out of your relationship with Erin. Three's a crowd. All right?"

Kate nods. She looks so nervous, so scared, that all Amy wants to do is squeeze her tight. "I've asked Erin and Eliana to move in with me."

Amy gasps her surprise. Surprise but also joy. "Well, I hope they were smart enough to say yes."

Kate laughs. "They were."

Amy hugs her friend. "You've surprised me, Hendy. And I could not be happier for you. For Erin too. You're doing the right thing."

"Thanks, hon. It means the world to me that you're okay with this."

"Okay? Hell, I'm going to throw you a party."

Kate laughs. "I think we've had enough parties for a while, though Erin and I are going to throw a big Christmas bash at my—" She rolls her eyes playfully. "*Our* place. And if you don't ask Ellis Hall to come as your date, I will be asking her on your behalf."

Amy could play dumb, but she doesn't want to, not anymore, and especially not since Kate has confided in her. She needs— wants—to tell Kate the truth. "I'm pretty sure I can handle that part myself. And I'm pretty sure she'll say yes."

"Well, I *have* noticed you two are pretty friendly these days."

"Actually, a little more than friendly."

"Seriously?"

"Yes. And yes, it's serious."

Kate blanches as though she's seen a ghost. "Holy crap, I had no idea."

"That's kind of the way it has to be. A secret, I mean. Until she's finished her report, some time around Christmas, I expect. I'm a shit for not telling you sooner, and I'm sorry. I...we can't have anyone finding out at the hospital or it could compromise the job she's doing."

"If you're happy, Ames, I could give a shit when you decide to confide in me."

"I am. Happy. Very happy. I love her."

"Good. You're forgiven." Kate links her arm with Amy's again. "Look at us. Guess we can drop our contingency plan now, huh?"

"What? Oh... God, I hope so. I mean, nothing against you or our master plan, but..." They'd joked a year ago about shacking up together as a couple of old, platonic spinsters if they were both single by the time they turned sixty-five.

"No offense taken. It was our Plan B, after all." Kate suddenly halts their progress. "Wait, maybe it would be a good thing if word got out about you and Ellis and her report got compromised. Then they'd have to start the review all over again."

"What?"

"If Ellis is basically recommending that the hospital be gutted, then buying us more time would be a good thing, right?"

"Nah, I don't think you have to worry about that."

"Why not?"

"Hendy, you gotta promise me you won't—"

"Do you even have to ask? Ames, you know I'd walk on burning coals for you. Now tell me, I'm dying to know what the hell is going on."

Amy tells her about Ellis's plan to add programs to the hospital that will bring in more funding, so that they can keep what they have. No guarantee the regional board will go for it, Amy cautions, but adds that the community will go nuts if the board doesn't go for it and chooses to make cuts instead. "It's a solid plan, a spectacular plan," Amy says. "If I need to, I'll leak her report to the media. Isn't Erin's twin sister married to a newspaper editor?"

"She is, and that's a masterful idea. Jesus, I'm so damned relieved. I don't want to leave this hospital, especially since Erin plans to set up her own practice in town by spring."

"I don't think anybody's going anywhere."

"This calls for a celebration. An epic one."

"It does, but not until everything's official. I'm not doing anything to jinx it, you know?"

"Boy, do I ever."

They're about to rejoin the party when Amy notices Erin and Ellis chatting amiably. She halts Kate in her tracks, points to their girlfriends. "Goddamn, will you look at those two beauties?"

Kate's shaking her head, but she's grinning. "How the hell did we get so lucky?"

"I don't know, but I'm not going to question it. I'm going to hold on like hell."

"I'll second that, my friend."

Amy's eyes take in the crowd: her parents, her friends, her girlfriend, Mia. This is her life now, these people. The hospital, her patients, they're her life too, but they pale in comparison to this—her family. She knows without question that she'll follow these people anywhere, whether the hospital continues to exist or not. Because when it comes down to it, the hospital is just bricks and mortar. It's the people, the community, that make everything worthwhile.

"You know what?" she says to Kate. "No matter what happens, we're going to be okay."

"You're right, we are. We're survivors."

Being a survivor has never felt so promising. Or so damned good.

EPILOGUE

Three consecutive Christmas songs are usually enough to put Amy out of the holiday mood—too much syrupy cheer—but tonight she hums along to every tune, twirls Ellis around Kate's living room to "Rockin' Around the Christmas Tree." Even Mia and Susie have chosen not to make fun of the music; they're too busy holding hands and gazing into each other's eyes, oblivious to those chatting and laughing and dancing around them the way only two people newly in love can be. Kate and Erin have cooked up a storm. There's butter chicken, samosas, spanakopita, beef sliders, and an entire table of salads and desserts.

Kate and Erin are incredibly cute together, and with Eliana, they look like a real family. The kind of family Amy knows her friend has always wanted. Kate and Erin have also become stand-in aunts to Mia, who's made no secret of the fact that she wants to stay living here until she finishes high school at least, but forever if that's possible. Ellis has been coy, assuring Mia their stay is indefinite for now, but Amy wants more, so much more. She wants Ellis and Mia to move in with her. She wants them to create a family together, to make this town their lifelong home, but it's too soon to ask. Ellis has completed her hospital review, but it will be early February before the regional board decides what to do with her report. They could act on all of her recommendations and quickly. Or they might send it back to a committee for further study, prolonging any decisions. Worst-case scenario, they'll reject Ellis's recommendations and decide on something entirely different, something out of the blue. No matter what happens, Amy's going to ask Ellis and Mia to be with her. To be her future.

Kate sidles up to Amy, refills her glass with the bottle of chilled Prosecco she's carrying around like a trophy. Ellis steps next to Amy and holds out her glass.

"So," Kate says, glancing between them, "you never did tell me when you two first knew you were attracted to one another."

Amy shares a glance with Ellis, notices the barest trace of a smile at the corners of Ellis's mouth. She's trying not to giggle.

"I mean," Kate continues playfully, "did you see each other in the hallway one day at the hospital and like, that was it? Or was it at that first board meeting, when you stared into each other's eyes for the first time and thought, 'Wow, I want that woman.' Hmm?"

"Um…" Amy stalls. She and Ellis have decided to keep the true source of their coming together their own little secret. Well, Natalie has an idea, since she was out with Amy for dinner when Ellis and Mia and her former in-laws walked into the restaurant. Amy knows there's no fooling her sister, that she won't buy the lie that the first time they met was at the hospital. Luckily, Natalie's too scattered and preoccupied to give it much thought.

"Well?" Kate persists. "This is one romance story I don't want to miss out on."

In the last week, they've quietly told their friends and family about their relationship, editing out most of the details.

Amy can't resist a little fun at her lover's expense. She bites her bottom lip to hold back from smiling. "Um, I'll let Ellis tell that story. You tell it so well, honey."

Ellis is going to kill her; her eyes are promising it. "Well, um, let's see. I, ah, well…." Her eyes have gone from threatening to pleading, and Amy takes pity on her.

"All right, I'll tell the story," she says to Ellis. "But, honey, you have to promise me something."

Ellis grins and whispers, "Anything you want, lover."

Kate rolls her eyes, but she doesn't mean it. She and Erin are every bit as goofy around one another.

Amy cups Ellis's chin, stares into her eyes. "Anything I want, huh? All right, how about that report of yours. I hope you put in there that we need to hire a replacement for Dr. Atkinson. So I'm not on call every other weekend. Oh, and I want a kiss."

Ellis rises on her toes and kisses Amy. "Done and done."

"Whew. Thank you. Are you always a step ahead of me?"

"Yes."

Amy laughs, kisses Ellis again and almost spills their refilled glasses of sparkling white wine.

"Hey," Kate interjects. "I'm still here, and still waiting for my answer."

"Fine," Amy replies, affecting a bored tone. "It was in Collinsworth, during that working trip." Not totally a lie, because it was in Collinsworth that they came to realize they didn't want to be apart.

"I knew it," Kate says triumphantly. "A little hanky-panky on the company dime, eh?"

Ellis's face is as red as Amy's feels, but they don't deny the accusation. Amy adds, "Oh, don't worry, we worked hard. Very hard."

Kate shakes her head, laughs as she says, "I'm sure you did," before resuming her mission of filling more glasses.

* * *

Valentine's Day is a week away when Ellis's report is accepted and voted on by the Essex County Regional Hospital Services board. She attends the meeting to be on hand for any questions, nervously holds her breath as the board goes around the table and votes unanimously to accept every one of her recommendations. It takes a moment for her to remember how to breathe again, and when she does, she smiles like someone who's been pardoned from a death sentence. For once, she knows she's earned every penny they're paying her for the review, because Erie Shores Hospital will continue to exist now. More than that, it will thrive and serve more people, become even more of an integral part of the community in the years to come.

Amy has been texting her every ten minutes, asking for updates. The minute the meeting is over, Ellis texts that she's on her way back to town and will be at Amy's house in an hour. She ignores the pleas, the begging, to tell Amy what the board has decided, because she wants to tell her in person. In the car, she takes pity on Amy and texts her a smiling emoji.

When she pulls her car into Amy's driveway, Amy is on the porch waiting impatiently for her, hugging herself against the cold.

"Dammit, you're killing me," Amy says, her teeth chattering. "That smiling emoji you sent me better mean good news."

Ellis leaps onto the porch and hugs Amy fiercely. "Come on, let's get you inside. You're freezing."

"I don't care about that, I want to know what the hell happened."

Ellis leads them inside, tugging Amy by the hand. As soon as they're in the door, she says, "They voted to implement every single recommendation. Not even a moment's hesitation. What's more, they think Erie Shores could be a model for small hospitals. They think this hospital can set the bar for other hospitals struggling to make ends meet."

Amy yelps, pumps her fist, and hugs Ellis so hard her insides feel like they're oozing out of her.

"I knew they'd love it. How could they not? That report is perfection personified!"

"Hmm, if you were so sure, how come you were standing outside waiting for me, nearly catching your death of cold?"

"Um...well, I might have been a little worried." Amy laughs because she knows she's been busted. She's been a ball of worry lately, but only in Ellis's presence. To everyone else, she's been the picture of confidence because she's wanted to set the tone for her colleagues. Kate's been insufferable, pestering Amy constantly for updates.

Ellis hands Amy her coat, lets Amy get her a glass of wine from the kitchen. When she returns, she's holding a bottle of expensive champagne and two glasses.

"Ooh, so it wasn't an act, you really were confident the board would pass my recommendations."

"Not exactly. If it had gone the other way, I've got a bottle of whiskey in the cupboard."

Amy pops the cork, pours them each a generous glass. They clink glasses.

"Oh my, this is good," Ellis says.

"Only the best for the best." Amy's eyes are twinkling, and Ellis swears it's the happiest she's ever seen her. "Oh, sweetheart, I can't tell you what this means to me. This is the best news I've ever heard. And all because of you."

"No, not all because of me. It's you, too, darling. All of you...Mia, Kate, and Erin, too. You all kept chipping away at my defenses until I finally listened, until I found another way. And it's the right way. I feel like I finally did something good, you know? I feel like I'm helping to build something, not tear it down."

Nothing this rewarding has happened in her work life before. Usually her recommendations involve downsizing, cutbacks, amalgamations, trimming, forcing things to work in the face of enormous opposition. But this, this is making a sustainable future for the hospital. For herself, too. This is building something, and Amy makes her want to build a life and grow roots. For too long she's ignored her own happiness.

For too long she's put things ahead of people, put her own fears ahead of progress. Not any more.

"I'm so tired," Ellis says, and Amy gives her shoulders a massage before guiding her to the sofa. "Thank you, love, but that's not entirely what I meant."

Amy sits next to her. Their bodies touch, because they can't be this close and not touch. It's been that way almost since their first Thursday afternoon.

"I mean," Ellis continues, "that I'm tired of running."

"So don't run."

She loves Amy's directness, her way of simplifying things. "It used to be a thrill when I ended one project, when it was time to move on to another. A fresh start. A chance to reinvent myself, choose another future." She reaches for Amy's hand because she needs her steadiness. "I don't want to do that anymore. I don't want to run ever again."

"So don't. Stay here. With me. With Mia. Make a life, a family, the three of us."

Amy's looking at her with such passion, such conviction, that Ellis lets herself fall headlong into it. And it feels, for the first time in years, like she's truly free. "I think I would like that. A lot."

She hadn't noticed the fear in Amy's eyes until it was gone, wiped away with her words. Amy lifts their joined hands, kisses Ellis's fingers one by one. "Move in with me as soon as possible. You and Mia. Or we'll sell my place and buy something together."

"Wait. Sell this place? Are you nuts?"

"All right, then we'll keep it. Will you? Move in with me?"

"Oh, sweetheart." Ellis can no longer hold back the tide; tears course down her cheeks. She's laughing, she's crying. She doesn't know what she's feeling, other than incredibly happy. And grateful. "How can reversing the course of your life feel so freaking good?"

"Easy. Because you're home now."

"You're right. I am. But we need to talk to Mia."

"Right. Do you think she'll say yes?"

"Are you kidding? She'll be booking the movers as soon as I tell her." Ellis tilts her chin, waits for Amy to kiss her. It's a soft kiss, like the falling of a gentle, warm rain.

"I love you," Amy says.

"I love you too, darling. Can you handle having a housewife?"

"I would love nothing better, if that's what you want."

"Well, I'm unemployed now."

"I think somehow we'll manage."

Ellis laughs. Of course they'll manage, with her fat bank account and Amy's high six-figure salary. "I do want to work again, at some point."

"I might be able to help with that."

"The hospital needs to add to their cleaning staff?" Ellis isn't entirely joking.

"Very funny. You remember Donna, our chief financial officer?"

"Uh-huh."

"She's pregnant. She'll be going on maternity leave in about four months. That sounds about the time you'll start climbing the walls around here, itching to get back to work."

"You think so?"

"I know so. Besides, that brilliant mind of yours is too, well, brilliant to stay unemployed for long."

"Why do I get the feeling you've got everything figured out?"

"Because I do."

"I see. And did you have something to do with Donna getting pregnant, too?"

Amy's face reddens for a fraction of a second, and then she's laughing and pulling Ellis onto her lap. "There's one more thing I want you to say yes to."

Ellis feels her heart slow until it's almost not beating at all. She knows she'll say yes to anything Amy asks her.

"Next Thursday," Amy says around a grin, "happens to be Valentine's Day."

"Well, isn't that a coincidence that it falls on a Thursday." She's pretty sure she knows where this is going.

"I've booked the day off. And I've booked our hotel. Do you happen to be free?"

Ellis feels her heart lifting, soaring like a kite. The hotel. In the city. Where they first met nine months ago. "I happen to be free as a bird."

A look of horror flashes across Amy's face. "Not *that* free, I hope. As in, you're taken."

Ellis laughs, kisses the frown off Amy's forehead. "Yes, I'm taken, and happily so. But my day is wide open. My life, too."

"Ooh, I love the sound of that. I hope there's lots of room for me in your big old life."

"Darling." Ellis looks into those liquid gray eyes, wants nothing more than to dive into them. She'd do it too, but then she wouldn't get to look at them. "You are my life."

Amy kisses her, trails her fingers up and down Ellis's back, leaving warm tingles along their trail. Ellis deepens the kiss, her impatience growing because she needs Amy in bed. She needs them both naked; she needs them touching one another, loving one another, consummating their new plans.

"I think," she says when she comes up for air, "that we need to move this celebration to your bedroom."

Amy kisses the tip of her nose, gives her a hungry look. "Can you stay the night?"

"Let me text Mia. I'm sure she won't mind."

They get up from the sofa, Ellis to find her phone, Amy to retrieve the champagne and their glasses. Already it's starting to feel like this is her home. Ellis corrects her thought. No. Already it's starting to feel like it's the beginning of the rest of her life.

Bella Books, Inc.

Women. Books. Even Better Together.

P.O. Box 10543
Tallahassee, FL 32302

Phone: 800-729-4992
www.bellabooks.com